Truth or Dare

Truth or Dare

©Barbara Knight 2022

Cover illustration: Original artwork by Ryan Curtis

Proofing and typesetting: Ryan Curtis and Julia Knight

Published by: Sculptural Images

Printed by: Ingram Spark

Dedication

This book is dedicated to the XLS (ex-library staff),

wonderful workmates and great friends for decades.

Truth or Dare

The Beach House 1988

Jenny felt an overwhelming sense of power as she steered her new red Celica around the sharp bends and then accelerated when she came to a long straight stretch in the road. She'd only had her licence for a month, so it was still a novelty to be driving without her mother twitching nervously in the passenger seat or her father bellowing unnecessary instructions. God, she'd got sick of that. They were both such pains. Anyone would think she didn't know what she was doing.

Her friends all told her how lucky she was to have parents who would buy her a brand new car for her seventeenth birthday, but she saw it as her due. Her father could afford it anyway, and it gave him something to brag about to his friends. When he'd handed her the keys he'd said, 'Nothing's too good for my Princess.'

She had hugged him and thanked him prettily, but her show of affection was all a sham. Beneath this surface display she felt nothing but disdain for him. As a little girl she had adored her big handsome Daddy and beautiful gentle mother, but when she was about twelve she learnt what they were really like. Her father's main interest in life revolved around business and making money and her mother's role was as hostess to his business partners and associates. She was his trophy wife and had always seemed content to fill that role in exchange for a life of wealth and leisure. Jenny sometimes wondered if they had ever actually been in love, or if their marriage had been one of convenience right from the beginning. Although they appeared a loving couple when in public, Jenny saw little sign of affection between them in the home. She had seen how loving Annie's parents were with each other and was enough of a romantic to wish she lived in a house with that much love around. Sheila's folks were pretty tight too, but Georgie's were even worse than hers. Her father was a horrible small-minded man and her mother a wimp.

She had been thinking it's the luck of the draw who you cop as parents when she noticed that the long flat stretch she had been driving along had ended and the road ahead was steeper. She changed down a gear as the road rose before her. Next to her Annie removed the Whitney Houston cassette they had been singing along with and replaced it with a U2 one. Annie began singing dreamily with the first track, 'With or Without You', and in the back seat Georgie groaned. 'Not that one again. The next thing we know you'll be saying how much you miss Joel.'

'Don't be mean Georgie. You just don't understand true lurv.' Jenny gave a laugh, but patted Annie's knee to show she wasn't really making fun of her. 'I for one think it's great to have you to ourselves again, much as I love Joel.'

Annie stopped singing. 'I do miss him, but it is good to be just with you lot again. He had to go home to help his father with apple thinning or something, so this trip's come at a good time for me.'

The next tune on the cassette was, 'I Still Haven't Found What I'm Looking For,' and the four girls joined in, singing at the top of their voices, the sound wafting behind them through the open windows of the car.

They didn't know the words of the next couple of songs and chattered about what they planned to do during the coming week of freedom from the world of school and adults. This would be the first time they had been together at the beach house without Jenny's parent's there watching their every move, and filling the house with their boring old friends. Jenny had promised not to have wild parties or to let any boys stay overnight. She had made these promises, and thought they would probably keep them. She and her friends were looking forward to this time for just being together and enjoying their close-knit companionship that they all felt was beginning to unravel slightly. They had been best friends since first year high school and loved each other like the sisters none of them had. Jenny and Georgie were only children, and Sheila had a young brother and Annie had two. Now that Annie was going steady with Joel, and Jenny was always going out with one or another of her numerous boyfriends the other two saw far less of their friends. This week was seen by all as a time for the 'Gang of Four' to touch base.

Annie changed the cassette and the joyous sounds of 'I've Had the Time of my Life', filled the car. They knew all the words of this song for they'd seen 'Dirty Dancing' several times and, except for Georgie, thought Patrick Swayze the sexiest man alive. Even Annie had swooned at the sight of him dancing, although she had felt a bit guilty having sexual fantasies about another man when she loved Joel so much.

When the song finished Annie rewound the cassette and they were singing at the top of their voices as Jenny turned into the white-gravelled drive that led to the beach house.

The house was a large white weatherboard dwelling with a wide verandah running across the front and along one side. It was set on a big slightly sloping block. There were trees planted along the fence lines to give privacy from neighbouring houses, but in front of the house was only a large expanse of lawn that gave an unimpeded view of the beach nestled between large outcrops of grey rock topped with orange lichen and the sparkling cobalt blue water beyond.

As soon as Jenny parked the car in the carport at the side of the house the girls scrambled out. Georgie stretched, for she was a tall girl and had been a bit cramped in the back seat. The other three ran giggling down the drive and across the road to the beach. By the time Georgie caught up with them they had thrown off sandals and sneakers and were splashing around in the shallows. She kicked off her sandals and joined them, and for a while they cavorted around like children, splashing each other until they were all thoroughly soaked.

Annie, the practical one of the foursome, eventually said, 'We'd better get the food out of that hot car or the ice cream and butter will be starting to melt and the milk will go off.'

Giggling they made their way up the drive and began unloading the food from the boot. Jenny unlocked the front door and grabbed a pile of towels from the linen cupboard in the passage. They scattered boxes of food and dillybags of clothing haphazardly on the verandah, then discarded their sodden clothing and wrapped themselves in the big soft towels. Georgie, who had long dark hair and smooth olive skin, looked like an island princess with a white towel wrapped like a sarong around her tall shapely body. Sheila said enviously, 'You look good in anything, don't you,' and Georgie laughed self-consciously.

'Let's get this stuff inside and then we can go for a swim.' Annie picked up one of the boxes as she said this and headed towards the kitchen.

Jenny followed behind her and put a box on the table before busying herself opening the refrigerator and the large pantry cupboard next to it. 'It looks as though Mrs Jones has been in and done a good clean and stocked up on the basics for us. Mum said she'd organise for her to do that and for her old man to mow the lawns.'

Sheila looked around appreciatively. 'Everything looks great. I'd sort of forgotten how big it is, or perhaps it just looks bigger because we're the only one's here. God, we'll be able to have a bedroom each instead of bunking down together in the kid's room.' At the mention of this they all made a dash for the bedrooms that lined one side of the house. Sheila was the last to stake her claim so got the bunk room at the end of the passage. She spent the rest of the holiday bemoaning the fact that she was the only one sleeping in a single bed.

They set to work putting away the food, filling the refrigerator with meat and vegetables, soft drinks and bottles of green ginger wine. Once this was finished they unpacked rather haphazardly then changed into bathers and met up in the lounge dining room. This enormous room adjoined the kitchen and ran along the other side of the house. It had folding glass doors that opened onto the side verandah from both the kitchen and the lounge room.

Jenny grabbed fresh towels from the cupboard and they once more ran down to the beach. They spent over an hour swimming, having competitions to see who could do the best somersaults and who could stay under water the longest. When the sun went behind a cloud and the water changed from sparkling aqua to a dull grey they began to feel chilled and decided they'd had enough of the water for one day.

They raced each other across the lawn to see who would get the first shower because they knew from previous holidays that the water temperature could be erratic if too many showers were used at the same time.

Jenny was first to be showered and changed and had set out nibbles and tall glasses of icy west coast coolers on a glass-topped cane table out on the verandah. When the others joined her she handed around the drinks and said, 'A toast to us and a fabulous holiday.'

They clinked glasses and sat around in the cane chairs, feeling sophisticated, grown-up and very, very happy.

In later years they remembered this holiday as one of the most perfect times of their lives, and for the most part it was really good. They had swum every day, walked the beach and the surrounding bushland, lounged around on the verandah reading and chatting. They had eaten when hungry and kept meal preparations to a minimum, making sandwiches or salads for lunch and barbecuing each night. Some evenings they watched television or videos selected from the small collection for hire at the general store; other times were spent playing cassettes and dancing and singing along to their favourites.

None of them forgot the last night they spent at the beach house, but they didn't let the sorrows and secrets disclosed that night affect their good memories of the holiday.

They had sat on cushions around a low coffee table in the lounge room. No-one had felt like cooking on their last night so they'd ordered in pizzas. On the table were the empty pizza boxes, several crumpled crisp packets, four glasses and an empty bottle of chardonnay. When they ran out of west coast coolers Jenny had raided her father's wine racks. The girls were dressed in casual beach wear; Georgie in shorts and singlet, Jenny and Annie wore sarongs and Sheila had on a white long-sleeved blouse and a full-length green cotton skirt. While the other three were happy to wear revealing clothes that showed off their tans

Sheila hid her freckled peeling skin beneath concealing layers.

Georgie had picked up the empty bottle saying, 'Have you got any more bottles of this stashed away Jen?'

Jenny grabbed the bottle and said, slightly slurring her words, 'Course I have. One thing I can rely on with my Dad is a well- stocked cellar.'

She had risen awkwardly, tripped over Sheila's bare feet and with a mumbled, 'Sorry Sheil,' walked to the refrigerator and removed a bottle of wine. She put the empty one is the rubbish bin, and was struggling with a bottle opener when Georgie joined her at the breakfast bar, took bottle and opener from her hands and said, 'Let me do that Jenny. You go and sit down.'

As Jenny staggered back to her place in the circle Georgie opened the bottle efficiently then refilled everyone's glass.

'Well done Georgie,' Annie said. 'Now what are we going to do?'

"Let's play Truth or Dare,' Sheila suggested quickly. 'We haven't played that in ages.'

'Okay,' Jenny agreed. 'And as it's your suggestion you can ask the first question Sheil.'

Sheila had looked around the circle and then her eyes returned to Jenny. 'Right, will you take truth or dare?'

'I'll take truth.'

'Alright. Why did you ask me to cover for you last Saturday? Did you spend the night with Nigel?'

'Strictly speaking that's two questions, but I'll answer the second.' Jenny had given a drunken giggle. 'Yes I spent the night with him, and he sure knows how to treat a girl.

First we had dinner at this fabulous French restaurant and then we went back to a room he'd booked at The Bayside. It was all very classy; gorgeous room with a view over the water and champagne in a bucket on a little table. The sex wasn't bad either.'

Annie looked a bit shocked. 'But he's too old for you. He must be at least thirty-five.'

'Oh, don't go on so Annie.' Jenny said slightly defensively. 'I'm not planning on spending the rest of my life with him, but he was fun for a night. And what's wrong with dating older men. At least they generally have the money to give a girl a good time. My mother says, "Better a rich man's darling than a poor man's slave." In fact that's her mantra; not that it's bought her much joy. I don't think she expected an older husband to be a skirt chaser. Anyhow the rules of the game are that you don't criticise anything someone tells you so you shouldn't criticise who I choose to date.'

Annie had said a quiet, 'Sorry,' and taken a sip of wine.

'Right Annie, you're next. Truth or dare?'

Annie knew it would be a question about her and Joel, and probably to do with their sex life because they all tease her about how he can't keep his hands off her. She and Joel had been going together for ten months petted heavily almost from the time they met, but had only gone all the way during the past four months. What they feel for each other is so special and she doesn't want to discuss their lovemaking. Although she knew her friends would be peeved she said, 'I'll take the dare.'

The three other girls groaned, and Jenny said rather sarcastically, 'Frightened we'll ask something about you and your precious Joel.'

Sheila urged, 'Come on Annie, take the truth. Surely there isn't anything you couldn't share with us?'

Annie had always blushed easily and now she flushed beneath her golden tan. 'It's not that. I'd just rather take the dare.' There were things she and Joel did that she doesn't want to share with these best friends, and they were making her feel as though she is being disloyal to them in some way.

Abruptly Jenny asked the others, 'Okay, what will we dare her to do? It has to be something pretty horrible as she doesn't want to share truth with her three very best friends.'

Georgie had been silent, watching the repartee between the others, but now said, 'Let's mix up some foul concoction and dare her to drink it.'

Sheila giggled. 'Yes, something with raw eggs. They're pretty hard to swallow.'

Jenny reached down and pulled Sheila to her feet as she said, "Come on Georgie. Let's see what we can mix up.'

The three girls spent a while breaking two eggs into a glass, then adding tomato sauce, several drops of Tabasco sauce, a large sprinkle of salt and topped it off with some milk. It looked disgusting and they giggled as they put it on a tray and carried it with much ceremony back to the table.

Jenny said, 'We dare you to drink our wondrous cocktail,' while the other two fell in a giggling heap.

Annie looked at the curdled mess in the glass and almost gagged, then with false bravado said, 'I accept the dare,' and attempted to scull it. She almost got it down, but then retched and ran to the bathroom where she had been violently sick. Georgie followed her in and put an arm around her shoulders as she heaved up the last of the mess, then helped her white-faced friend back to the circle.

They all looked a bit shamefaced and Jenny said, 'Sorry love. We didn't think it would have that effect.'

Annie smiled wanly, 'It's okay. I chose to take the dare so I got what I deserved.'

Georgie said, 'Well it's your turn to ask now, so you can get back at one of us.'

Annie was a gentle soul and wouldn't ever deliberately put anyone on the spot. She turned to Sheila and asked, 'Truth or dare,' and when Sheila chose truth she asked what she thought would be an uncontroversial question. 'If you could change something, what would it be?'

'God, that's easy. I'd change the way I look. I'm so tired of being the plain one amongst you lot.'

Annie had put a comforting arm around Sheila. 'But you're not plain. You have the most beautiful hazel eyes and a lovely figure. I wish I was tall like you.'

'You don't have to be kind Annie. I know how I look. My hair's a ghastly carroty colour, my nose is too long and I'm a freckled, peeling mess after a few days in the sun, no matter how much sunscreen I put on. And look at you lot. Georgie's stunning and you two are both beautiful, golden blondes. No wonder I can't get a boyfriend. I'm ugly, ugly, ugly.' She burst into loud weeping and her three friends crowded around her patting her back and making soothing remarks.

Finally she wiped her eyes and said apologetically, 'Sorry I made such a show of myself. God this was meant to be a bit of fun and so far Annie's been sick and I've made a fool of myself. Let's have some levity around here.

Anyhow, it's my turn to ask, and Georgie is the only one who hasn't been put on the spot so far, so truth or dare Georgie?'

Georgie laughed, 'I don't like to think what you lot would cook up for a dare so I'll take the truth.'

Sheila had thought for a while and then asked, 'Is there any boy you really like?'

This is something she had wanted to ask her friend for a long time. At school Georgie always seemed to be talking to boys, and at parties and dances she was popular. Occasionally she dated a boy, but rarely more than once, and she never raved about certain boys the way Jenny did and Annie used to before she got so hung up on Joel.

For a long while Georgie was silent, so long that Jenny urged, 'Come on. It can't be that hard to think of a boy you like. Have you got a secret crush on some guy you haven't told us about?'

Georgie looked around the circle of faces. These were her very dearest friends, and there was something she knew she must tell them, but was afraid of how they would react. Perhaps the point of this rather silly game was that it gave you the opportunity to be honest with your friends.

She gave a big sigh and said, 'No Jenny I haven't got a secret crush, not on a guy, and Sheila there are lots of boys who I like as friends, but not romantically. I just don't feel that way about boys.'

'What are you trying to tell us?' Annie asked quietly.

'That I think I'm a lesbian.'

'Whatever makes you think that? You don't fancy any of us do you? And you enjoy kissing boys, don't you?' The questions had tumbled out of Jenny, but then she paused, a look of total bewilderment on her face.

'I've known for a long time I don't feel the same way about boys as you lot do. Sure I like boys. I enjoy talking with them and I like the way their minds work, well some of the brighter one's that is. But I don't want to kiss them or cuddle up with them, and the thought of actually having sex with a guy almost makes me puke.'

Annie looked really worried. 'Perhaps you're just a late developer. You are only sixteen and we're all seventeen.'

'And you three were all interested in boys a year ago. I haven't known how to tell you this without making you uncomfortable around me. I find some girls sexually attractive. Sometimes I'll be talking to a girl and I wonder what it would be like to kiss her mouth, or the way a girl moves attracts my attention and I imagine holding her body and caressing her.'

'Perhaps you should talk to the student counsellor or a doctor or someone,' Sheila suggested tentatively.

'I'm not sick, and I have talked to the student counsellor. She was very understanding and accepting, but warned me about the problems associated with coming out. I don't know if I'll ever be able to tell my parents, but I hope it won't change things between us.'

'As if it would.' Annie had put her arms around Georgie and given her a big hug.

Sheila and Jenny both stood and walked to where Georgie was seated. They too patted her arm and said of course it wouldn't make any difference, but Georgie had felt there was a slight wariness in their touch. She was hurt by this, but accepted that it would probably take a while before they truly came to terms with the fact that she was different from them. She loved Annie for her spontaneous and natural acceptance, and hoped the other two would get over their feelings of trepidation around her.

Later that night when they were in their comfortable double beds in separate rooms all the girls had lain awake, thinking about the game and what had been said. Sheila was cross with herself for her display of self-pity. So often she felt the odd one out amongst her friends, for Georgie was tall, tawny-haired and absolutely gorgeous, Jenny a petite, pretty blonde and Annie had long fair hair, a beautiful complexion and a smile that lit up her face. Compared with them she felt so plain, but she regretted her outburst for she didn't want her friends feeling sorry for her.

Jenny wondered why she had revealed faults in her parent's marriage she had previously kept hidden from her friends. She knew she mentioned that her father was a skirt chaser, and made her mother sound rather mercenary.

When she found out about her father's infidelities two years ago she had been shocked and upset but hadn't talked about it with her friends because she was ashamed of him. She learnt what her father was like when she overheard a conversation between her mother and her mother's sister, Jenny's Aunt Beth. Her aunt had been saying she didn't know why she put up with her husband's philandering and her mother answered weakly that she didn't have much choice. She had added that Jenny and her father were so close she might choose to stay with him if there was a divorce, and anyhow she wasn't prepared to give up her comfortable life because of his little flings. Since then Jenny had felt a lack of respect for her mother and positive detestation for her father. He was so old, over sixty, and to think of him having sex with other women made her feel ashamed and rather sick.

Now as she thought about what she had said she didn't really regret it. At least her friends would understand now why she was critical of her parents and seemingly ungrateful for all they gave her.

Annie thought of Joel, and how her love for him was creating a divide between her and her friends. They had been such an important part of her life for so many years, and she had talked openly with them about previous boyfriends. Now she didn't want to tell them about the times she spends with Joel. She felt what she and Joel shared was special and precious, but she knew her friends felt she was shutting them out by not confiding in them about it. She must make sure they realised how important they still were to her, even though her love for Joel was taking her away from them.

Georgie was glad her friends now knew why she wasn't interested in boys. She had kept secret her sexual feelings towards women for she had feared these very dear friends would not understand and might even distance themselves from her. She hoped it would not affect their friendships but she wasn't sure. Annie had been lovely, but the other two seemed uncomfortable; or was she just imagining that they didn't seem to want to touch her?

In the morning they were all a bit hung over and ate hurried breakfasts of coffee and toast before commencing the cleaning up and packing. No-one mentioned the game of the night before. Georgie was pleased her friends now knew her secret, and Jenny felt relieved she would no longer have to pretend about her parents. For Annie playing the game had brought home to her the divide that was developing between her and her friends and made her a little sad. Sheila remained slightly embarrassed about her outburst and was pleased no-one referred to the game or what had been revealed.

They piled into the car; Jenny started the engine and beeped the horn as a farewell to the beach house and the other three waved. They giggled at their foolishness and all agreed they must return the following year, but many summers passed before they would.

Georgie

Georgie trips as she walks up the stone steps and curses softly. Perhaps she shouldn't have worn such high heels to a funeral, but then she didn't have much choice. She'd given all her old shoes to Vinnies when the fashions changed. As she straightens she can see inside the church and it's full. Mark had been a popular guy, but she'd never understood why people found him so attractive, let alone why Jenny married him. Georgie had always felt there was something insincere about him, as if he were putting on an act, and that behind the façade of loving husband and father and successful businessman was a spoilt child who would retaliate with violence if he didn't get his way.

She is late because of a stupid mix up at the airport with the car rental people. She had told them definitely that she wanted a manual but they had delivered an automatic. Getting her a replacement had taken an overly long time and has made her late. Every seat is taken so she leans against the cold stone wall as she peers towards the front of the church where she knows Jenny and her sons will be seated. Above the crowd she catches a glimpse of her friend's blonde hair partly concealed by a small black hat. Seated either side are her two big dark-haired sons who tower over her. One has an arm draped protectively around her shoulders. Georgie hasn't seen the boys for several years, and in that time they have changed from gangling, scruffy boys to young men. Because she has no children of her own Georgie is always being taken by surprise by how quickly children change from one year to the next.

This is her first trip back home in over five years although she has seen Jenny more recently when her friend visited her in Sydney two years ago. She'd come alone; had called the trip, 'her escape from domesticity,' refusing to discuss Mark or the boys at all. Georgie had felt her behaviour strange; had wondered if there were problems in the marriage or if one of the boys was in some sort of trouble, but she had accepted her friend's edict. She had, in fact, been quite happy to keep their conversations to the present moment, for she didn't want to talk about her own personal life. At the time she was still getting used to living without Ruth, and trying to come to terms with how suddenly their three-year relationship had ended. Ruth's suggestion that they adopt a child had forced Georgie to face the reality of the relationship, and recognise the many compromises they were both making in order to make it work.

Georgie shakes her head to rid herself of those painful memories and instead thinks back on that time she spent with Jenny and how much she had enjoyed her company. They'd gone to shows and galleries, restaurant and boutiques, and had shared the same closeness that they'd enjoyed as teenagers. At the time of the visit Georgie had been living alone and when they returned to her penthouse after an evening out they had sat over a last glass of wine, gazing over the lights of the city while they giggled and chatted like carefree girls, never alluding to problems they might be experiencing. After Jenny left she had wished they had been able to open up to each other more and had regretted the way they had avoided talking about the really personal stuff that was important in their lives.

There is a sudden hush in the church and Georgie realises the music that was playing when she arrived has stopped. The minister steps forward and says in a solemn voice. 'Mr Herman Jones, Mark's long-time friend and business partner, would now like to say a few words.'

Georgie hates churches and everything to do with them. She particularly hates funerals and is only here out of love and concern for Jenny; she really has no interest in the proceedings. Somewhere in this crowd she knows Annie and Sheila will be sitting, probably together, and she tries to find them amongst the heads. The man at the front of the church is now talking about Mark's philanthropy and Georgie thinks cynically how unnecessary this is, for Mark had never been a shrinking violet regarding his largesse to the various causes he assisted. Even in Sydney she had heard every time the great Mark Stein put money towards some worthy cause.

Finally the longwinded eulogy comes to a close, and the minister thanks him before introducing the next speaker. Georgie's eyes and thoughts had been wandering, but now she looks interestedly to the front as Stephen, Jenny's oldest son, stands and walks to the lectern. He is impressively tall, well over six feet, and immaculately dressed in a smart navy suit, white shirt and dark tie. In the five years since Georgie last saw him he has become a man, and a stunningly handsome one at that. He has inherited Mark's size but he looks very like Jenny's father who was extremely good looking, despite the fact that he was quite old. Even though Georgie had never been attracted to men she had recognised the appeal of his good looks and forceful personality.

Stephen speaks fondly of times spent with his father. He has a deep resonant voice and speaks with humour and self-assurance. He finishes by thanking everyone for coming and then takes his seat back next to his mother. Finally the minister says those words Georgie has heard so often at funerals about the departed person not really leaving but just being in another room. She sneers inwardly at the foolishness of that message; when you're dead you're dead, not hiding away in some room waiting for your loved ones to join you. She braces herself for the most horrible part where the coffin slides behind the curtain. Always she imagines the flames reaching up and enveloping the coffin and destroying the body inside. She is sure she can smell burning flesh. God how she hates funerals! She is glad to be near the door and is the first person out when the last song is played.

It is a relief to be out of that cold dreary church and into the sunshine once more. As the rest of the congregation files out through the heavy wooden door Georgie stands to one side watching the departing figures as she waits for Annie and Sheila to appear. They have spoken on the phone and arranged that Annie will stay in town for the night after the funeral and Georgie will follow Sheila's car to the wake. Jenny and her family moved during the past five years since Georgie has been back and she isn't quite sure how to find the new house. She is wondering how to get to the wake if something has happened to prevent the two of them being here when she hears her name shouted. Annie greets her with an enveloping hug and Sheila grabs her hand and kisses her cheek. Their noisy greetings attract the attention of the other mourners and some cast critical glances in their direction.

Sheila is the first to step back from the loving tangle and says joyously, 'God it's good to see you again. And you're looking gorgeous.'

Annie looks her over. 'You're certainly looking very smart. You make me feel like a country cousin.'

Georgie hasn't seen these two friends for over four years. They have kept in close contact through emails and on Face Book, but the last time they were together was when they came to Sydney to celebrate Georgie's thirty-fifth birthday. It was meant to have been a get together of the 'Gang of Four' as they'd called themselves back in their high school days, but at the last minute Jenny had to pull out. Her younger boy, Alec, had broken his arm in a rugby match, and evidently Mark was incapable of looking after him for the few days she would have been away.

In a way Georgie had been glad Jenny wasn't there because the visit hadn't gone well. She'd been looking forward to her friends meeting Ruth but they hadn't been able to hide their obvious discomfiture at seeing her with a lover. Ruth hadn't helped matters by being overly demonstrative, touching her intimately and kissing her passionately in front of them. She guessed it was Ruth's way of showing these old friends that she was now the most important person in Georgie's life, but she had found it embarrassing just the same. She had enjoyed the later visit when there had only been her and Jenny, but now she is so pleased to see Annie and Sheila again and is looking forward to really catching up for she has planned to stay for ten days.

She looks at these two dear friends, noting Sheila's stunning new hairstyle but also that Annie's pretty face is beginning to show the signs of aging. She has worry lines around her eyes, her skin looks dry and parched from her life lived much of the time out of doors and she does indeed look like a country cousin in a rather shapeless black dress and sensible court shoes.

As they walk towards the car park Georgie asks quietly, 'How's Jenny taking it? From what you've told me I gather the last couple of weeks were pretty horrendous and that he insisted on staying at home.'

'I think she's glad it's over. I dropped in to see her last week and she looked exhausted. A nurse came in the mornings to help bathe him and to adjust his medication.' Sheila sighs before continuing. 'During the last weeks he was on a pretty high dosage of morphine, but he still seemed to be in a lot of pain. I never liked the man much, but you don't want anyone to suffer, and I know seeing him like that took a lot out of Jen.'

'Jenny says the boys have been wonderful. They've grown up to be such lovely young men. I came up to town to see her the day after Mark died and she told me they were making all the funeral arrangements. She's very proud of them.'

As she says this Annie stops beside Sheila's BMW and gives Georgie another quick hug before settling herself in the passenger seat. Sheila follows suit then says, 'I'll wait until you're in your car before taking off, and make sure I don't lose you. See you there love.' She slides gracefully into the leather seat and turns on the ignition.

As Georgie follows Sheila's little silver car through the once familiar streets she thinks about her friends. When she had initially planned a trip back home the main reason for her return had been to catch up with them. Growing up they had been such an important part of her life, and in all the years in Sydney she has never developed any friendships as close. She has several colleagues at work whose company she enjoys and has had a few lovers who have been important to her, at least for a while. With the exception of Ruth none of these has been as important as Jenny, Sheila and Annie, for the easy camaraderie is still there and their shared memories bind them together even though life has pulled them apart.

She has taken ten days off work, but now wonders if she'll stay that long. Before Mark's illness and subsequent death they had talked about taking off together, tripping around the state or staying at Jenny's beach house, but now what should have been a time for them to celebrate being together again has become a time of mourning for Jenny. As she watches closely the silver car in front of her moving along new and unfamiliar streets Georgie wonders what the next few days will bring.

Tomorrow she will visit her mother; get that out of the way at the start. She hasn't seen her for five years, and before that there had been an even longer time when she had no communication with her parents. For years she had kept her sexual proclivities a secret from her parents. She had known her bigoted little father would be horrified to learn his daughter wasn't straight or 'normal' as he put it. He often sounded off about dirty poofters and militant dykes and almost had an apocalyptic fit the first time he heard about the Gay Mardi Gras.

Shortly before she left to take up a position with a law firm in Sydney her mother had been rabbiting on about all the nice professional men she would meet. Unable to stand the deception any longer Georgie had blurted out, 'Mum, I'm not interested in men, not romantically at any rate, and I never will be. Surely you've realised that by now.'

Her mother had said stupidly, 'Mr Right just hasn't come along, but he will dear, and then you'll settle down.'

Her father had not been so obtuse, for he had lowered his glasses and peering across the top of them had asked, 'What exactly do you mean by that Georgia?'

'I think you know what I mean Dad.' She had stared back at him belligerently, a sense of relief flooding through her as she spoke. 'I'm what you'd call a 'dyke' or a 'lesso'. Neither of you has ever really understood me or even tried, so I don't expect you to start now. I find women attractive and have met a few like me who have found me appealing. Some have been my lovers, and if I ever settle down, as you call it Mum, it will be with another woman.'

Her mother had sat staring like a rabbit caught in a car's headlights, but her father had jumped to his feet scattering the paper he had been reading all over the floor. He shouted frantically, 'Get out. Get out. Get out of my house you depraved creature. You're no daughter of mine.'

Georgie had looked to her mother hoping for support, but not really expecting it. Her mother had sat silently quivering in her chair as Georgia turned on her heels and left, not even bothering to collect any of her belongings that were still stored in the house. She heard later that her father bundled up everything of hers, spare clothes, photos, books and papers and burnt them on a bonfire in the back yard.

A week later she left for Sydney, feeling free and unencumbered. Only her three best friends were there to see her off and, as the plane taxied along the runaway then lifted into the air, she knew that their companionship was the only thing she would miss.

Five years ago she returned for her father's funeral. She had felt hypocritical doing so for she wasn't sorry he'd died, but she still harboured a residual sense of duty towards her mother. She knew she was a weak woman who had allowed herself to be totally dominated by an ignorant unthinking bigot, but she had tried to be a good mother. She'd been gentle and caring while Georgie was growing up, and since her father's death had tried to mend the rift that her confession created, but the hurt from her mother's rejection remains. Georgia can never quite forgive her for going along with her father's edict and shutting her out of her life.

Occasionally they talk on the phone and tomorrow she will make a duty visit. They will sit in the kitchen and drink tea, and try to mend the gap that has widened through the years of separation. She will never respect her mother and her mother will never understand her. All very sad, but that's how it is.

Georgie sees that Sheila's car is turning into a wide sealed driveway and she follows her through high metal gates and towards the large two-storied house at the top of the rise.

Annie

As she settles herself into the passenger seat of Sheila's car she gives a luxuriating sigh, and when Sheila gets behind the wheel Annie says enviously, 'Oh, I do love your car. The smell of real leather is just so special.'

Sheila laughs, 'Yeah, I love my car too. I think Silver is the favourite of all the cars I've owned.'

'You seem to change cars nearly every year so that's saying something. I think you've probably had six in the ten years since I bought my Datsun.'

'I think I'll stick with this one for a while. I really love it. But that's enough about cars. Doesn't Georgie look great? She just seems to get more glamorous with the years, and she still looks so young. It's hard to believe she's only a year younger than we are.'

Annie grimaces and flicks a stray lock of hair back from her face. 'You still look great too. I'm the one who's aged. I sometimes look at Jamie and Phoebe and Sam and can't believe I'm their mother. They're adults now, and seem to inhabit a different world and speak a different language. I'm only forty but I feel so old and dumb compared with them.'

'You're not dumb love.' Sheila takes a hand off the wheel and pats her friend's knee. 'You were so young when you had them, but they'll soon be off your hands and then you and Joel can have some time to yourselves. Mine will still be around when I'm fifty and Scott has retired.' She adds a silent, 'If he's still alive.'

Like Jenny, Sheila married an older man. Her husband Scott is fifty-five, and Mark's illness and subsequent death at sixty has caused Sheila to worry. Lately he has been stressed out by the abusive calls from his bitch of a daughter, and his health is being affected. He isn't sleeping well and is terribly depressed. At times Sheila gets angry with him for continuing to listen to these harangues, but doesn't want to put any more pressure on him than he's already experiencing. She just wishes he'd be more decisive for she still loves him. It had taken her such a long time to find him, and a lot of heart-ache before they could be together.

To banish morbid thoughts she changes the subject back to Georgie.

'Do you realise this is the first time we've seen Georgie in over four years?'

Annie gives a girlish giggle. 'That holiday we had with her when Ruth was around. We couldn't stand her and wondered what Georgie saw in her.'

'Not only did she seem a bit of an airhead, but she was so clingy. Constantly stroking and touching Georgie all the time, and do you remember how she'd give her great sexy kisses in front of us. I'd only ever seen women kissing once before in some film and I found it embarrassing. I think Georgie was embarrassed as well'

'That Ruth was certainly over the top. I think she may have been staking her claim; showing us she was more important than we were.'

'Well I found it all pretty gross. We've known for years that Georgie's a lesbian, and couldn't care less about her sex life, but the way that woman carried on was too much. She just couldn't seem to keep her hands to herself for more than five minutes. She behaved like a randy teenager. I was glad to leave.'

Annie nods in agreement. 'Me too.'

She is silent while Sheila drives the car expertly around a series of sharp bends, checking in the rear vision mirror to make sure Georgie is still behind them. Sheila's cutting remark about 'a randy teenager' has hit a nerve with Annie, reminding her of the derogatory comments Sheila had made frequently about Joel when they were courting.

When she and Joel first hooked up the other three had all been really bitchy. They saw him as a threat to their friendship; an interloper who was breaking up their quartet. She had found their attitudes hurtful, and eventually told them if they didn't stop slagging off about him they could no longer be her friends. They had all finished up in tears, and from that time accepted Joel as part of their group. He came with them to parties and dances, looked out for all of them if they were being bothered by some yobbo, and spent time with any one of them if they seemed to be being left out of things.

Annie glances sideways at Sheila's profile, noting her long thin nose and determined chin and the deep auburn chignon pulled high on her head. She is a stunning looking woman now, but as a teenager her features looked too big, her hair was a carroty colour and her face and body had been covered in freckles. Often she was the wallflower at dances and left alone at parties, and Joel had always been so sweet with her. They are still great friends, and greet each other with affection on the rare occasion when Sheila and Scott meet up with them for a night out.

'You're very quiet over there. Are you thinking deep dark thoughts about death and funerals and whether there's a hereafter?' Sheila raises a questioning eyebrow.

'No. Not at all. I was actually thinking back to when we were young and how mean you girls were about Joel when we first got together. Your remark about Ruth behaving like a randy teenager set me off.'

Sheila gives a deep delighted laugh and smiles at her friend. 'Well you did seem to find it hard to keep your hands off each other. I guess we were jealous and thought he'd take you away from us. Anyhow he handled it all so well, became a part of the group. I think eventually we were all a little in love with him, and he's still one of my favourite men.'

Annie smiles at her friends remarks and says fondly, 'He is a luv. He's always been so calm and capable. We had some rough times during our first years of marriage, but he was always my rock.'

She wonders if she has emphasised 'was', and hopes she hasn't, for she is not yet ready to confide in her friend how she really feels about Joel at present. She also doesn't really consider Joel was always her rock and wonders why she continues to hide her true feelings.

Annie had never confided in any of her friends about just how bad the first years of married life had been, and is dubious about talking about her current problems. Almost from the start they had known there were difficulties with Joel's mother, Margaret, but she had never told them just how bad things became.

When she and Joel told his parents that they were expecting a baby and were getting married she had lashed out at Annie; had called her a slut and accused her of ruining her son's life. Joel told her not to dare talk to Annie that way; that he wanted to be with her and was proud she was carrying his baby; that if his mother couldn't be civil to the woman he loved more than anyone in the world he would leave, and she would never see him again.

Margaret appeared to give in gracefully, but had harboured hatred towards Annie until the day she died.

Annie's parent's had been much more accepting of the situation. Her father only said it was a shame she'd have to forget about going to university and studying to be a teacher. Her mother said she knew how much Annie and Joel loved one another and was confident they would make a good life together. She'd added comfortingly that Annie could always go to uni later once she'd had her family. Her two young brothers accepted the news laconically that their big sister was pregnant, and looked forward to being uncles when they were only ten and twelve.

She and Joel finished their final year of matriculation and a few weeks later were married in the little church at the top of the street Annie had lived in all her life. Her mother made her a long white dress with a panel in the front that hid the rapidly growing baby bump. Only close family and her three best friends plus a couple of Joel's mates attended the wedding and the reception in the local pub.

The following year, while Sheila, Jenny and Georgie were enjoying the challenges and fun of being first year university students, Annie became a mother. Joel had planned on attending Agricultural College, but now would help his father on his farm instead, and she and Joel began their married life in a very small worker's cottage situated on the edge of the property.

Margaret was forced to accept the situation, but she made life hell for Annie. In front of her husband and son she showed a veneer of polite friendship, but when they were alone she never missed an opportunity to belittle or criticise everything her daughter-in-law did, and to bemoan the fact that Joel had been unable to complete his education.

Her reminisces are interrupted by Sheila saying, 'Almost there. Will you check and make sure Georgie turns in at the gates?'

Annie swivels her head around and sees the little red Corolla make the turn. 'Yes she's just behind us.'

Sheila pulls to a stop in the big parking lot next to the house and almost immediately Georgie is pulling up beside them. They get out of the cars and link arms as they walk towards the rather imposing doorway.

Georgie

As the three women walk up the wide front steps they see Stephen standing at the entryway to greet new arrivals. Next to him is a small, slim blonde girl in a short black dress. He hugs them each in turn then turns to the girl. 'Lindy, meet my Mum's three oldest friends, Sheila, Annie and Georgie.

Sheila gives him a playful punch on the arm and says, 'Enough of 'the oldest. We're her three best friends, and it's lovely to meet you Lindy.'

Georgie joins in the mild teasing. 'Are you too old to call us your aunties any longer?'

He grins, a bit self-consciously. 'Mum said once I turned eighteen it was okay. Annie and Sheila are cool with it.'

'So am I you big lug, just as long as you still love me like an aunt.' She gives him another hug then steps back. 'You've certainly grown up since I last saw you, and you spoke so well today. Jen must be very proud of you.'

He looks a bit embarrassed and brushes a hand through his hair before saying, 'Mum will be so pleased to see you three, especially you Georgie. She was saying how much she was looking forward to catching up with you again. She's in the front living room and Alec will get you a drink.'

The three women walk along a wide passage with Sheila leading the way. She has been a frequent visitor to the house and is familiar with its layout. Alec is standing near the doorway and as they enter the room he comes forward and gives Georgie a hug. Like Stephen he inherited their father's height, but he also has his rugged good looks. He will never be as handsome as his older brother, but once he finishes growing he will be a formidable-looking man.

'It's great to see you Auntie Georgie. It been years since you last came home.'

Georgie hugs him back, but feels a mild sense of dismay. Alec had always been her favourite out of all her surrogate nieces and nephews, and he now seems almost like a stranger. During her years of absence he has changed from the gawky, affectionate boy who she loved so much and who had loved her. He is now a young man and she has missed all those years when he was growing up.

She pulls away from his arms and says trying to laugh, 'At least you still call me auntie.'

He grins. 'You three will always be my very best aunties.

Annie steps forward and pats his hand. 'And you'll always be special to us. I'm sorry about your Dad sweetie. It must be hard to lose your father when you're only seventeen.'

She thinks how distraught her seventeen year-old Sam would be if anything happened to Joel.

'The last few weeks were rough. The doctor had assured Mum they could control the pain levels, but the old man suffered a lot and he wasn't the most patient of patients.'

The three women know he is trying to make light of what has undoubtedly been a horrendous time, but they can see the sorrow in his eyes.

He moves towards the drinks table and says, 'Now, let me get you something to drink and I'll see where Mum's got to.'

He pours a whiskey and soda for Sheila and a white wine for Annie before once more turning to Georgie and saying in an affected voice, 'And what can I get for you Madam?'

He grins mischievously and the smile lights up his face the way it did when he was a little boy. Georgie thinks, 'Perhaps he hasn't changed all that much.'

She asks for a white wine and then they follow Alec through the crowded room to where Jenny is seated on a long, black leather couch. She is surrounded by people, but when she catches sight of her friends approaching she leaps up and runs into Georgie's arms.

'Oh, it's so good to see you again. It's been ages.'

She disentangles herself then turns to the other two women and clutches their hands. 'You don't know what it means to have you all here. I have to circulate, but please, please stay until everyone else has gone so we can have a good long talk. You three are really the only people I wanted to see.'

She leaves and the three friends move to a clear space near a window.

Georgie looks around the room. 'I don't think I know anyone here except you two. And everyone looks so old.'

'I guess a lot of them are people Mark worked with and their wives,' Sheila says. 'Scott came to the funeral, but he left by a side door. He had to get back to work, and he also thought we four would like to get together without him hanging around.'

'Joel thought the same, but he also hasn't ever had much time for Mark. He's never liked the way he was with Jenny; thought he dominated her too much.'

'Which of course he did.' Sheila grimaces. 'I know one shouldn't speak ill of the dead, but he was also serially unfaithful. He didn't even try to keep his infidelities a secret half the time. Scott and I saw him out with other women on several occasions, and the way he behaved with them you could tell they weren't business associates. I'm sure Jen knew, but turned a blind eye to his carrying on.'

Annie feels uncomfortable. She too hadn't liked Mark or the way he had treated their friend, but this really isn't the time or place to criticise him.

To change the subject she says, 'Let's get another drink and go out into the garden until everyone leaves.'

Alec pours them each a drink and tells them there are nibbles in the next room. As they pass through the kitchen they each take a smoked salmon tart and a mini quiche from the long bench before stepping through the French doors that lead to a courtyard garden. Citrus trees flank one side of the area and a water feature sends jets of spray into the warm spring air. The three women settle on the padded seating that runs along one of the stone walls.

Annie sighs. 'Isn't this lovely. Those pots of bougainvillea and the trees covered in oranges and lemons remind me of some Mediterranean courtyard. Not that I've ever seen any except in magazines.'

Georgie, who has made several trips overseas says, 'It certainly has the look of some of the ones I saw in Spain and Italy. It's amazing what you can grow when you create the right microclimate.'

They sit chatting quietly while the sun disappears behind a nearby hill, and they hear people saying their goodbyes and the sounds of cars driving away.

Jenny comes through the door with a glass of wine in her hand. She is followed by the tall silver-haired man who had been sitting next to her on the couch when they arrived. She looks slightly tipsy as she walks towards them and says, 'Everyone's gone so you can stop hiding out. Frank's insisting I introduce him to my three best buddies before he'll leave.'

She giggles and pulls him forward. 'Girls, this is Frank. I don't know how I'd have coped without his support during the past few weeks. And Frank, meet Georgie, brilliant Sydney lawyer, Sheila, accountant extraordinaire and Annie, who with her husband has the most beautiful orchard and vineyard in the state.'

He bends and shakes each of their hands in turn before saying, 'Jenny's told me so much about you all, but I know you want to catch up so I'll leave you to it.'

'I'll see you to your car,' Jenny says and they walk away together.

There is a familiarity between the two as he holds open the door and Jenny smiles up at him that catches the attention of the three watching women. They raise their eyebrows and Georgie asks, 'Is something going on there I don't know about?'

'Search me. He was there the day after Mark died, but everything was in such a turmoil I didn't get to meet him. I thought he must be connected to the funeral parlour.'

Sheila chortled, 'Well somehow I don't think he's an undertaker. They look pretty cosy to me. Perhaps our girl Jen has finally taken a lover.'

'I don't think you should be jumping to conclusions Sheila. The poor darling's just buried her husband. She's been through hell during the past weeks, and it's good if she's had someone to lean on a bit.'

As Annie is speaking Jenny reappears at the door. They don't know if she has heard them gossiping about her and Frank, and hope she hasn't. After all if she has taken a lover she would have told them, surely.

Jenny

As Jenny comes through the door to the courtyard she hears Annie saying, 'it's good if she's had someone to lean on a bit.' She guesses they have been discussing Frank and her; probably wondering if he is her lover. Well they'll have to wonder for now. On this of all days she's not going to divulge something she's been determined to keep secret. No, she'll play the bereft widow for a while; at least for as long as she's able to.

She smiles and says, 'Come on you three. It's getting a bit chilly out here. Let's see what's left to eat in the kitchen and I'll open another bottle of wine.'

The kitchen is a long room with white vinyl cupboards, granite bench tops and stainless steel appliances along one wall and opposite is the wide preparation bench which is still covered with several plates of food. There are elegant steel stools topped with black leather along either side of this bench and Jenny says, 'Take a seat and I'll heat up some of these quiches and pies.'

'Don't worry about heating anything up. You must be exhausted and they'll be just as good cold.'

Georgie puts an arm around Jenny's shoulder and steers her towards a stool, then opens a bottle of wine and pours a glass for each of them. They clink glasses but no-one makes a toast; there doesn't seem to be anything to say that would be appropriate.

Annie looks through the adjoining doorway. 'Where have the boys got to? There's far too much food here for us to get rid of.'

'Stephen's taken Lindy home and Alec has gone up to his room.' Jenny sighs. 'He's too young to have gone through this; watching his father die and seeing him in pain. It's been hard on both the boys, but Stephen seemed to handle it better.' She rubs a hand across her eyes as though erasing a painful memory and says, 'It would've been so much easier on them if Mark had gone to hospital for those last ghastly weeks, but he was adamant about dying in his own home, and he always got his way. Oh, I'm so glad it's over. I just wish he could have died sooner.'

Her voice is harsh when she says these last words. Her friends find her tone of voice unsettling, and look at her with questioning, worried eyes.

'Don't look at me like that, as though I've said something I shouldn't. You all know he was far from the perfect husband and he railed against being sick the whole time.' She takes a long drink of wine. 'It's all been completely intolerable, and I'm glad it's over and I'm free.'

Sheila, who is sitting next to Jenny, pats her arm and says sympathetically, 'We understand love, and we're here for you. What you need is a change of scene. Go somewhere to relax and recuperate.'

'I thought I'd go and spend a few days at the beach house. I always feel happier there than anywhere else. The thought of escaping to there is the only thing that's kept me going through these past ghastly weeks. I've talked to the boys about it. They don't want to come, but they assure me they can cope without me around.'

'I should think so,' Georgie says emphatically. 'God, they're almost men.'

Annie looks worried. 'But you shouldn't be alone at a time like this. Would you like me to come with you? With Sam boarding in town and Phoebe on the mainland we've only got Jamie still at home, and he and Joel can batch quite happily for a few days.'

'Why don't we all come?' Georgie jumps up and pours another wine for everyone. 'It would be like old times, the four of us together again at the beach house.' She pauses, remembering that Sheila's children are still young. 'Can you get away Sheil?'

Sheila looks pensive. 'Oh, I'd love to come. It will take some wrangling, but they can do without me at work for a few days, and I guess Mum would help Scott out with the kids. She already picks them up from school most days. I'm pretty sure she won't mind hanging around until Scott gets home from work.'

'Right, we're all in.' Georgie claps her hands and grins. 'I've got ten days off work so I'm a free agent, but when can the rest of you get away?'

'I'll need to clear up a couple of accounts at work, and let Mum know what's going on, but I reckon I'll be right to go by the weekend.'

Annie grins. 'When I get home tomorrow I'll have already been away for a couple of days. They'll probably carry on about me gallivanting around the place, but all I'll need do is pack and perhaps make them a casserole or two to salve my conscience. Yep, I can be ready to go by the weekend.'

Georgie gets up and gives Jenny a hug. 'There sweetheart, it's all arranged. You don't have to go alone. And what's more I'm putting myself in charge of the catering. I'll buy all the food and wine, and Sheila and Annie will help me with the cooking so you can have a complete rest.'

'You're too generous Georgie,' Sheila says fondly. 'You can buy the food but I insist on the wine being my contribution. Scott is great buddies with a guy who runs a wine wholesalers and I'm sure he'll pick me out some goodies.'

Jenny looks around at the eager faces of her friends. She has been silent during the sudden burst of planning as she sees her plans for a quiet time at the beach house disappearing. She loves these three women, but at this time in her life doesn't necessarily want to be with them. There is no way she can say this though. They would be hurt, and wouldn't understand.

She forces a smile. 'You're all so wonderful. I'll go up tomorrow to air out the house and have the welcome mat out for you when you arrive on Saturday.'

'And it's time we left and let you get to bed.' Sheila stands, kisses Jenny on the cheek and then turns to Annie. 'You're not driving all that way home tonight are you?'

'No. I'm staying with Georgie at the hotel and driving home in the morning. Come on Georgie. We'd better be off and let this poor tired girl get to bed.' She kisses Sheila, gives Jenny an extra hug then says, 'See you at the beach house.'

As they let themselves out Sheila turns to Jenny. 'I'll be off too.' She pauses at the door. 'You were pretty quiet when we were doing all that planning. We haven't railroaded you into something you don't want to do have we? Perhaps you'd have preferred to go to the beach house by yourself.'

'No silly. It will be lovely having the four of us all together again. I look forward to seeing you all on Saturday.'

She walks Sheila to the door and watches as she expertly turns her little silver car and drives quickly down the driveway. She shuts and locks the door. Stephen isn't home yet, but he has his own key. Once more in the kitchen she covers the left-over food with plastic wrap, puts the last of the plates in the dishwasher and rinses the glasses before pouring herself a final glass of wine. She carries it outside and sits on the bench in the courtyard. The moon is full but dark clouds keep scudding across it creating a pattern of light and dark on the stone walls.

Jenny takes a long deep breath and lets it out with a sigh that is almost a moan. She feels so exasperated with herself. Why hadn't she spoken up and told her friends what she really wanted to do? But then how could she have turned them down? Annie's concern about her being alone was motivated by love and kindness and Georgie's wholehearted enthusiasm at the thought of them all being together again was so infectious. Only Sheila was sensitive enough to realise that it mightn't be what Jenny wanted to do. They have spent more time together in recent years so Sheila knows her better than the other two, but even she might not understand what she had originally planned to do once Mark died. Well it's too late now. They will have a girlie get-together and of course it will be fun, but just not what she wanted.

She sculls the remaining wine in her glass and goes to bed.

Annie

As Georgie turns the car and begins heading down the driveway Annie turns to her. 'Do you need me to navigate?'

Georgie laughs. 'Nah! One thing I have got is a good sense of direction. Once I've been somewhere I can always find my way back. You just relax little one and enjoy the ride.'

The Corolla hasn't quite the comfort of Sheila's BMW, but Annie is tired and soon finds herself drifting off to sleep. It has been a long day, for she had chores to do around the house before making the trip up to town. She'd also met Sam for a quick coffee in the little café opposite the college where he'd asked her to intercede between him and his father about what he wants to do. After that she'd spent a considerable time driving around the block before finding the entry to the parking area beneath the Sheraton. The emotional stress of the day has worn her out. Although she hadn't liked Mark much it was sad to think of him dead, for he was such a vital, energetic man. He wasn't much of a husband, but Jenny must have loved him to stay with him all these years, and the boys would certainly miss their father. He could be bombastic and domineering but he had seemed to be good with his sons and very involved in everything they did. Jenny had told her how he'd coached both of the boys' soccer teams, taken them fishing and surfing when they were young and attended all their parent/teacher nights.

Thinking of Mark as a father leads Annie to make the inevitable comparisons between him and Joel. Unlike Mark, he has been a loving and faithful husband, but when the children were younger he left most of the parenting to her. The farm has always been a seven days a week job, so

Annie naturally took the children to their weekend sport and to play dates. She also generally attended parent/teacher nights alone because Joel would be so tired by the evening.

She loves Joel; has loved him from the moment he first walked into the classroom at matric, a shy gangling boy from the country looking slightly lost amongst the more self-assured city kids. Her love for him is both passionate and maternal, and she admires his calm steady ways, but often lately she wishes he was a bit more understanding about their children's differing ambitions and that he would discuss things with her. He was very happy about Jamie opting out of going to agricultural college and joining him full-time on the farm, and couldn't understand why Phoebe was so keen to do the degree course in viticulture and wine making at the TAFE institution in Melbourne. He'd thought she could learn all she needed to know from local winemakers. Sam is doing brilliantly at matric and has told Annie he wants to go to university to study either engineering or architecture. He has tried to talk to Joel about what he might like to do, but Joel just fobs him off. Sam knows his father expects him to join him and Jamie on the farm and hates to disappoint him, but now he has enlisted her help to intervene on his behalf.

Annie has been sitting back with her eyes closed but opens them when she feels the car slowing and turning into the underground car park. As Georgie parks the car then gets out and opens the boot to get her case Annie says, 'I booked us in earlier and have the key card in my handbag so we can take the lift up from here. We're on the third floor and have a nice view over the waterfront.'

Once the two women reach the room and open the door Georgie throws her bag on the nearest bed then heads straight for the window. She stretches her arms wide and says, 'People rave about the view from my apartment in Sydney and I know it's fabulous, but somehow this touches my heart more.'

Annie laughs. 'Guess you're still a small town girl then.'

'Oh, don't get me wrong. I love Sydney, and at this stage in my life wouldn't want to live anywhere else, but so many good memories are tied to this place. Watching the yachts finishing in the Sydney to Hobart race, pub crawls with you three, going to the market on Saturday mornings and later lunching outside one of the restaurants in the sun with a sea breeze wafting in across the water; all good times.'

Annie looks pensive. 'Don't forget, I missed out on most of that. You shared those times with Jenny and Sheila when you were at uni together. I was stuck on the farm with a tiny baby, a husband who worked from dawn till dusk and a harridan of a mother-in-law.'

Georgie puts a comforting arm around Annie's shoulder. 'Oh Sweetie, I thought you were happy. You always seemed to be, on the few occasions when you escaped temporarily and came out with us.'

'I didn't like to moan to you three because it would have felt like I was being disloyal to Joel or criticising him, and I loved him too much to have you thinking there was anything wrong with him. Part of my problem was I wanted both lives. I wanted to be married to Joel and I adored our baby, but I couldn't help wishing I was also at uni and enjoying the freedom from responsibility you all still had.'

Georgie opens the tiny fridge and inspects the miniature bottles lining the rack. 'You look as though you need another drink, something to cheer you up. How about one of these tiny champagnes and we'll drink a toast to a resurgence of freedom. It won't be long before your three will all be making separate lives for themselves.'

The two women place the two comfortable chairs near the window and sit looking out as they drink the champagne.

Annie finishes her little bottle then stands and stretches. 'Well I'm off to bed. I want to get away early in the morning. I bet those two men of mine haven't done any washing while I've been away, or anything else in the house for that matter. On Friday I'll do some extra cooking, and then drive up to Sheila's on Saturday morning and go to the beach house with her.'

Georgie laughs, 'Annie the planner. You always were the one who organised things while the rest of us were inclined to just go with the flow.'

Annie flushes slightly and says defensively, 'Well you have to plan when you've got other people to think about.'

'I know love. And I guess I'd better work out what to buy for this jaunt of ours, and what to do with it once I've bought it. Tomorrow I have to go and see my mother, something I'm not looking forward to, and then I'm having dinner at Sheila's tomorrow night. You know I haven't seen Mia since she was a baby and now she's five.'

'Well that only leaves Friday for shopping.'

'Yes. I think I'll book out of here Friday morning, do the shopping and then drive up to the beach house in the afternoon. Jenny will be there by herself and she might need company.'

Annie grins smugly. 'So now you're organised too.'

The two women laugh together then walk towards the bathroom. They reach the door at the same time and there is an awkward moment until Annie steps back and says, 'You go first.'

While Georgie cleanses her face and brushes and flosses her teeth she can hear Annie moving around in the adjoining room. When she comes out of the bathroom Annie is standing at the window dressed in a long cotton nightdress. From the back she looks as young and slim as she had as a girl. Georgie is always amazed at how women's bodies can change so much during the childbearing months, and then revert back to normal. This metamorphous is something she knows she will never experience, and it fills her with wonder but not regret.

She puts on cream silk pyjamas while Annie is in the bathroom, reaches for one of the books in her case, and then puts it back. Usually she reads for a while before going to sleep, but perhaps Annie will want the light out. She lies back in the big double bed and thinks how strange it feels to be sharing a room with a woman who is not a lover; strange and a little bit awkward.

Annie walks from the bathroom and settles herself in the other double bed, turns off her bedside light and says with a luxuriating sigh. 'Oh, what bliss, to have the whole bed to myself. You don't know how lucky you are.'

Georgie switches off her bedside light and turns to face her friend in the darkened room before saying, 'I guess I take it for granted, but it can be a bit lonely at times you know.'

Annie just says, 'I guess,' in a quiet voice.

Her friend's brief and slightly guarded response makes Georgie worry that perhaps she has interpreted Georgie's remark as a come on. But then she thinks to herself, 'For goodness sakes, this is Annie. She's not going to take me the wrong way.'

Georgie has become ultrasensitive, for she has found how easily relationships can become complicated when you're gay. Often women with whom she's had an easy-going friendship have behaved differently with her when she's told them she's a lesbian. A few have unexpectedly come on to her and been hurt when she rebuffed their overtures. Most of her male friends have handled the situation well, although some avoided her after learning she is gay while others have wooed her, convinced they can change her by their persistent attentions.

She knows it is highly unlikely that Annie will have seen her remark as suggestive, but feels the need to clear the air. Turning towards her in the dark Georgie says, 'You've gone awfully quiet. Are you still awake over there?'

'Course I am. I was just thinking about what you said about being lonely at times. I was sort of surprised because I know you have a pretty full social life and have made lots of friends in Sydney. I just hadn't imagined you being by yourself very often.'

'Oh love, there are lots of nights when I'm home alone, and it would be nice to have someone to wind down with at the end of a particularly obnoxious day, or to share a nightcap and a chat when you return home after a night out to dinner or a film.'

'You've had that with several women though, haven't you?'

'Yes, but I've never been with anyone for very long, except Ruth of course. I sometimes envy couples like you and Joel. You've had the stability of loving and being there for each other your entire adult lives. Neither of you would know what it's like to be lonely.'

Annie sighed. 'Don't you believe it. You can feel lonely as hell when you have an expectation that your partner will be there for you and he's not.'

'But Joel's such a dear, and he positively dotes on you.'

'Yes I know, but he's not perfect. There've been plenty of times in the twenty-two years we've been married when he's let me down, and then I've felt so alone because I've expected support or understanding from him and haven't got it.'

Georgie stares across the darkened room and says in a worried voice, 'Things are okay between you two though, aren't they?'

Annie laughs. 'Yes, I guess so. We still love each other, and it's hard to imagine life without him, but we don't always see eye to eye. Anyhow, we'd better get to sleep. We both have busy days tomorrow. Goodnight love.'

Long after Annie is snoring quietly Georgie is still awake thinking about her friends. There is something not quite right about the way Jenny is behaving; something false and brittle, as though she is holding her emotions in check. Now Annie has hinted that there may be problems between her and Joel. Hopefully both of them will relax and share with Sheila and her any problems that may be bothering them once they're together at the beach house. After all isn't that what friends are for?

Sheila

When Sheila pulls into her driveway she is surprised to see the house in darkness. On the rare occasions when she goes out at night without him Scott invariably stays up until she is home. He hasn't been sleeping well since his first wife, Joan, died and their daughter has become so abusive towards him. She looks at the time on the dashboard clock, noting that it is only ten o'clock, and thinks, 'Poor Darling, he must be worn out to have gone to bed this early.'

As she opens the front door she hears soft music coming from the lounge room, and finds him sitting in the dark. A faint glow from the street light filters through the curtain and she can see the shape of him slumped in his armchair. She walks quietly across the room, thinking to wake him with a kiss, but as she bends down she sees that his eyes are wide open and that he is staring into the blackness.

'What on earth are you doing, sitting here in the dark darling? If you were tired you should have gone to bed.'

When she turns on a light that sits on the coffee table near his chair she sees the tumbler of Scotch in his hand and the half empty bottle next to the lamp. She is about to say something flippant about drinking alone when she notices his eyes. They are red and swollen, and it is obvious he has been crying, something she had never seen him do until recently.

'What's the matter Scott?' She leans forward and hugs him rather awkwardly around the neck.

'Vicki rang again. She gets more abusive every time she calls. She positively screamed at me on the phone; called me every insulting name she could think of. I just can't take this any longer Sheil.'

'I don't know why you keep putting up with it. Just hang up next time she calls. It's ridiculous for her to think that your leaving her mother more than eight years ago could be responsible for her getting breast cancer six years later.'

'Well I just don't know what to think. When she gets going about how I behaved I can't help wondering if perhaps I was somehow to blame. Joan was very stressed out when I left, but she seemed to pull herself together pretty quickly. At the time both Vicki and David seemed okay about it. They were old enough to see we weren't happy together.'

Sheila shrugs impatiently. 'For God's sake. They were twenty-two and twenty-four. You did what you felt was the right thing, and stayed around until they finished uni despite what it was doing to us. You haven't anything to feel badly about, and it's just not fair of Vicki to hang this guilt trip on you now. I've a good mind to ring her up and tell her to stop.'

'Oh, Sheila, it wouldn't do any good. And she was as drunk as a coot so she's probably sleeping it off now. I know I shouldn't let it get to me, but it does. She was all right when Joan was first diagnosed, but then they read some article about stress being a major cause of cancer. From that day both Vicki and her mother decided I was the cause of all the pain and suffering Joan was going through, and now I'm responsible for her death.'

'Well you mustn't let her get to you darling. David thinks she's being ridiculous so perhaps we could get him to talk some sense into her. If that doesn't work I'm getting our number changed so she can't harass you any longer.'

'Perhaps I am to blame though. Once they started making those accusations I did some checking on Google, and several doctors say that stress lowers the immune system and could be a contributing factor towards subsequent health problems.'

'Look, I know you think I'm being hard-hearted about this, but it didn't strike me that Joan was all that stressed out after you finally left her. She was dating before your divorce went through, and would have married that Carl fellow if he hadn't had a heart attack and died. Why didn't she and Vicki blame the stress of that as the cause of her cancer? No, Joan wanted to get back at you for leaving her, and at the same time turn Vicki against you. You've got to stop beating yourself up about this. Now come to bed.'

As she walks up the stairs and into the bedroom Sheila feels so angry. She's angry with that snivelling malicious woman and her benighted daughter but most of all she's angry with Scott and the way he is letting it affect him and their marriage. She washes her face, cleans her teeth and is in bed with the light out by the time he joins her. When he reaches for her she turns away. She hears him sigh as he turns over, and they lie rigid in the bed, back to back.

Long after Scott is asleep Sheila lies on her side of the bed feeling wide awake. For many years she hated Joan. She had known Scott was married from the first time they met, for he told her his wife had done the accounts when they'd only owned one shop. Once the business expanded and he had three men's wear boutiques they needed a professional accountant. The firm for which Sheila worked had been overseeing the accounts and preparing his tax returns for some time. When Mr Goldman, who originally handled Scott's account, retired his clients were split between the remaining partners. Sheila became Scott's accountant and shortly after his lover.

At the time she was twenty-six and fancy free. She had topped her year in accountancy at uni and been offered a junior partnership with one of the most prestigious accountancy firms in the city. She had also metamorphosed from a very plain freckly teenager into a strikingly attractive young woman. Once she reached her twenties her carroty hair darkened to auburn, her freckles faded and she had the height and figure to wear the designer clothes she could now afford. By the time Scott came into her life she'd had several lovers, but none of them were serious enough for her to consider marriage.

From the moment he walked into her office she knew she wanted him. Everything about him appealed to her; his tall, rangy body, the way his hair flopped over his forehead as he sat down, his dark hazel eyes and unwavering expression as he looked at her as he spoke and his long slim fingers as he pointed to figures on the accounts sheet. She'd noted the gold wedding ring before he mentioned his wife. Normally for Sheila married men were out of bounds for she considered marriage an all-important commitment. When she met Scott all her previous principles in this regard vanished.

He was her last client for the day and when he invited her for a drink she readily accepted. They went to a nearby bar and shared a bottle of red while they filled each other in on their lives. He talked proudly of his son David, who at eighteen had just commenced an economics degree and his sixteen year-old daughter, who was doing her first year at Matriculation College. Sheila knew from the start that he loved his children very much and felt very responsible for their well-being. She had also known Scott found her attractive and felt the same sexual tension building between them as she did.

When they got up to leave he held her arm and looked as though he wanted to say something, but then let his hand drop. They walked in silence to the footpath where he had shaken her hand and said, 'Thank you. It's been lovely meeting you.'

Sheila had wanted to grab his arm and say, 'Come home with me. Don't leave now when we're just getting to know each another.' Instead she'd simply smiled and said something daft like, 'See you next year at tax time,' and walked away.

She hadn't been able to forget him; had mooned around her apartment like a love-sick teenager, racing to answer the phone when it rang and being disappointed when it wasn't him. Before Scott came into her life she'd had several men friends who she dated, as well as enjoying nights out with girlfriends. Now she became almost a recluse, hurrying home after work in case he might ring and at night dreaming of him. She knew she was being stupid. She reminded herself that he was married with children, and probably thought of their meeting simply as a pleasant interlude, but she couldn't forget him.

Several weeks after their first meeting she came out of work to find him standing on the footpath. They walked towards each other and he put his arms around her. She had clung to him feeling that she didn't want to ever let him go, unaware of the curious glances from people passing by. All she cared about was that he was there and whispering urgently, 'I couldn't stay away. I just had to see you again.'

They went straight to her apartment and made passionate love for hours. Afterwards she made them omelettes, opened a bottle of champagne and as they ate they toasted each other, vowing never to be apart so long again. That was the joyous beginning of their love affair, but there was much unhappiness during the following years.

After they had been seeing each other for six months Scott told his wife he had fallen in love with another woman and wanted a divorce. Joan refused, saying the children were both at important stages in their lives where they needed the security of a stable home life. She played on his strong sense of responsibility, asked him whose happiness was more important his or his children's. She was cunning and manipulative and succeeded in making him feel guilty about their love.

This continued for years. Whenever Sheila became insistent that he get a divorce it seemed either Vicki or David was at a crucial stage in their life. At times she railed against the way he gave in to Joan's emotional blackmail; a couple of times she broke up with him, had called him weak and spineless and refused to see him. But always they got back together again and Scott would promise to file for divorce.

Eventually he did, and now they have been married for eight years and have their two beautiful children, William who is seven and Mia who is five. They had been happy years until Joan convinced Vicki that the stress of Scott's defection caused her breast cancer. Before she died she managed to create a rift between Scott and Vicki, and since her mother's death his daughter has become downright neurotic. Scott had been upset by Vicki's coolness towards him, but for the past three months that coolness has turned into hatred and she rings him regularly abusing him drunkenly.

When the abusive calls first started Sheila was sympathetic. She knew how he loved his first daughter and how hurt he was by her changed attitude towards him, but as the abuse continues and he has become more depressed she is getting angry. Sheila would like to shake the wretched girl for the grief she is causing, but she also thinks Scott should refuse to listen to her tirades.

After knowing and loving him for so long she is finally realising why Joan's emotional blackmail worked. His first wife knew something she has just discovered; that he is a weak man who allows others to manipulate him when he is faced with an emotional situation. She'd known how difficult he'd found it to extricate himself from his first marriage, but she had never quite understood why. Now as she is seeing him being emotionally manipulated and harassed by his daughter she is losing respect for him. Perhaps he is weak and spineless as she once accused him of being.

Annie

Annie and Georgie are breakfasting together in the hotel dining room. This is quite a novelty for Annie, and she has let Georgie talk her into ordering eggs Benedict. Normally Annie only has tea and toast for breakfast, and now she looks with dismay at the plate in front of her. There are two poached eggs sitting on whole slices of toast and covered in a creamy sauce. Besides this there are several rashers of bacon and some fried mushrooms.

'I'll never get through this lot,' she says in a slightly apologetic voice.

'You don't have to eat it all love. No-one's going to tell you off if you leave some.'

'Oh, I know, but I've spent so many years telling children to finish up everything on their plates I feel I should do it too.'

'Promise I won't tell on you, now just enjoy.'

Annie gives a little self-conscious laugh. 'I am a twit aren't I? Always the mother. It would be nice if I could simply be me again.'

'Hopefully once we get to the beach house you can be just that. It will be fun. Do you realise this'll be the first time we'll have been together, just the four of us, since that holiday when Jenny got her first car?'

'Yes, I was thinking that last night. How we'd said we would come back the next year but by the following summer I was pregnant with Jamie, and an old married woman.'

Georgie hears the wistful note in Annie's voice and reaches for her hand across the table. 'You and Joel are okay though aren't you? You were both so young when you got married and started your family, but you've always seemed pretty happy.'

'Yeah, we're okay, but there are a couple of problems at the moment, and sometimes it's hard to get through to Joel. Sam has been trying to tell him for weeks now that he wants to go on to university, but Joel doesn't listen. He thinks Sam should follow in Jamie's footsteps and join them on the farm, and he doesn't want to.'

'I'd have thought Joel would be pretty easy going about something like that.'

"Don't you believe it.' Annie gets quite a set look on her face. 'I had the same problem when Phoebe wanted to study viticulture at college on the mainland. Joel was firmly convinced she could learn everything she needed to know from vignerons in the district. It took a lot of talking to convince him otherwise. Fortunately for me Phoebe had done her homework, knew exactly what she wanted to do and which institute offered the most comprehensive course. She also plans on coming back to work on our property, helping in the vineyard and making our own wine, so Joel finally saw the advantages.'

'And what does Sam want to do?'

'Well, that's a bit of the problem. He's not sure. At present he's tossing up between engineering and architecture, so he can't put his case as forcefully as Phoebe could. All he knows is that he doesn't want to work on the land and Joel doesn't, or won't, seem to understand this, so Sam's asked me to talk to him about it.'

'I'm sure you'll be able to talk him round. Now eat up, and then we'd better get moving, you to tackle Joel, and me to try and get through a couple of hours with my mother, without feeling like strangling her.'

Later while Annie is driving home she thinks of Georgie's words, and considers 'tackle' was very apt, for it implies a battle of wills. She and Joel have had few arguments during their marriage. He grew up in a house with his quiet, gentle father and his harridan of a mother. When she was in one of her moods his father would take himself off to the furthermost part of the property until she calmed down. Like his father Joel usually shies away from any possible confrontation. Annie's parents never rowed so she hasn't learnt how to deal with disagreements either. This has led, in the main, to them having a very peaceful marriage. It has also led to many contentious matters being ignored on the surface, but some have festered.

She has never quite forgiven Joel for the lack of support he gave her when his witch of a mother bullied and blamed her for forcing him to curtail his studies. She was even more resentful after learning from Joel that he hadn't even wanted to go to agricultural college. He only told her this some months after both of his parents had been killed in a car accident; not a time for recriminations but she had always thought one of the things they shared was that they had both given up the opportunity of furthering their education because she was pregnant. She felt somehow cheated to learn it hadn't mattered to Joel, particularly as she had borne the brunt of his mother's recriminations for years.

Because he has made a success of the farm without the benefit of a higher education he thinks his children can do the same. Jamie happily followed in his father's footsteps, but the other two don't want to, and Joel refuses to see this. They had some minor arguments before he agreed to Phoebe enrolling in the viticulture course, even though she will probably return and work on the family property.

Sam wants something entirely different, and somehow she has to make Joel see this.

There is another problem festering away inside her, but this concerns only Joel and her. Over the years she has always put the welfare of her children first, so she will deal with Sam's problem first and discuss the other matter with Joel after that's settled.

As she drives up to her house through an avenue of espaliered apple trees Annie remembers how Jenny described the property to her friend Frank as 'the most beautiful orchard and vineyard in the state.' On this bright clear day it certainly looks a picture and a testament to Joel's long years of work and planning.

After his parents died he grubbed out many of the oldest trees and replanted with varieties more popular on the Japanese market. He espaliered these new trees to make pruning and picking easier and to simplify mowing between the rows. Next he turned some of the cleared land into paddocks where free range pigs now graze, and the final addition had been the vineyard, planted ten years ago and at last producing a profitable crop. They currently have their wine made by a local vigneron, but the long-term plan is for Phoebe to take over this task once she completes her degree.

In a way she can understand Joel's attitude that a university education is not an essential ingredient if one is to succeed on the land, but it might have prevented some of the pitfalls they experienced. He is inclined to say, 'You learn by doing,' but in saying this he is minimising the amount of research and study he needed to do before commencing each new project.

She parks her car at the side of the house, gets out and walks towards the steps that lead up to the verandah.

When she turns at the top she can see Joel and Jamie working side by side along one of the distant rows of apple trees. She smiles at the sight, for it gives her inordinate pleasure to see these two together. They are so alike, in looks and mannerisms, and also in their attitude to working on this land for which both have a deep and abiding love.

As she opens the front door her smile turns to a frown as she thinks once more about Sam and his plea to her to explain to his father that he doesn't want a life on the land. The problem is that at seventeen he knows what he doesn't want, but his ideas and ambitions of what he does want are still somewhat amorphous. He has tried to explain his feelings to Joel but his father always fobs him off saying, 'We'll talk about it when you finish matric,' or 'When you're a bit older you'll see what's the best thing to do.' Annie has seen her younger son turn away, a look of frustration on his normally cheerful face. Sam loves his father, but Joel's current attitude is creating a wedge between them, and she knows she must intervene before the barrier widens.

Sighing loudly she wanders into her bedroom where she unpacks her overnight bag and puts soiled clothes in the laundry basket. She changes into jeans and a tee shirt and walks barefoot into the kitchen to begin preparing a salad for lunch. Joel and Jamie will have been working for at least four hours by the time they take a break, and she knows they will be hungry. She makes a salad, slices big chunks of ham made from one of their own pigs and puts out pickled onions, cheese and her home-made green tomato pickles.

The two men walk through the back door as she is slicing a fresh crusty loaf of bread she bought at the local bakery on the way home. They are red-faced and sweaty from their exertions in the early summer sunshine. She kisses them both before they go off to wash up and she smiles to herself about how alike they are. It is almost as though they managed to produce a clone of Joel when they conceived their firstborn. Phoebe inherited Annie's blonde hair and dimples but is considerably taller, having inherited Joel's height. Sam looks like neither of his parents but takes after Annie's father who has dark hair and soft brown eyes. Before his recent retirement her father had been the top marine biologist with the CSIRO and Sam also seems to have inherited his fiercely enquiring mind. He is doing brilliantly at matric and should be encouraged to continue with further study, even if at present he isn't exactly sure whether he wants to study architecture or engineering or even a combination of the two.

Annie pushes thoughts of Sam's future from her mind, and when the two men return from the bathroom and are seated she passes them the bread and they all help themselves to salad and slices of ham. They chat about the work they are doing in the orchard, and Joel asks her about the funeral and how Jenny and her boys are coping. She tells them about the planned holiday with her friends and Joel jokes about her always gallivanting around. And it is a joke, for she rarely spends a night in town alone, and has never been apart from Joel for more than a few days during their twenty-two years together.

She spends the afternoon catching up with the washing, doing some tidying up and cooks roast lamb with lots of baked vegetables and an apple crumble for dessert. She knows Joel and Jamie will be hungry after an afternoon working in the orchard. Both of them have hearty appetites and seem to be able to eat vast quantities of food without putting any surplus weight on their tall, lean bodies.

After the meal Jamie kisses them both goodnight and heads off across the orchard to the little cottage where she and Joel began their married life. He moved into it soon after his twentieth birthday and is slowly fixing it up. He is engaged to Betty, whose parents own the adjoining property, and they plan to make this their home after they marry next June. She and Jamie have been sweethearts since high school, and the cottage has been their refuge from the time they were teenagers. Here they could escape the prying eyes of parents and inquisitive younger siblings when they wanted to make love. It is now recognised as Jamie's place, but he still has many of his meals in the parental home and is not averse to having his mother do his washing. She says she is going to give him a new washing machine as a wedding present, but she doesn't really mind.

After he leaves for the evening Annie loads the dishwasher and joins Joel on the couch where he is reading a book about organic vineyards. Phoebe has said this is the route she would like to take, and he wants to find out what changes would need to be made to their current practices.

When she sits down next to him on the couch he puts down the book and pulls her into his arms. 'You look tired Darling. Did you and Georgie have a late night?'

She curls into his side, enjoying the familiar feel of his body. 'Not really late, but yesterday was pretty full on, what with the drive up, meeting Sam for coffee and then the funeral and its aftermath. I'm looking forward to an early night in my own bed.'

'How was Sam? He hasn't been home the last couple of weekends. Is everything alright with him?'

Annie is feeling tired and had been looking forward to a quiet night. She had hoped to avoid the argument she anticipates will follow once she broaches the subject of Sam's future, but knows she must speak up.

'Actually he's not all that happy. The last couple of times he's been home he's tried to talk to you about his future plans, but you don't seem to want to listen.'

'What do you mean? Of course I listen to him, but he is still so young. He's always enjoyed working with Jamie and me on the farm. How can he be sure he wants something different?'

'Joel, you have to realise not everyone wants what you do. You've been so lucky to have Jamie who is completely happy to follow in your footsteps. But Sam's not like you two. He doesn't want a life on the land. He wants to design houses or bridges or castles in the air. He's young, so of course he's not sure what he'll finish up doing, but he is sure it's not farming. He loves you and doesn't want to hurt your feelings, but you're not listening to him. You fob him off about being too young to know because you don't want to face the fact that he isn't interested in working on the family farm.'

'How can he be so sure at his age? Perhaps he thinks he should go on to university because you've always told him how clever he is. My mother did that to me and I never wanted to go to agricultural college. Perhaps you're doing what she did to me.'

Annie can feel her self-control slipping. She doesn't want to argue, but being compared with her ghastly mother-in-law is just too much. During the early years of their marriage she had blamed and harassed Annie for ruining her son's life. At the time Annie had been angry with Joel for not speaking up and supporting her against his mother. Often during those early years she felt he let her down and after he told her he'd never wanted to continue his studies she was furious. This has continued to rankle with her as she had contained her fury at the time because his parents had just died and he was grieving. Now when he is comparing her to that domineering witch, and continuing to refuse to take any notice of what Sam has been trying to tell him for months, all those pent-up emotions rise up again and she loses her cool.

'Don't you dare compare me with her.' She stands up and feels herself shaking with fury that has been suppressed for too long. 'You let her blame me for preventing you from doing something you hadn't even wanted to do; weren't man enough to stand up for me or to tell her the truth. Now you insult me by comparing me to her because you don't want to believe that Sam wants something different from life. Well he does, and it's nothing to do with what I might or might not want for him. He needs to find his own path and you have to stop making it so difficult for him.'

She stalks across the room and turns at the door. 'You're the one behaving like your mother. You think you know what's best for Sam and you don't.'

As she leaves the room she slams the door, then goes to the bathroom and cries tears of anger and frustration.

That night Annie sleeps well over on her side of the bed and when Joel reaches for her in the dark she shrugs him off. For the first time in their marriage they don't cuddle up.

Georgie

After watching Annie's aging Datsun drive away Georgie checks her watch. It's not quite ten o'clock and she's expected at her mother's for lunch so has a couple of hours to kill. She crosses the street and wanders aimlessly through the main shopping mall. It is mid-November and all the shops are decorated with bells and baubles and streamers, and big signs touting Christmas specials.

Georgie isn't really interested in anything the shops have to offer; from the little she has seen the clothes are a season behind those in Sydney, and she isn't interested in buying a camera or computer or even a new CD. She passes a toy shop and thinks perhaps she should buy something for Sheila's two children. She always sends them a card with money inside for their birthdays, but it would be nice to have something to give them when she goes there tonight for dinner.

For a long time she wanders around the store. She picks up a game that looks interesting, but it says for eight and over and she decides it may be too hard. Aimlessly she checks out guns, dolls and fluffy animals, but has no idea what would be suitable for a seven year old boy or a girl of five. Eventually she throws herself on the mercy of a lively young shop assistant who actually seems to know what she's talking about. She says she has younger brothers and a sister, and suggests a thing called a Diablo for the boy, and assures Georgie she can't go wrong with a Barbie doll for the little girl. Georgie happily accepts her advice, and leaves the store with her purchases that the girl has gift wrapped for her.

Georgie still has at least an hour to kill so she walks down to the wharf area and wanders past the old stone buildings that were once warehouses but now house restaurants and galleries. She stops at a small café and orders a coffee. She goes outside and sits at a small table, sipping her drink and watching the people passing by. Sitting in this familiar place reminds her of the many times she spent here with her friends and she feels a brief sense of loss and regret that this is no longer her home. It's such a lovely little city and at times she misses it so much, but she knows this is stupid sentimentality. She also knows that here she would have had to face the unspoken discrimination that being different would bring, even though it might be hidden beneath a veneer of acceptance. No, she likes her life in Sydney. She has achieved a level of success in her profession that would have been impossible in her home town, has a beautiful apartment and a busy social life. Living there also gives her the perfect excuse for having minimal contact with her mother, and that suits her.

Thinking of her mother she checks her watch and sees it is almost lunch time and her mother is a stickler for punctuality. She finishes her coffee and walks quickly back to the hotel to get her car.

When she pulls up outside the nineteen-sixties bungalow where she spent the first two decades of her life she casts a critical eye over the faded and peeling paintwork. The squares of grass either side of the path are mown and the surrounding flower beds bright with colour. Obviously her mother is still interested in her garden, but the exterior of the house has a definite look of neglect. As she walks up the path Georgie decides to talk to her mother about this, and offer to pay for a tradesman to come in and paint it. Before his death her father always did this job; painting one wall each year during his time off work. Georgie smiles to herself because she has mentally used the same term her father did to describe his holidays.

Most people went on holidays but her father only had 'time off work.' To call it a holiday would have conjured up a time of leisure and enjoyment that was beyond his comprehension.

She no longer has a key to her mother's house and is about to knock on the door when it is flung open. Evidently her mother had been watching from the front room and has seen her arrive.

Her mother walks forward tentatively for a hug and as Georgie puts her arms around her she is surprised by how tiny the woman in her arms feels, and shocked to see how thin and white her hair has become during the five years since she last saw her. Her mother turns her face up to look at her, and Georgie is surprised to see tears streaming down her lined face. As she disentangles herself she is hit by the thought that she should have bought her mother a present; something tangible that she could keep and imagine was given with love. Instead she has bought only herself; has thought her presence would be sufficient, even though she knows in advance that memories of this visit may not be all that comforting.

Georgie's mother leads her into the dining room where the table is set with what Georgie knows is the best crockery. There are slices of ham and pieces of cold chicken carefully arranged on a platter and salads in the bowls that were usually only brought out for Christmas dinner.

'I got everything ready in advance so I wouldn't have to waste time cooking while you're here.' Her mother, the tears now surreptitiously wiped away, looks around the table with pride. 'Would you like a glass of wine darling? I bought a bottle especially for you, and the nice young fellow at the bottle shop said it would go well with a cold collation.'

Georgie doubts very much that the 'nice young fellow' would even know what a cold collation was, has probably fobbed her mother off with the first bottle he laid his hands on. She looks at the label and sees it is a very dry Riesling, and guesses that her mother, whose drinking has always been limited to a sweet sherry at times of celebration, will find it almost undrinkable.

'I'm sure it will be wonderful Mum,' she says and instantly feels hypocritical.

Once they are settled with platefuls of food and glasses of wine her mother asks, 'How's Jenny holding up? I sent her a card but I didn't think it as my place to attend the funeral. In my day it wasn't the done thing for women to go to funerals. It was considered unladylike. I suppose you and the other girls all went though.'

Georgie decides to ignore the implied criticism of her and her friends 'unladylike' behaviour. 'Yes Mum we all went; and Jenny doesn't seem too bad. Mark was evidently in a lot of pain towards the end and she just seems glad it's over.'

'Poor girl. So young to be a widow, but that happens when you marry someone so much older than yourself.'

Georgie spent years listening to her mother making seemingly innocent but snide remarks about her friends, so she changes the subject. She asks her mother what she has been doing lately and listens to a boring monologue about a visit to the Botanical Gardens with her friend Alice and of a rare trip to the cinema.

Georgie has seen the same film in Sydney and for a while they discuss it, but then there is an awkward silence. She really has very little in common with her mother, and the years of separation have strengthened this feeling of alienation.

She finishes her wine and pours herself another, noticing as she does so that her mother's is almost untouched.

The conversation continues, stilted and awkward. Georgie thinks, 'This is not the way a mother and daughter should be talking with each other', but there is nothing she can do to make it right.

'Where are you staying?'

'At the Sheraton.'

'You know you could have stayed here.'

'I know Mum, but I didn't want to put you to any trouble.'

'It wouldn't have been. Anyhow how long are you back for?'

'Probably another week. We're going to the beach house for a few days, Jenny, Annie, Sheila and me. Jenny was going, and we thought she could do with the company.'

'It will be nice for you girls to get together again. Will I see you when you get back?'

'Of course Mum. I'll drop in before I head home to Sydney.'

'Before you leave today there's something I want to give you. I found it a few years ago when I was sorting through the last of your Dad's papers.'

'You've got me curious. What is it?'

Her mother takes a sip of the wine that she obviously is not enjoying and says tentatively. 'Do you remember how I told you that you looked like your father's sister Joanna?'

Georgie nods and her mother continues. 'Well I found a photo of her and I'd like you to have it.'

After her mother leaves the room Georgie sits back sipping her wine remembering the day, so many years ago, when she first heard about her Aunt Joanna. She was about fourteen, and for a long time had felt she didn't belong with these people who were meant to be her parents. Except for being tall like her father she didn't look like either of them, and she already knew she was much more intelligent than both of them. For some years she had fantasised that she must have been adopted and one day she had got up the courage to ask her mother if this was so. It had been disastrous, for her mother had been deeply hurt; had told her in graphic details about the long labour she endured when giving birth, and had cried at Georgie's implied rejection of them as her parents.

Although Georgie felt guilty at causing her mother such pain and had tried to comfort her, she had still excused herself by saying, 'But I don't look like either of you, or feel the same way about things.'

Her mother had shrugged her narrow shoulders sadly. 'That happens in families. I know you don't look like either your father or me, and that you think you're so much cleverer than us, but according to your father you're a dead ringer for his sister Joanna.'

Georgie hadn't heard of this aunt before and asked about her only to be fobbed off with an abrupt, 'She died before you were born.'

Georgie had virtually forgotten about this long-lost aunt, but now is quite interested to see if she does in fact resemble her.

Her mother returns to the dining room a small snapshot clutched in her hand and thrusts it in front of Georgie, who looks at it in amazement. It could be a photo of her taken when she was about twenty, but she knows it isn't. It is black and white and old and crumpled. The young woman in the photo wears wide baggy knee-length shorts topped by a loose peasant blouse and on her feet are white old-fashioned sandshoes. Standing on a rocky outcrop smiling into the sun she looks a picture of health and beauty. She has the same thick mane of hair, big dark eyes and full curved lips that Georgie sees every day in the mirror. She instantly feels a bond with this woman and a sense of loss because they never met.

'You told me she died before I was born, but she must have been terribly young. What did she die of?'

Georgie's mother sits down again, rubbing her hand across her face as though wiping away some unpleasant memory. 'Your father told me she committed suicide when she was only twenty-two. She had gone to a rather dangerous surf beach with some friends. She swam out further than the others, but they weren't worried about her because she was a strong swimmer. Evidently she had continued swimming out and then just disappeared. Her body was never recovered. I hadn't met your father at the time, and he didn't like to talk about it. He told me she had been very beautiful and clever, but had never seemed happy. She was a couple of years older than he, and I don't think they were close. Your father said her suicide devastated their parents so much that neither of them lived for very long after her death.'

'Did he say why she committed suicide?'

'As I said he didn't like to talk about her, but I got the impression she might have been like you in other ways as well.'

Her mother falters as she says this and Georgie says angrily, 'You mean queer like me. You still find it embarrassing that I'm a lesbian, don't you Mum.'

'No, not really, though I don't understand the sort of life you lead. It doesn't affect the way I feel about you. You're still my daughter and I love you. Your father could never come to terms with you being the way you are, but he also worried that it could only lead to unhappiness for you. But you are happy aren't you? I couldn't stand it if you felt the way his sister did.'

'Look Mum, you may find this hard to believe, but I'm happy with the way I am.' She looks down at the small likeness in her hands and says, 'I'm surprised he kept this.'

'So was I. Anyhow, I thought you might like it as you look so like her.'

'Oh, I do. Thanks Mum.'

'Here, I'll get an envelope for you to put it in.' Her mother opens a drawer in the old-fashioned sideboard and fumbles around amongst the mess of papers, old cards and letters that have always been kept in this drawer. She pulls out a slightly crumpled envelope and hands it to Georgie who carefully slips the photo inside it before putting it in her handbag. As she does this she surreptitiously looks at her watch, but her mother notices.

'I suppose it's time for you to go.' She says this dolefully and Georgie feels the familiar sense of guilt her mother can always engender in her. She would in fact like to leave immediately, give her mother a tentative kiss and go, but she has only been here for a little over an hour and can't think of an excuse for needing to leave after such a short visit.

72

She knows she is a disappointment. Despite her mother's protestations she knows she isn't the daughter her mother wanted; one who was normal and got married and gave her grandchildren to enjoy like other women of her age. Her mother's lack of real acceptance of her as she is has destroyed what little love she once felt for this woman, for without acceptance there can't be love, but she will stay a little longer out of filial duty.

She picks up their empty plates and carries them towards the kitchen saying, 'I don't have to leave yet. Let's clear this up and make a cup of tea, then you can show me what you've been doing in the garden.'

They spend a not unpleasant time wandering around the garden, sipping their tea and talking about the garden. Georgie tells her mother about her small collection of potted herbs she has started growing on her balcony, and her mother suggests others she might like to try. When Georgie makes the offer to pay for someone to come in and paint the house she is pleasantly surprised that her mother accepts readily.

Georgie leaves at three o'clock, saying she has things to do before going to Sheila's for dinner. Her mother says to remember her to Sheila and Georgie smiles at this old-fashioned term she hasn't heard for years. Her mother is certainly still living in the past in many ways. They say their goodbyes, and Georgie is almost to her car when her mother comes running down the path, clutching the half empty bottle of wine.

She thrusts it towards Georgie, saying breathlessly, 'Here darling, you might as well take this with you. There's still half a bottle left.'

Georgie accepts the bottle graciously, gives her mother one final hug then gets into the car and drives away. In the rear vision mirror she can see her still standing at the gate looking small and forlorn, and knows she will stay there until the car is out of sight.

When she arrives back at the hotel she parks the car and takes the elevator to her room. It has been serviced and has the immaculate, sterile look shared by all rooms in first class hotels. She finds a cold wine glass in the mini-fridge, unscrews the cap on the bottle and pours herself a drink before positioning herself in an armchair near the window. She kicks off her shoes and breathes a sigh of relief to be once more alone and with the dreaded visit behind her. When she thinks back on it she feels it wasn't so bad after all. They had been awkward together to start with, but things had improved as the afternoon progressed.

She rummages around in her handbag and pulls out the envelope containing the photo. As she sips the wine she looks at the young woman in the photograph and once more feels surprised by the close resemblance and saddened by the thought they will never meet. She would dearly love to know more about her. Was she in fact also gay? She would have been a young woman in the fifties. Georgie knows that at that time homosexual men were treated like social pariahs; their proclivities were considered an abomination. Many were subjected to shock treatments to cure them of their illness, while others were gaoled for their criminal activities. Little has been written about lesbianism during that time, but it must have been difficult for Joanna if she was indeed gay. Despite these perceived difficulties Georgie doesn't believe her father's story about her committing suicide. She looks far too vital and positive to have taken her own life.

Georgie sighs for this lost aunt as she slips the photo back into the envelope. Even now, when there is much greater acceptance of homosexuality, she has encountered problems because she is 'different' and she can imagine how difficult it would have been for Joanna growing up in that time of intolerance. As she sips her wine and gazes out over the view of docks and water and distant yellow hills she wishes this lost aunt had lived. They would have been such a solace for each other.

After finishing the last of the wine Georgie showers and puts on a lightweight wool green dress and twirls a colourful scarf around her neck. She takes a jacket from the wardrobe, for although it is a mild late spring evening she knows it will probably be cool when she leaves Sheila's place. Before leaving the hotel room she picks up the presents she has bought for the children and smiles at the thought of seeing their little faces light up when they open them.

Sheila

As Sheila dashes into the kitchen and puts her packages on the bench she hears sound of childish laughter coming from the bathroom. Obviously her mother is giving the kids an early bath. This is one less thing she'll have to do before Georgie arrives and she feels grateful for her mother's thoughtfulness.

She had planned to leave work early but her last appointment went on for longer than anticipated. Realising she wouldn't have time to make a dessert she stopped at the patisserie on the way home and bought a French tart, rich butter pastry filled with custard and topped with glazed fruit. She takes it from its box and puts it on a plate before placing it carefully in the refrigerator, then removes the chicken that is now thawed and rinses it before rubbing the skin with oil and salt and placing it on a rack. She turns on the oven and peels potatoes that she puts in the bottom of a baking dish with a little oil and butter before placing the chicken on top. As she places this in the oven she checks the time on the oven clock and sees it is already six o'clock.

While she is crouching down getting carrots and beans from the crisper drawer Mia dashes into the kitchen and flings herself at her, nearly causing her to lose her balance. She drops the vegetables on the floor and enfolds her small daughter in her arms, enjoying briefly the feel and smell of this tiny person who she loves so much. William also comes over for a cuddle and Sheila's mother follows him into the room a doting smile on her face.

'They've been very good. Mia did a drawing for you while William read his home reader to me and now they're both nice and clean and looking forward to meeting their Auntie Georgie.'

After disentangling herself from the children Sheila picks up the vegetables and puts them on the sink before giving her mother a hug. 'Thanks Mum. I got held up at work. I don't know what I'd do without you.'

Her mother Chloe gives a smile that lights up her still handsome face. At sixty-four her face is almost unlined and there are only touches of grey in her thick black hair. Although their colouring is different there is a strong family resemblance between these two women. There is also a strong bond of love for theirs has been a happy mother/daughter relationship. Sheila feels her mother has always been there for her, reassuring her when she was a plain, gawky teenager, and giving her emotional support when she agonised over her relationship with Scott.

'I'm glad to be of use, and they're such good kids it's a pleasure to be with them. Helping you out gives me something worthwhile to do now I've retired.' She looks at her watch. 'But I'd better be off. Your father said he'd put on the dinner, but he really can't be trusted in the kitchen.'

She gives each of the children a hug and kiss and Sheila walks with her to the door where they kiss goodbye. 'Give Georgie my best wishes Darling, and I'll come and collect the kids at nine on Saturday morning so you and Annie can get away early.'

The children have followed them to the door and wave to their Nanna as she backs out of the drive. Sheila picks up Mia and holds Williams hand as they return to the kitchen. 'Let's do the vegetables together and then we'll have time for a story before Auntie Georgie gets here. Mia, you can wash the beans after I get them ready and William can scrape the carrots because he's a big boy now.'

'Do I know Auntie Georgie?' Mia was very shy as a toddler but has become more outgoing since starting school. She is still a bit wary of strangers though, and her pretty little face squeezes into a frown as she asks this question.

'She doesn't know you, but she knows me because she's my godmother.' William says this proudly, but he's not all that sure he remembers this aunt. She always sends them cards with money in them for birthdays and Christmas so he knows she likes them. He thinks he might remember what she looks like, but perhaps that's only because there is a photo in the lounge room of Mummy with Auntie Jennie and Auntie Annie and another lady who Mummy says is Auntie Georgie.

Mia looks a bit worried. 'Why isn't she my godmother too? Doesn't she like me Mummy?'

'Auntie Jenny is your godmother because Auntie Georgie wasn't here when you were christened. She came all the way from Sydney to see you though when you were born and thought you were beautiful.'

'But I'm big now and she mightn't still like me.'

Sheila hugs her daughter and says, 'Of course she'll like you. You're such a good little girl, and you've done a wonderful job with those beans. Now let's put them in a pot then I'll help William with the carrots. You can go and choose a book while we finish off here.'

The have just settled on the couch with the book when the doorbell rings.

'That'll be Georgie. Come on kids. We'll all go to let her in.'

William slides off the couch and runs eagerly to the door, but Mia hangs back so Sheila picks her up and carries her. They reach the door just as William opens it and there is a flurry of greetings. Mia hides her face in her mother's shoulder when she is introduced to the tall lady with the smiley face. She peeps out when the lady says, 'You must be Mia and you're as pretty as a picture. Do you want to see the present I've brought you?'

Mia nods shyly and Georgie turns to William and says, 'And I've got something for you too, my little man. My, how you've grown since the last time I saw you. You were just a little tacker and now you're a big boy.'

Soon the children are excitedly opening their presents and Sheila looks on benignly as Georgie helps William undo the tags holding the Diablo in place while simultaneously admiring Mia's Barbie doll. Georgie has always had a way with children; Annie's and Jenny's children adored her when they were little, and she already has Mia and William laughing and at ease with her. At times the three friends have commented to each other that it is such a pity she will never have children of her own, but they would never say this to her.

Georgie sees the open book on the couch and says, 'Come on kids. It looks as though Mummy was reading you a story. Oh, Angelina Ballerina, one of my favourites. Would you like me to read to you while Mummy finishes getting dinner ready?'

Sheila gives her a grateful grin. 'That would be wonderful sweetie. I still need to get the veggies on and I think I smell cooked chicken.'

She checks the chicken, which is indeed cooked, and removes it from the oven before putting the carrots and beans on to steam. After putting the chicken onto a platter and surrounding it with the potatoes she returns them to the cooling oven and starts making gravy. It is bubbling away nicely when she hears the front door open and Scott saying, 'Georgie, it's good to see you again.'

Sheila feels a bit nervous as she walks to the lounge room to watch this meeting. When she told Scott that Georgie was coming to dinner he had said how nice that would be, but there was a wariness in his voice. Her husband and this best friend have always been a bit uncomfortable with each other. Sheila and Georgie were sharing an apartment when Scott first came into her life, so Georgie saw the frustration and heartache that loving him caused her friend. At times Georgie had told Sheila to forget him and move on. She hated seeing her suffer, and because of this behaved coldly towards Scott when they encountered each other at the flat. Although that's so many years ago there is still a barrier between them, and he has never felt quite as comfortable with Georgie as he does with Annie and Jenny.

As Sheila watches from the doorway Georgie smiles up at him from the couch and says, 'Hi Scott. Long-time no see. I'm keeping these two little darlings amused while Sheila puts the finishing touches to dinner.'

He gives each child a quick kiss before turning to the kitchen saying, 'I'll see if she needs a hand.'

Sheila walks towards him and gives him a brief kiss hello before saying, 'Everything's ready, but you can open the wine while I set the table. Those bottles of pinot you got from your friend actually have corks, not screw tops.'

'Yes, you don't see that much nowadays. Evidently they come from a vineyard owned by an old Italian guy who still believes corks are better.'

While Sheila and Scott busy themselves with final preparations of the meal Georgie finishes the story. Both children want to sit next to her at the table and a chair is moved to make this possible. She feels a bit cramped, but really doesn't mind and cheerfully obliges when Mia asks her shyly, 'Will you cut up my chicken for me Auntie Georgie.'

William tells her proudly, 'I can do my own now because I'm a big boy.'

Scott and Sheila exchange grins, for it is not that long ago that he learnt this skill. Georgie is pleased to see their smiles for she had thought they seemed less affectionate with each other than they used to be. She thinks this is probably to be expected after eight years of marriage.

The meal continues with the children dominating the conversation. They tell their father about the new toys Auntie Georgie has given to them; Mia doesn't like her beans and has to be cajoled to eat them with promises of a yummy dessert and William brags about being the first one finished. The adults are pleased with their diversions. Sheila is still angry with Scott but doesn't want to show this in front of Georgie, although she thinks her friend may have sensed something is amiss between them.

When Sheila brings out the dessert she apologises for not making it herself and for a while the two women reminisce about the lavish desserts they used to make when they shared the apartment. One of the big things they had in common was their love of cooking, and during their years flatting together had experimented with many different cuisines.

Not wanting to be left out of the conversation William asks, 'Could you've made this Mummy.'

'Of course she could William.' Georgie grins down at the little boy's serious face. 'Just give us a cook book, the right ingredients and plenty of time and your mother and I could make anything. We were good cooks back then.'

'Mummy's still a good cook,' Mia says loyally.

'I know she is darling.' Georgie gives the little girl a hug. 'That chicken was delicious. I'm just saying that when we were younger we had more time to mess around in the kitchen and try out new things.'

With her mother's abilities recognised Mia returns to her slice of tart. She is beginning to take the strawberries and apricot slices from the top of her slice of tart with her fingers when Scott says abruptly, 'Don't play with your food Mia.'

'I'm not playing with it Daddy. I just want to keep the fruit for last.'

'Don't answer back Miss.' Scott scowls angrily across the table at his little daughter. 'And you're meant to be using a spoon, not your fingers.'

'Oh, let her be Scott. It doesn't really matter how she eats it as long as she finishes it all.'

'Why do you always let her have her way? It's time she learnt how to eat properly.'

'God she's only five Scott. She does a very good job for her age.'

Since the phone calls from his daughter began Scott has been more edgy around the children, and Sheila often finds herself having to defend them against what she considers to be unfair criticism. Often this leads to arguments, but she doesn't want this to happen in front of Georgie. Obviously Scott feels the same. He sighs and looks as though he wants to say something more but refrains. He remains silent through the rest of the meal. Mia picks up her spoon and eats the fruit with the rest of the tart even though she would have liked to leave the fruit till last. She casts worried glances at her Daddy while she eats.

Scott is sorry his edginess has put a damper on what had been an enjoyable meal. He knows how much Sheila had looked forward to being with Georgie again and having her meet Mia, and now he has upset both his wife and daughter. When everyone has finished their desserts as a peace offering he says, 'I'll clear up and put the kids to bed so you two can spend time together. Come on kids. Help Daddy clear the table and you might get another story.'

Sheila and Georgie carry their wine glasses into the lounge room and settle themselves down on the couch. Sheila kicks off her shoes and tucks her legs underneath her. She sighs. 'It's been a long day, and I didn't sleep very well last night.'

'You must have changed over the years. When we were in the flat it used to amaze me how you would be asleep the minute your head touched the pillow.'

Sheila sighs. 'I still could until recently.'

Seeing the sadness in her friends eyes Georgie asks, 'What's the matter love? Things are okay between you and Scott aren't they?'

'Oh, I guess so. There's something bothering him though, and he's letting it get him down. He's always been so good with the kids, but lately he's like a bear with a sore head; picks on them about little things like he did tonight, and we finish up at loggerheads.'

'Do you know what's worrying him?'

'Oh, I know.' Sheila sighs and takes a sip of her wine. 'Look love, I don't want to talk about it tonight. He'll probably walk in when I'm in the middle of telling you about it and think I'm being disloyal. I'll fill you in on what's been going on when we're at the beach house. Now let's change the subject. Have you worked out what food you're taking?'

'Pretty much. I thought I'd buy lots of steaks and chops for barbecues and perhaps a chicken and a leg of lamb to do roast meals when the weather's too cold to be outside. I'll also get heaps of fruit and vegetables and cheeses and pates. Is the Wursthaus still going?'

'Yes. And it's still in the same place.'

'Where's the best place to buy fruit and vegetables now. Remember how we used to always go to the market on Saturdays and buy from the Hmong's' stalls? Do they have any other outlets for their produce?'

'There's only one family of them left in Tassie now. All the rest moved to somewhere in Queensland; better job opportunities and of course a warmer climate. The remaining family still has a stall at the market, and I think they might supply some stuff to that big food store in Salamanca. They have a good range of fruit and vegetables there.'

'I thought I'd shop tomorrow morning and drive up to the beach house in the afternoon. Jenny was going up today and I don't like the thought of her being alone too much at a time like this.'

'I'd give her a ring before you arrive. Jen doesn't always like surprises. Annie and I should get there about midday on Saturday. Gosh I'm looking forward to it. I know I'll miss the kids, but it will be fun, just the four of us together again.'

Georgie smiles. 'The old 'Gang of Four'. I'm really looking forward to it too. I just hope the weather's nice.'

'It's not going to be as warm as you're used to in Sydney, but I checked the long-range forecast and it looks pretty good. There are showers expected later next week though, but if it gets too cold there's that lovely big fireplace in the lounge room. We can toast marshmallows on the log fire.'

'I don't think I'd like them anymore,' Georgie chuckles.

'Garn, of course you would. We do them for the kids some times, and they still taste as good to me.'

'So kids not only keep you young, they also help you retain your juvenile tastes. Anyhow I'd better remember to put marshmallows on my list, just in case.'

The two women are laughing together when Scott puts his head around the door. For a while he stands there looking tense and sad but then says, 'I've tidied up in the kitchen and put the kids to bed, now I'm off to bed too. Nice seeing you again Georgie.'

Before Georgie can answer he is gone. She turns to Sheila and says, 'What's wrong with him? I thought he'd come and join us. Surely he's still not holding a grudge against me because of how I was with him during your early years together?'

'It's not you love. He's probably had another phone call from that bitch of a daughter.' As she says this Sheila looks grim and angry.

'What's going on there?'

'Look, I'll tell you all about it later. I don't want to talk about it tonight.'

'Okay love.' Georgie looks at her watch. She is beginning to feel uncomfortable being in this house; thinks that perhaps Sheila and Scott need to talk about whatever it is that is getting them both so upset. 'Anyhow, it's time I hit the road. I want to get an early night. Busy day tomorrow.'

The two women walk to the door and hug and kiss before Georgie leaves. For Sheila the evening has come to an abrupt end, but she can understand why her friend wanted to go. Besides picking on Mia at the dinner table Scott has been totally unsociable. It's no wonder Georgie left early.

Sheila takes the two empty glasses to the kitchen, rinses them at the sink and puts the bottle in the recycling bin. She goes up the stairs and into her bedroom. Although the room is in darkness she knows Scott won't be asleep so she turns on the light. He looks at her and she can see he has been crying again. Furiously she goes to his side of the bed and pulls back the doona shouting, 'God, I've had enough of this. You're letting that little bitch destroy you, and us as a family as well. What do you think Georgie thought of you; picking on Mia like that, and then not even having the common courtesy to spend time with Georgie and me? Too busy listening to that whining woman abusing you on the phone. I've had a gut full. If you don't tell her where to get off and to stop harassing you by the time I get back I'll deal with her myself.'

She throws the doona back over him, turns out the light and stomps to the bathroom where she scrubs her face furiously, telling herself she will not cry. When she is finished in the bathroom she undresses in the dark and slips into bed. For a long time they both lie in the dark, not sleeping. There are only a few inches of bed between them but it feels like an enormous chasm across which neither can find their way.

Annie

On the Friday morning Annie and Joel are quiet and distant with each other. After breakfast Joel makes sandwiches and a thermos of coffee, he says because he and Jamie will be too busy to break for very long. She knows he is doing this to avoid further confrontation, and it only adds to her annoyance with him.

After he leaves she pours herself another coffee and sits brooding about their argument of the night before. She is still angry with him for comparing her with his mother, and feeling like this towards him is so alien she doesn't know how to deal with it. She had hoped he would apologise this morning, but obviously he just hopes his insult will be forgotten, swept under the carpet as any previous disagreements have been. As she walks to the sink to rinse out her cup before putting it in the dishwasher she sighs for she knows this is probably what will happen. When he returns tonight she will act as though his insult and her angry response had never happened, for neither of them knows how to deal with disagreements.

She takes some beef from the refrigerator to defrost, then makes a large egg and bacon pie. When it is cooked she'll slice it and put it in the refrigerator for Joel and Jamie to have for lunches while she's away. While the pie is cooking she decides to check out her clothes to see what is suitable to wear at the beach house. She opens the wardrobe doors and casts a jaundiced eye over its contents. Her three friends wear fabulous, expensive clothes, but she had never had much money to spend on herself. During the early years of their marriage Joel worked for his father for wages and after he died they ploughed much of what they made back into the property.

The children have also been quite an expense particularly in recent years when first Jamie, then Phoebe and now Sam have had to board in town while attending matric.

Her lack of an extensive collection of glamorous clothes has never bothered Annie, but she had felt dowdy compared with her friends at the funeral and wake. What does she have that is suitable to take on this holiday?

She pulls out a favourite dress that she bought a few years ago for a dinner in town with Sheila and Scott. It is a lovely silky fabric in a colourful abstract pattern and has a low scooped neckline and a wide, floaty skirt. It also packs into a tiny space without creasing so she puts that on the bed. They are sure to go to the only restaurant in the seaside town at least one night and it would be totally suitable for that. There are also a couple of long cotton skirts she wears when she and Joel have friends to dinner and they will come in handy with different tops. She puts her two best pairs of jeans and some tee shirts with these on the bed, and then begins rummaging through her drawers to find her one and only pair of bathers.

The nearest beach to their property is about twenty kilometres away so as a family they haven't spent much time there. There is a pool in the town where the kids learnt to swim and where they still hang out with their friends during the summers. Annie has rarely used the pool since her children have been old enough to go by themselves, so she hasn't worn bathers for years. She's not even sure where they are likely to be.

She bought them over ten years ago for a holiday at the beach house with Jenny and their children. Jenny had inherited the house when her father died and this will be the first time she has holidayed there since. At that time her two sons were seven and eight and Annie's three children had been eleven, nine and seven. Both of their husbands had been too busy to take a holiday and the two friends looked forward to a relaxing time together; at least as relaxing as a holiday can be with five children.

It had been fun. The children had all got on well together and spent a happy week playing beach cricket and making enormous sandcastles and swimming in the sea, which was quite a novelty for Annie's children. One night they took them all to the local restaurant, but most other evenings were spent around the barbecue.

Now as Annie searches for the bathers she bought especially for that holiday she remembers she had felt dowdy and matronly in them. They were a blue and white patterned one piece and had looked alright on her in the shop, but then she'd seen Jenny dashing around the beach in gorgeous brief bikinis. Compared with her she'd felt so drab. She had also secretly envied her friend's smooth, unmarked stomach, for despite having borne two babies Jenny had no stretchmarks, whereas Annie's stomach is covered in fine silvery lines which cause her to feel self-conscious changing in front of anyone except Joel.

While her thoughts have been busy she continues her search for the missing bathers and finds them at last, tucked away at the bottom of her underwear drawer. They are made of a flimsy nylon fabric and when she holds them up to the light she sees that they have a worn look around the bottom area and the bra cups have flattened from being crushed away in the drawer. She's darn sure she's not going to wear them in front of her friends.

Angrily she carries the bathers to the kitchen and pushes them into the rubbish bin before slipping into her shoes that are near the front door and grabbing up her car keys and wallet. She has always been so careful with money, putting the needs of the farm and the children in front of her own. Now she feels misunderstood and unappreciated by Joel and is still angry with him. For once she will put herself first.

She drives rather too quickly down the drive and along the quiet main street, where she stops outside the only shop in town that sell clothes. It also sells household linen and towels and has a large selection of wool and needles, fabric and patterns, for many of the local women spend what free time they have knitting and sewing.

Ruby Smithers, the co-owner of the shop, is standing behind the counter and Annie says a falsely cheery hello to her before making her way through the rather cramped shop to the women's clothing section. Here there is a small rack of swimwear, but as she looks through the collection she knows that she won't find the kind of bathers she wants here. There are a few pairs of plain Speedos, like the ones she wore when the children were learning to swim, and some hideous one piece suits in bright floral patterns. Ruby and her partner Jill are middle-aged country women and the stock represents their tastes.

When the children were young Annie bought most of their clothes here, but once they hit their teens they wanted designer jeans and trendy tops. She has continued to buy most of her own and Joel's clothes from this shop for she believes in patronising local businesses, but the children insisted on shopping at the trendier boutiques in town for their gear.

As Annie is walking out the door Ruby asks in an offhand way, 'Couldn't find what you're looking for?'

Annie answers with an abrupt, 'No.'

She knows she is being ungracious, but the anger she feels towards Joel is bubbling over into everything. Now she feels cross with Ruby and Jill as well. How can they expect people to patronise their store if they don't move with the times? They haven't undated the shop in the twenty-two years she has been living in the district, and must choose their stock from catalogues that are years out of date.

When she arrives back home Annie packs the clothes she has left on the bed into a small suitcase. She'll pack her toiletries tomorrow, and leave early enough to have time to buy new bathers in town.

The beef she left out earlier in the day has now defrosted and she cuts it into cubes before browning it with onions and garlic. She tosses the lot into a casserole, adds carrot cubes and capsicum slices and a tin of tomatoes before putting it in the oven on a low heat. It will cook away slowly during the afternoon and she'll serve it with potatoes and green beans from the vegetable garden.

Originally she had planned to prepare a couple of other dishes for her men to have while she's away. Now she feels she can't be bothered. If Joel thinks she's as bad as his mother was then she will be. Let him see what it's like having to fend for himself without her around. Jamie will be alright because he'll just go and have his meals with Betty and her parents if there isn't food readily available. She knows she's being childish, but his remark has cut deep and she can't forgive him, particularly as he hasn't asked to be forgiven.

Annie scrubs the new potatoes and puts them in water, then goes to her vegetable garden and picks the first of the green beans. After preparing them she collects the current book she is reading and settles herself on the couch on the verandah for a lazy afternoon. She knows there are chores she should be doing, but refuses to think about them. She's going on strike.

When the men arrive back at the house tired and hungry she is still engrossed in her book. Normally she would be waiting for them with a cold drink and the tea ready to go on the table. Joel goes to the fridge and gets out two beers before joining her on the couch with an amiable, 'Dinner not ready yet love?'

Without answering Annie puts aside her book and leaves the two men drinking on the verandah while she puts the vegetables on to cook and gets the casserole out of the oven. Through the open door she hears Jamie ask, 'You and Mum okay Dad?'

She fumes silently when she hears Joel say, 'Yeah, just something I said last night upset her a bit, but she'll get over it.'

During the evening meal the men talk about what they plan to do the next day. Annie doesn't even try to join in the conversation, but sits eating her meal in silence. Jamie is uncomfortably aware of a chilly atmosphere between his parents. As soon as he finishes his meal he leaves the house saying he is going to see Betty. He hopes that once they are by themselves they'll sort out what's wrong.

After Annie has filled the dishwasher and set it going she puts a cover over the remainder of the casserole and puts it in the fridge. She hears the sound of the news being reported on the television, pours herself a glass of white wine from the cask in the refrigerator and goes outside to sit on the verandah couch. She is being deliberately unsociable, for usually she and Joel watch the news together and discuss points of interest, but she's annoyed about what she overheard him say to Jamie. She won't just 'get over' being compared to his witch of a mother, for the comparison is so unfair. As she sips her wine she remembers all the times that woman ranted at her about how Annie had ruined her son's life. At the time she'd taken it, for she was young and pregnant and learning to adjust to a very a different life. This should have been her first year at university. She should have been studying to become a teacher, something she had wanted to do since she was in high school. She would also have been with her friends on a daily basis, instead of catching up with them about once a month when she went up to town. Instead she was being harassed by that woman on a daily basis. On the few occasions when she tried to talk to Joel about it he had offered her bland comfort. He hadn't wanted to see how difficult the situation was for her, and in the end she'd given up trying to make him understand.

She is brushing away the hot self-pitying tears that are streaming down her face when Joel comes out to the verandah and sits next to her on the couch. He puts a tentative hand on her shoulder and asks, 'What's wrong Darling?'

All the anger that has been boiling up inside her during the day comes steaming forth and she snaps, 'Don't you touch me. And you know damn well what's wrong. I'm tired of having to decipher what the kids want, I'm sick of the way you think you can deal with a problem by just ignoring it, and comparing me with your mother was the last straw. And you probably don't even realise why it was so insulting, because you never did face up to how ghastly she was to me. I'm going to bed now and you can sleep in Phoebe's room.'

As she is leaving the verandah she turns and adds. 'And you can get your own breakfast in the morning because I want to get away early.'

Later, lying in bed, Annie is unable to sleep because of the turmoil of emotions she is feeling. She hates that she has widened the gap that has opened up between them, for Joel and she have rarely argued during the many years they have been together. It would have been easy to accept his tentative approach; to have wiped her tears away, smiled falsely and 'got over it' as Joel had expected her to. This is what she has always done to prevent mild disagreements from turning into full blown arguments, but she is tired of always being the one who steps back; the one who makes allowances. Until yesterday she hadn't realised that the years of being the peacemaker have been slowly building up within her a sense of injustice, and it has only taken Joel's hurtful comparison of her with his mother for it all to come fuming out. She feels like a volcano that has sat quietly for years and is now erupting to spew out fire and bitter ash.

She hears Joel's footsteps in the passage; hears him pause at the door to their bedroom, and then continue quietly to Phoebe's room.

Georgie

Georgie wakes to a quiet knock on the door and looks around at the unfamiliar surroundings. She had been sleeping soundly and in her half-awake state it takes a while for her to remember where she is, and that she had ordered breakfast in her room before going out last night. Wiping a hand across her eyes she stumbles from the bed and picks up her silk dressing gown from the chair near the window. She calls, 'Coming,' as she puts it on and ties the cord around her waist. She opens the door and a small Chinese woman dressed in the hotel uniform smiles brightly up at her and says, 'Your breakfast Miss. I'll put it on the table for you.'

She walks lightly across the room, places the tray on the small round table and gives another bright smile accompanied by a slight bow before leaving the room and shutting the door quietly. Georgie wonders briefly about the Chinese woman and how she has come to be employed in this capacity. Usually service staff in this hotel chain are either home grown Aussies or migrants from one of the middle European countries. She muses that perhaps she is related to one of the chefs in the Asian restaurant that is part of the hotel complex.

Georgie removes the silver lids covering the various dishes and sees that the fruit is freshly prepared and the eggs and bacon are still hot. She hadn't wanted to eat alone in the dining room, but sometimes room service breakfasts can be a bit disappointing. With a contented sigh she settles herself in one of the chairs facing the window and eats the hearty breakfast as she looks out over the sparkling water and plans her day.

After completing the meal she showers and dresses in jeans and a light cashmere sweater before packing her case. She looks around the room one last time to make sure nothing has been left behind before catching the lift to the ground floor and checking out. Humming softly to herself she opens the back door of the little rental car and puts her case on the seat; this way there will be plenty of room in the boot for all the food she plans to buy. Georgie is feeling good; the day is bright and sunny, she is looking forward to shopping for treats for her friends and to the days ahead when they will be together again.

As she manoeuvres the car out of its rather cramped parking spot and joins the traffic on the one-way street that leads towards the wharf area she thinks about the time she has spent with them so far during this visit. She is a bit perturbed about how all of them seem to be, and wonders if she is imagining problems where none exist. Jenny isn't behaving in quite the way Georgie had expected, there is definitely something going on between Sheila and Scott that is damaging their relationship and even Annie isn't quite as contented as she has always seemed to be.

Georgie is thinking about what Annie had said about being lonely at times. Although he has always appeared to be the most loving and caring of husbands Joel has evidently not always given Annie the support she could have expected during their marriage. Georgie is thinking about this and the nature of loneliness when she realises she has missed the turnoff to the wharf area and is heading in the wrong direction. Fortunately she hasn't gone far and remembers there is a left turn that will get her back to where she wants to be.

It is still not quite ten o'clock and there are plenty of vacant parking spots on the cobbled road across from the shops and galleries. She feeds coins into the meter and puts the card facing out on the dashboard before heading towards the big food store where she hopes to do most of the shopping. Besides having a large range of fruit and vegetables there is a meat section at the back of the shop and Georgie is pleased to see that the chicken and pork are free range and the beef hormone free. There is also a section containing free range eggs and next to that are the milk, cream and butter.

By the time she has circled the store she has a trolley full to the brim. She has bought every kind of fruit and vegetable available, several large steaks, two packs of chops, a chicken and a loin of pork as well as eggs and all the dairy products she thinks they might want. After paying at the checkout she realises there is too much to carry and is asking if she can take the trolley over the road when a tall young man steps forward and says, 'I can give you a hand with those.'

Before she can refuse his offer he picks up several bags, so she collects the last three and follows him out of the store.

'Where's your car?' He smiles at her. 'You've certainly bought up big. Are you planning a barbecue?'

Georgie is feeling a bit overwhelmed by the way he has taken over, but he seems such a nice young man it would be churlish to be unfriendly. 'Several I hope. I'm going on holiday with three friends.'

She opens the boot and he stows the bags carefully inside before taking the ones she is holding and stacking them in as well. When he straightens up she thanks him for his help and he says rather cheekily, 'God, you're beautiful. I don't suppose you'd have a coffee with me? '

Georgie feels flustered. He is looking at her eagerly and she is grateful for his help, but she really isn't interested in wasting either his time or hers. Men often try to strike up an acquaintance with her, but she has never learnt how to turn them down graciously. Sometimes she just feels like saying, 'You're wasting your time buster. I'm a lesbian.' Instead she mumbles that she still has lots to do, before turning and walking away. She knows he will be watching and that she has been rude, but it can't be helped.

As she walks towards the Wursthaus she feels unsettled by this encounter. At times she gets thoroughly fed up with a world so full of heterosexuals and their expectations that everyone should feel the same as they. Even Craig, one of her dearest friends in Sydney, seems to think that one day the perfectly lovely platonic friendship they have might somehow change and she will find him sexually attractive. This attitude is spoiling what they have, but so far she has been unable to make him see this.

He does, however, take her rebuffs amicably which is more than can be said of other male friends she's had. At least two accused her of leading them on when she told them she had no sexual interest in them, and what she had considered to be good friendships finished abruptly. She knows men find her attractive and she likes their company, but after a while sex always seems to rear its ugly head. When she first heard about pheromones, back when she was about seventeen or eighteen, she remembers wishing that she secreted ones that were only attractive to other women.

She is still thinking about the encounter with the young man and wondering how she could have handled it better when she arrives outside the Wursthaus. She pushes open the heavy glass doors and is assailed by the delicious smells of ripe cheeses, ham on the bone and freshly ground coffee. When she lived in Hobart this had been one of her favourite places to shop. Everything is so good, but also so expensive. In the past, when Sheila and she were still poorly paid, they had shopped here very carefully, buying small quantities of pates and cheeses and home cured ham. Now she can buy whatever takes her fancy and she soon fills a basket with several different varieties of cheese, tubs of pate and some quince paste. At the counter she selects several different kinds of sausages and has the assistant slice off a kilo of ham from the leg that rests, pink and glowing on the cutter. She also takes a bag of her favourite coffee beans, watches as the girl puts it into the grinder and sniffs the air as the marvellous aroma is released.

When she returns to the car with her purchases she checks the time and sees she still has half an hour on the meter. She would dearly love a coffee but fears she might run into the nice young man again. So far she thinks she has everything she needs except for bread that she plans to buy it at the little country bakery she will pass on the way. She'll also get a cup of coffee there, for they have a small dining area.

There is little traffic around and it's not long before Georgie has turned onto the road that winds its way up the East Coast. She turns on the radio and flicks through the few available stations until she finds some jazz. Although she is not a great fan of this kind of music it is better than the various offerings on the other stations. If she'd thought about it she would have packed some of her own CDs. Too bad, this will have to do.

In less than an hour she has reached the bakery. She suddenly realises she is hungry as well as in need of a caffeine fix. Often when she's had a large breakfast as she has today she will miss lunch, but buying all that lovely food has wetted her appetite. It is years since she last drove past here but Joe's bakery is unchanged, and still smells as delightful as she remembers. She wonders if Joe is still baking or if he has moved on or died and new owners have kept the name.

The girl behind the counter is young and pretty and gives Georgie a big dimpled smile when she asks if she can help. Georgie orders a loaf of crusty white bread, a multigrain and several different kinds of buns and rolls, and then selects a scallop pie to have with her coffee. While the coffee is being made and the pie heated she takes her purchases to the car and puts them on the back seat, for the boot is almost full and she doesn't want to crush the bread. This done she returns to the bakery and sits near the window, watching the passers-by as she sips the good hot coffee and eats her delicious pie.

There are a few who are obviously tourists, for they have cameras slung around their necks or are busy taking snaps of one another. Most of the people she sees are locals, women in track suits or rather shapeless dresses, the occasional child going home for lunch from the nearby school and a couple of old men with fishing rods slung over their shoulders and buckets in their gnarled old hands. Sometimes when she is passing through a small town she tries to imagine what it would be like to live there. In a way it might be nice to know everyone you meet, to have space around you to grow your own vegetables and fruit, and to work at a job where you didn't have to worry about the competition or whether you could maintain the high standard of work expected of you. In reality she knows she would hate it, but sometimes it amuses her to consider this alternative life.

She has already paid and could just walk out when she finishes her snack. Instead she picks up her cup and plate and takes it to the counter in order to thank the girl who served her and to compliment her on the coffee and the pie. She is rewarded with another lovely dimpled grin and a cheery, 'So glad you enjoyed them.'

Georgie settles herself into the car once more and checks the time on the dashboard clock. It's nearly one o'clock and she only has about another forty kilometres to go so should arrive at about half past. There will be plenty of time for her and Jenny to unpack the car and put the food away, then have a swim and a nice walk along the beach before drinks, a relaxed dinner and time to talk. She drives at quite a leisurely pace because this is a particularly beautiful stretch of coastline and she has looked forward to seeing it again. There are several small beaches along this part of the coast and she catches brief glimpses of them through the silvery-grey needles of the she- oaks that grow here in abundance. In one place there is a rocky outcrop that conceals a small curved beach until the road winds steeply then reaches a plateau. From above Georgia can see there are black rocks at both ends of the silver curve of sand and huge dark blue waves roll in, smashing onto the rocks and sending lacy white spray into the sunny air. The place draws her to take a closer look and she parks the car at a spot where there is a pull-off, obviously placed there for people to stop and enjoy the view. She walks across a paddock of springy dry grass until she is standing on the headland above the beach. Looking down she can see thick coils of shiny kelp swirling in the dark water as each wave recedes after battering against the rocks. For a while she watches, mesmerised by the constant swirling and battering of the water beneath her. It fascinates her but also fills her with dread, and she realises she has wrapped her arms tightly across her chest as though to protect herself from danger.

Georgia loves to swim, either in pools or the sea, but she fears waters that are rough and wild. She likes to look at them, but shivers as she imagines what it would be like to be at the mercy of those wild waves and feels a brief surge of panic as she stares at the sea beneath her feet. Suddenly a cockatoo flies close overhead screeching noisily as though warning her not to go too close to the edge. It wakes her from her moment of panic but still she can't help thinking how glad she is that the waters below the beach house are more benign. Shivering and with her arms still clamped tightly across her chest she returns to the car.

From the point above the little wild beach the road is flat and straight and in only a few minutes Georgie has reached the outskirts of the little coastal town where the beach house is situated. She drives straight through and is looking for the spot where she must turn into the driveway when a long black car cuts across in front of her. She has to brake suddenly to avoid a collision. She catches a glimpse of a silver-haired man at the wheel, but the car is going very fast and soon disappears around a bend. Shaken by the near miss Georgie sits for a while to get her bearings, then realises the driveway to the beach house is just in front of her. Whoever the madman in the black car was he must have been visiting Jenny.

Georgie turns into the driveway and can see Jenny's car in the carport at the side of the house. There is a gravelled area next to it where other cars can park and she drives the Corolla into there. She steps out of the car and breathes deeply, enjoying the tangy smell of the sea overlaid by the sweet fresh scent of newly mown grass. After opening the boot she takes out the bags containing the dairy products and some of the meat. Jenny must have heard the car arrive for she is standing on the verandah. She looks a bit flustered, and Georgie is wondering if perhaps she should have rung and told her she'd be coming early when Jenny hurries towards her and hugs her saying, 'What a lovely surprise. I wasn't expecting you and the others until tomorrow.'

'I couldn't see much point in hanging around a hotel room for another night when I could be here, and this way we'll get a bit of time together, just us.'

'Let me take one of those.' Jenny reaches for one of the bags but Georgie laughs. 'I'm alright with these but there are lots more in the car. I've had a wonderful morning shopping and bought stacks of goodies. Let's get these into the fridge and we'll unpack the rest together.'

Jenny walks quickly in front calling out as she enters the house, 'Georgie's arrived early. Make that two glasses Stuart.'

When Georgie follows Jenny into the kitchen she sees a muscular young man dressed in brief shorts, a khaki shirt and Blundstone boots standing near the sink pouring wine into two glasses. An opened bottle of beer is sitting on the table. There is something wild and untamed about this man that reminds Georgie of the way Mel Gibson looked in the film 'Mad Max 3'. He has the same strong features and longish curly hair although he seems much more relaxed than that character had been. She is wondering who he is and why he's here when Jenny makes hurried introductions, 'This is Stuart Jones. Stu meet my friend Georgie. Stu's just finished mowing the lawns for me and is having a beer to cool off. I thought I'd join him with a wine, but now we can make it a welcome drink. Just pile that stuff in the fridge and we'll sort it out later.'

Georgie is concerned about the other perishables being left in the car and says, 'I think we'd better bring the rest of the food into the house before we have that drink. I don't want any of it going off.'

Jenny turns to Stuart and says with a smile, 'you'll bring it in won't you Stu?'

'No problems. You two go and sit on the verandah with your wines and I'll unpack the car.

He sculls the remainder of his beer and Jenny picks up the wine bottle and her glass saying, 'Come on Georgie. Relax and enjoy your drink. Stuart will look after the shopping.'

While the two women sit sipping their wine and Georgie talks about the trip up Stuart makes several trips back and forth to the car and brings in everything including Georgie's case. He is in the house for some time then comes out and says, 'I've stashed anything that would go off in the fridge and left the rest for you girls to sort out. I've put your case in the big end bedroom Georgie. Now I'll just put the lawn mower away and then I'll be off.'

When he is out of earshot Georgie turns to Jenny, a wicked grin on her face, and says suggestively, 'And where pray did you find that wild young man? He seems very obliging and friendly; quite at home around the place.'

Jenny blushes ever so slightly and answers a bit defensively, 'Yes he is familiar with the house and that's because he's a friend from way back; and I wouldn't call him young either. He's only a couple of years younger than I am. He's the son of the couple who looked after things up here for Mum and Dad. I used to play with him sometimes when I'd come up for the holidays. His father's got too old to care for the gardens and do the general maintenance on the house and Stu's taken over from him.'

'Okay, okay. You don't have to explain him to me. I was just teasing. He reminded me a bit of how Mel Gibson looked in 'Mad Max 3' and I suppose that set me off because you used to rave about Mel when we were teenagers.'

'He does look a bit like him, but he's nothing like that character though. In fact he's an uncomplicated, happy sort of guy. He's intelligent too, but didn't get much of an education because his parents couldn't afford to send him away to a decent high school. The local area school only went to grade nine and he's only done odd jobs around the district and a bit of fishing since leaving school. He's very good with his hands though and can fix anything.'

Georgie is tempted to make a teasing remark about Stuart being, 'good with his hands,' but thinks better of it. Jenny is after all a widow, and it wouldn't be in good taste to tease her too much about another man when her husband has virtually only just died. There did seem to be a very easy familiarity between her and Stuart though, but Georgie accepts this would be natural as they'd known each other a long time. She thinks perhaps she's seeing something that isn't there, the way Sheila had about that man Frank at the wake.

Thinking of Frank reminds Georgie of the near collision and she says, 'Incidentally, I was nearly wiped out at the bottom of your drive by a madman who drove straight out. If I hadn't braked hard he'd have sidelined me. Who was it? He looked a bit like your friend Frank.'

'It was Frank. He was in the area and stopped by to see if I was here.'

'Well he was driving like a mad thing. He came out of your drive like a rocket and was going like the clappers down the road.'

Jenny looks a bit embarrassed. 'He's usually a careful driver, but I think he had an appointment in town and was running a bit late.'

Jenny is not a good liar and Georgie knows her well. She knows her friend is hiding something, but for the life of her has no idea what it is. Perhaps Sheila's suspicions were correct, and there has been something going on between Jenny and Frank. Going by the furious way he drove away it looks like whatever it was may have ended, and Georgie's not going to spoil the afternoon by quizzing Jenny about it.

They finish the bottle of wine, and then spend a companionable half hour putting all the provisions away before changing into bathers and going for a swim. The water is cool as they swim across the bay. Both women are strong swimmers and they make a race of it to the end of the beach. Georgie finishes a couple of strokes ahead of Jenny and jokes about winning because she's younger as she offers her hand to help her older friend up onto the rocks. They lie on the warm rocks for a while, enjoying the warming sun and talking idly about what they will do during the coming week.

A light sea breeze ripples the water and begins to cool the air so they walk briskly back along the beach. They are both beginning to feel quite cold by the time they reach the house and head straight for the showers and to put on warm clothes. Georgie looks around the room she'd shared with the other girls when they came up here as teenagers. Until that last holiday, when they'd had a room each, they had slept in here together on two sets of bunk beds. Now there is only a queen sized bed and the room looks enormous. She unpacks her case and puts her clothes away in the wardrobe and drawers, her toiletries on the glass shelf in the ensuite and her books on the bedside table.

By the time she has completed these little chores the smell of cooking meat is wafting through the house.

Walking to the kitchen she sees that Jenny has already prepared a salad and is outside on the side verandah turning steaks on the barbecue. There is an opened bottle of Shiraz sitting on the glass-topped cane table and as Georgie comes through the sliding doors she turns and says, 'Pour the wine will you love? These will be ready in five minutes.'

'God, you've been quick. I'd have still been fiddling around washing the lettuce.'

Jenny laughs. 'You learn how to get a meal ready quickly when you have two hungry sons who're always on the go. Anyhow, I hope you're hungry. These steaks you bought are enormous.'

'I'm ravenous. It's amazing how a little bit of exercise and the sea air has stirred up my appetite.'

'You've had a busy day too. Doing all that shopping must have taken quite a while, and then the trip up. Now just sit back and enjoy your wine while I fetch the salad and some plates.'

The two women talk companionably while they eat their meal and drink the bottle of wine. Georgie comments on how different her room looks now, and Jenny says rather sadly. 'I left the bunks in there for a long time thinking they would be handy when the boys brought friends to stay, but that didn't happen much so I changed it a few years ago. You know you've got the biggest bedroom in the house.'

'My reward for doing all that shopping,' Georgie laughs.

Once the sun disappears from the sky there is a sudden drop in the temperature and they gather up plates and glasses and go inside to the warmth. They do a quick tidy up of the kitchen then enjoy a competitive game of scrabble before bidding each other goodnight and going to bed.

Georgie stretches her long body in the comfortable bed and sighs contentedly. She has enjoyed the day; shopping at her old familiar haunts, the pleasant drive up and the afternoon spent with Jenny. The only bad parts have been her moment of almost panic on the headland and her near collision with Frank's car. Why was he leaving in such a hurry? Jenny's explanation about him being late for an appointment didn't ring true. Had Sheila's supposition been true, and her arrival coincided with a lover's tiff or the ending of an affair? Of course Sheila's suspicions about Frank and Georgie's own idea that there is something more than friendship between Jenny and Stuart might both be totally wrong. They may be misinterpreting what are completely innocent friendships because of the way Jenny behaved when they were the girls of the 'Gang of Four'.

Back then Jenny was the most popular one in the gang. Wherever they went as a group she attracted male attention with her blonde hair, big blue eyes and petite curvy figure. She was also a terrible flirt, and would flutter her eyelashes encouragingly at any man around. Sometimes she had two or three boyfriends at the same time. Often a boy knew about the others, but would hang in there hoping she would choose him and discard the rest. She continued to be like that all through their time at uni, but when she met Mark the flirting stopped. She'd fallen for him hard and was thrilled when he asked her to marry him, even though he was years older and had been married twice before.

As far as Georgie knows she has always been faithful and loyal to him, even in the face of, according to Sheila, his numerous infidelities. Is it likely she would have acquired not one lover but two during the last months of her husband's life?

Jenny

Jenny dabs a rich night cream across her forehead, over her nose and cheeks and onto her neck and then proceeds to smooth it on with upward strokes. She remembers her mother showing her how to do this when she was scarcely fourteen and this has been part of her nightly routine ever since. Her mother was very pretty when young, and even now at sixty-two is an attractive woman. Since Jenny's father died she has had several admirers, a couple of whom have wanted to marry her, but she tells her daughter 'once is enough', implying that the love they'd shared was enough to last her a lifetime. In death her father has become some sort of a saint according to her mother, but Jenny learnt about his infidelities while in her teens and knows that far from being the perfect husband he caused her mother years of heartache.

She wonders why she is thinking about her parents and their unhappy marriage when there are so many more important things going on in her own life that need thought and attention. She is in such a confused state about the coming week. In a way a few days away with her dearest friends may be just what she needs after the months of watching Mark die slowly and painfully and wishing he'd just let go. During those last two months she often thought the sooner the better, but had had to go on pretending to be the caring wife. Now there are decisions she needs to make that can't be left to sort themselves out, but she'll have to leave them until this week is over. She feels she's been railroaded into spending this time with her friends, but perhaps they can help. She certainly enjoyed the afternoon with Georgie, for her easy companionship was a relief after the disagreeable visit from Frank.

His sudden arrival was a surprise and his fury at finding her there with Stuart was totally unexpected. He had been a marvellous support to her during the past ghastly months and she is very fond of him, but at no time had she thought of him as a potential lover. Obviously he misread her show of affection towards him and mistook her gratitude as signalling a possible romantic attraction. Now his feelings are hurt, probably also his male pride and she feels pretty sure he will no longer want to be her friend.

As she lies in bed she thinks about the day and plays over in her mind the meeting between Stuart and Frank. He had arrived just as she and Stuart were about to sit down with a drink, and she was getting ready to tell him her news. She should have told him last night but had put it off, not wanting to spoil the wonderful novelty of them being together after so many months apart. After knocking on the front door Frank had walked into the house calling her name. As she stood to greet him, wondering why he was there, he came into the kitchen and said, 'Hope I'm not interrupting anything.'

He had stood scowling at the door, obviously taken aback to see she wasn't alone.

For a second she was too surprised to speak, but then had run to him and hugged him saying, 'Not at all. Stuart and I were just going to have a drink.'

She made hurried introductions and the two men had shaken hands, eyeing each other off as they did so.

Previously she had told Stuart a little bit about Frank; that he was a friend of her husband and had been a wonderful help to her during the past trying months. Because she knows him so well she was aware Stuart would sense tension in Frank and wonder why it was there; wonder why this man who she had told him was just a friend was looking at her in such a possessive way.

Behind Frank's back Stuart had signalled to her that he would leave them alone to sort things out then said, 'I'll go and finish the rest of the mowing while you two have a chat.' He had ambled out the side door letting it bang behind him.

Once he had left Jenny turned to Frank and offered him a glass of wine before saying, 'What brings you to this neck of the woods?'

He had pulled her into his arms and said, 'Come on Jenny, we don't have to pretend any more. When you told me you were coming up here by yourself I knew you'd want me to join you. Now old Mark's gone we can let our real feelings show.'

He had clutched at her and tried to kiss her, and for a while refused to let her go when she tried to get out of his grasp. She was utterly taken a back for she had only ever thought of him as a friend. It had all been terribly awkward and although she'd tried to be tactful, had stressed how grateful she was for all the help he'd given her during a trying time, it was obvious he felt foolish for having misread the situation. He had responded angrily, accused her of leading him on, stomped out of the house and driven far too quickly down the drive. As soon as he left Stuart turned off the mower and re-joined her in the house, wanting to know what was going on. She suggested they have a drink and told him all about it. He'd opened a bottle of beer and was getting a wine glass for her when they heard a car in the drive. Thinking Frank might have come back she had hurried to the front door only to see Georgie getting out of her little rental car.

Then she'd had to pretend that Stuart and she were only friends, and she's not sure Georgie believed her. God, it had been a difficult day, and she still hasn't had a chance to tell Stuart she is expecting their baby but wants to have an abortion.

When she first learnt she was pregnant she considered not telling him at all and just going ahead and getting rid of the baby, but deep down she felt he had a right to be told. Although she thinks she knows him very well she is not quite sure how he will react. She is now nearly three months pregnant and has worked out that she must have conceived the baby during their last weekend together. Mark was back in hospital for what proved to be an experimental treatment that didn't work. She told the boys she needed to get away by herself for a few days after the months of caring for their father at home, and then days of being constantly be his bedside following his last operation.

Since that weekend she and Stuart hadn't seen each other until last night and it was so wonderful to be with him again she didn't want to bring up the problem of her pregnancy after being so long apart. She hopes he will understand why she must get rid of their baby, but fears he may not. During the three years they have been lovers he has often pleaded with her to divorce Mark and marry him. He hasn't been willing to see how this could affect her sons or to understand the lengths to which Mark would go to make her life miserable. Now Mark has gone, but how would her sons react to learning that their mother had been having an affair and getting pregnant while their father was sick and dying.

Stuart thinks nothing matters more than their love for each other, but then he has no-one else to consider. At times she feels so much older than he even though, as she pointed out to Georgie, there is only a two year difference in their ages. She has had so many more life experiences than he. She completed a university degree, worked in a high powered job, albeit for a short time, travelled widely and has been married for years and mothered two sons. In contrast he is undereducated, has mainly done manual work around the district, has never married or fathered a child and the furthest he's travelled was to Queensland for a surfing holiday with some mates.

Jenny sighs as she gets into bed, pulls the duvet around her shoulders then reaches out her hand to switch off the bedside light. She thinks about Stuart. They really need to talk and she had been hoping to get that chance today, but Georgie's unexpected arrival has put a stop to that. She hopes she managed to hide her feelings from her friend, but she had felt really pissed off seeing her here. First Frank and then Georgie prevented her and Stuart from having the talk they must have, and pretty soon at that. Now with the others coming tomorrow it will be nearly another week before she and Stuart will get a chance to be alone again.

She mumbles, 'Oh, why must life be so complicated?'

Annie

Normally Annie wakes early, but because she has spent a restless night it is eight-thirty by her little bedside clock when she opens tired eyes. She stumbles half asleep to the ensuite and stands under a hot shower until she feels ready to face the day. After dressing in good jeans and a blue, long-sleeved shirt she walks to the kitchen. Joel has evidently already breakfasted for there is a cup and plate rinsed and placed on the draining board. He can't have been gone long for the coffee in the percolator is still warm. Annie pours herself a cup, adds milk and sugar, then goes out to the verandah. She can see him walking through the orchard only a short distance from the house so knows he is deliberately avoiding her. He must have heard the shower going and left before he would have to face her and her anger, and it was probably wise though cowardly of him for she still feels misunderstood and cross.

After a hurried breakfast of toast and a second cup of coffee Annie rinses her cup and plate and places them next to Joel's on the draining board. For some reason that she doesn't quite understand the sight of them there together makes her feel sad.

Her case is packed except for toiletries and a couple of books she plans to take. She puts these in, closes the case and grabs her keys from the ring near the front door. It feels strange to be leaving home without anyone there to see her go, but she shrugs off this thought and is soon speeding along the highway to town. It is now after nine and she has to buy bathers before meeting up with Sheila at her house at eleven.

As she drives around the rather winding road she thinks once more of Joel, and her last view of him sauntering off amongst the trees. In a way she's glad he hadn't stayed around to say goodbye, but she also wishes he had thought it important to make peace before she left for the week; that he'd been able to bring himself to say the right words that would wipe away these feelings of anger that are making her feel quite sick.

She thinks back to the time when they were young and so much in love. She had absolutely adored him; had thought him perfect. He had also adored her and made her feel so special. When she had realised she was pregnant he couldn't have been more supportive and caring. This was why it was such a shock to her when very early into their marriage he hadn't stood up for her when that bitch of a mother of his began giving her a hard time. She remembers days when she had felt so alone and sad but he hadn't seemed to notice her unhappiness. 'I suppose I covered it up', she thinks, but still these last few months have made her realise she had never quite forgiven him. The problem is they have never learnt to discuss their problems calmly and sensibly as two adults should. Both of them simply vie away from talking about anything problematical. Has being so young when they married somehow stunted their ability to really develop a mature relationship? Perhaps you need to learn from your parents how to deal maturely with disagreements that crop up in any marriage and neither of them had witnessed this. Her parents had such a happy marriage. They seemed to agree about everything and she had never heard them argue. Joel's father had always just walked quietly away when he felt an argument brewing and Joel does exactly the same thing so nothing ever gets properly resolved.

She is engrossed in these thoughts and not paying enough attention to the road along which she is speeding, when she takes a sharp corner too quickly and brakes suddenly almost causing the car to spin. Her heart beats rapidly as she pulls out of the spin, and she turns on the radio to drown out unhappy thoughts as she continues more slowly towards town.

It is ten thirty by the time she arrives and has parked her car in the street on a meter. For once she wishes she had a mobile phone so she could ring Sheila and let her know she's running a bit late. Of course all the kids have mobiles, but she and Joel have never felt the need to own one. As she walks through the mall lined with expensive boutiques she thinks that if she hurries she won't be very late. She knows there is a swimwear shop somewhere here because Jenny and Sheila have mentioned it. Eventually she sees the shop which has a display of luxurious nightdresses and negligees in the window, and as she pushes open the heavy door she is assailed by soft music and scented air.

Annie knows that anything she buys here will be expensive, but she doesn't care. She has spent her whole married life being careful with money so that improvements could be made to the farm and later so the children could have what they wanted. This new, assertive Annie feels it's time she spoiled herself a little.

There is quite a large and varied swimwear collection and Annie soon finds several pairs of bathers she likes. The elegant assistant shows her to a dressing room and says to call her if she needs any help. The first pair she tries on is a beautiful aqua blue one piece with cut-outs at the sides. Annie had seen a similar pair in a magazine modelled by one of Australia's top mannequins and thought how lovely she looked. Now as she pulls on the bathers and looks at herself in the two-way mirrors she is thrilled. She regained her size twelve figure after having the children, but the years have added a couple of inches to her once tiny waist and she can't wear a bikini because of the stretchmarks on her stomach. This suit is more stylish than a bikini and makes her body look young and curvaceous again.

She tries on another one piece but it looks totally wrong, and then a two piece that has a bikini bottom and a top with a skirt that manages to make her look completely shapeless. Her last selection is a two piece that has a swirling white and gold pattern on a black background. The top has slightly padded cups that give her an amazing cleavage and the bottom just reaches to the waist and covers her stretch marks. It also has high cut legs so looks quite skimpy.

She is dressing when the assistant comes and asks how she is getting on and Annie happily hands her the two chosen pairs as well as the discards. When she comes out of the dressing room the assistant has finished wrapping her purchases and says, 'That will be three hundred and seventy dollars.'

Annie pretends to be unsurprised by this huge amount and hands over her credit card. She'd deliberately not looked at the prices, knowing they might have deterred her, but was determined to spoil herself just this once. As she leaves the boutique she can't help smiling to herself. Now she won't feel like the poor country cousin when she's with her friends, for she knows she looks good in both costumes. The retail therapy has done its job and she feels calmer and happier than she has for some time. As she packs the bathers carefully into her case she thinks of Joel; wishes once again they could have made up before she left. When she gets home she'll model the new bathers for him, and anticipates how his face will light up when he sees how curvy and sexy she looks in them. Then she remembers how he'd deliberately avoided her before she left and thinks perhaps she won't bother.

Sheila

When Sheila wakes she feels the weight of Scott's arm around her waist. During the night he has moved from his side of the bed to cuddle her, and she wonders if he had been awake or asleep when he made this act of reconciliation. She is sorry now for having spoken so harshly to him, but is sick and tired of the way he continues to try and reason with his daughter. Most of all she is worried about the affect these calls are having on him. Besides being edgier with the children he has lost weight and is not sleeping well, and Sheila fears he may crack under the strain. Last night, in her anger, she had threatened to talk to Vicki herself but she would see this as a last resort. She wants Scott to deal with his daughter; wants him to be strong enough to stand up to her emotional blackmail. If he doesn't Sheila knows she will lose all respect for him, and without that will love be enough to keep them together?

As the light edges softly through the closed blinds the bedroom door is pushed open and a rush of little feet announces the arrival of Mia. She is allowed into their bedroom once the sun is up and now she jumps onto the bed chirping happily, 'Time to get up.'

Sheila looks lovingly at this precious wee child and pulls her under the duvet for a cuddle. Her high happy voice has woken Scott and he looks across at Mia and says, 'Good morning Princess.'

She moves from Sheila's arms and squirms over the top of her and wriggles down between them before planting a kiss on her father's cheek. 'Morning Daddy. The sun's up.'

Scott hugs her to him and laughs. 'And so is Mia. Looks like we should all get up too.'

'Nanna said she'd be here early to take me and William to the park, so we gotta be ready.'

Scott looks at his watch on the bedside table and says, 'I don't think Nanna meant this early darling. It's only seven o'clock so there's still plenty of time. Tell you what. You go and wake William and I'll get up now and cook pancakes for breakfast.'

Mia says a quick, 'Okay Daddy', before sliding off the bed and running from the room. Normally William won't let her into his bedroom but now she has the perfect excuse for going there, and for jumping on him to wake him up.

Scott heads for the shower and Sheila is reaching for her dressing gown when she hears piercing screams coming from William's room. Still pulling the gown around her she hurries to her son's room and finds him holding Mia tightly around her body, imprisoning her arms.

'Let her go this minute,' she shouts as she advances into the room and pulls her screaming daughter into her arms. 'You know you're not allowed to hurt your sister.'

'She's not meant to be in my room.' William yelled defensively.

'Daddy said I could,' Mia says self-righteously as she snuggles into her mother's arms.

Sheila says sharply, 'Stop your arguing right now. Daddy's going to cook pancakes for breakfast and I want you dressed by the time they're ready William. And we'll go and see what pretty dress you want to wear today Mia.'

Left to her own devices Mia would put on jeans and a tee shirt, but today she's not going to get her way. Sheila's mother has bought her granddaughter several dresses and likes to see her in them. Mia is reluctant to choose, but finally makes a selection after Sheila tells her Nanna will be so happy to see her wearing one of the dresses she has given her. At five Mia is very pretty, with large hazel eyes, creamy skin with just a sprinkling of freckles across her small thin nose and a mass of red curls. From photos in her mother's treasured albums Sheila knows this is how she looked at five. Mia seems to be a carbon copy of her and Sheila worries about how Mia will cope when she goes through a plain stage as she did. All she can do is slather her with sunscreen whenever she is in the sun and build up her self-confidence. Now as Mia twirls before her in a yellow, full-skirted dress Sheila thinks she is the most beautiful sight she has ever seen.

By the time both children are dressed Scott is in the kitchen and Sheila sends them to him so she can have a shower in peace. As she stands under the stream of hot water she thinks it was a shame Mia came into their room before they'd had a chance to talk. Now they won't get another opportunity until she gets back from her holiday with the girls.

When she enters the kitchen Scott is turning the first batch of pancakes and the children are both shouting, 'I want the first one,' in unison. He looks harried and tired and snaps, 'If you both don't quieten down neither of you will get any.'

The children are instantly silent and sit at the table looking at their Daddy warily. It used to be fun to get breakfast with him, but lately he's been so growly and they are a little bit frightened of him. Sheila carries a plate to the stove and says, 'Daddy will put them all on the plate and we'll go shares.'

Pancake breakfasts should be fun, a treat to start the weekend, but today everyone is subdued and the children are careful not to take more than their share. Sheila thinks wistfully of how the whole atmosphere in the house has changed since Vicki began her harassing phone calls. She feels another surge of anger towards Scott for letting this happen, but tries to talk to him as though nothing is wrong for she doesn't want to worry the children.

She has told her mother about their problem and Chloe offered to have the children for the whole weekend. Her mother is fond of Scott now, although she had been quite hostile towards him when he'd strung Sheila along for all those years. Yesterday, before she left she'd said, 'The poor man looks worn out. Perhaps while you're away he could get out and play a round of golf with his mates or have a night at the pub; have a bit of down time, and see if he can get some perspective on how those calls are affecting him and the rest of his family.'

Sheila hasn't had a chance to tell him this earlier and now says, 'Mum's offered to take the kids for the whole weekend so you can also have a bit of time off.'

For a moment he looks nonplussed. 'What will I do without the kids? It's nice of your mother to make the offer but I don't particularly want to be alone.'

She sees this as a snide reference to the fact she is going away for a week and replies sharply, 'There's no need for you to be alone. Why don't you ring Harry and Ben and see if they'd like a game of golf?'

'I might just do that, and perhaps we'll have a night out on the town after the game.' He knows he has answered churlishly, but he is feeling judged and unloved. For years Sheila and he never argued, but now she seems angry with him all the time and he knows he is being impatient and bad-tempered with the children. Perhaps some time without his family is what he needs to help him decide what he should do about Vicki. Sheila had never got as close to her as she has to his son David and now only sees her as a troublemaker and lately as a drunk, but to Scott she is his daughter. He remembers her when she was as tiny and adorable as Mia is now. Later he'd been so proud of how well she had done at university and of her dedication to helping the disadvantaged in her position as a social worker. He loved the woman she became, but since her mother's illness and subsequent death she has gone to pieces. He is heartbroken at the rift that has come between them, but feels powerless to help her and doesn't know how to deal with her anger towards him.

He leaves the table and phones his friends who are both happy to join him for a game. After making the phone calls he goes to the garage to hunt up his clubs, for it is several months since he's had a game. He is checking to see that there are balls in the bag when he hears a car pull up in the driveway and opens the garage door just as Chloe is getting out of her car.

Seeing the golf bag she says with a grin, 'I see you're taking up my suggestion.' She walks into the garage and gives Scott a kiss on the cheek, then stands back and say, 'You're not looking well Scott. A day in the fresh air will do you good, and John and I are so looking forward to having our little darlings for the weekend.'

Scott had always liked Chloe and had been upset by her obvious hostility towards him during the years when he was still married to his first wife. Those feeling disappeared long ago and now they are good friends. She is only nine years older than he and he loves her more as an older sister than a mother-in-law. He puts an arm around her shoulder and says earnestly, 'Thanks Chloe, for thinking of me and for all you do for us. I don't know how we'd cope without your help with the kids.'

'You know how much I enjoy them.' She begins walking towards the front door then turns, 'And I'm only too happy to pick them up from school next week while Sheila's away. If you're lucky I might even cook dinner for you a couple of nights.'

As soon as she enters the house she is swamped by the children. Mia wants to be admired in her dress and William is anxious to know if he can take his new Diablo with him to Nanna's house. She tells Mia how lovely she looks and reassures William before pouring a cup of coffee and sitting down at the kitchen table where Sheila is finishing her second for the day.

Looking up at her mother she says, 'You're here earlier than I expected. I haven't even packed the kids clothes yet.'

'That's okay love. I'll help them with that after I've had my coffee, and that'll leave you free to get yourself packed and ready. I think it's great that you girls are going to get some time together, and you know how I love having my little darlings to stay.' Mia has come and stood beside her grandmother's chair and Chloe gives her a hug as she says this. 'We're going to have a great time. First we're going to the playground, and then Poppy is joining us for lunch at MacDonald's. After lunch we thought you might like to go for a game of mini golf.'

The children whoop with pleasure at the thought of the day ahead and Sheila says 'Well just don't let them tire you and Dad out.'

Her mother grins, 'We may have had to wait a while to become grandparents, but we're not in our dotage, and your father enjoys being around the kids as much as I do.' She finishes her coffee and rinses the cup in the sink before taking each child by the hand and saying, 'Now let's go and see what you need to take, and your Mum can get on with her packing.'

Sheila retrieves her case from the top shelf in her wardrobe and starts to pack the clothes she has planned to take. She can hear the eager voices of her children chatting away happily and her mother laugh at something William says. Although her parents were older than many of their friends when they became grandparents they are both fit and energetic enough to keep up with their lively grandchildren. During the years when Scott had 'strung Sheila along' as Chloe put it she bemoaned the fact that she'd never be a grandmother because Sheila was in a dead-end relationship and her younger brother Ben appeared happy to be a perennial bachelor. She was thrilled when Sheila and Scott married and finally gave her two beautiful grandchildren. Eventually, at thirty-five, Ben met Jillian and married her after a whirlwind courtship. Now, three years later, she is expecting their second child. Chloe is happy at the prospect of having another grandchild, but William and Mia will always be special because he was the first and Mia is so like Sheila was as a little girl it's like having her daughter back again.

While Sheila is busy in her bedroom she hears the door from the garage into the house bang and Scott shouts up the stairs, 'I'll be off. I have to meet the guys in ten minutes. Be good for Nanna kids and have a nice time Sheil.'

She hears the front door shut and goes to run down the stairs to say a proper goodbye to him, but just then the children and her mother come out of William's room talking and laughing, and she is caught up with their chatter. They all go down the stairs together. She kisses and hugs her children and mother before helping to pack their bags in the boot and fasten the children into the car seats that are a permanent fixture in her mother's car. With a last kiss for each child through the windows Sheila steps back and her mother drives off. Suddenly she feels bereft.

Annie

After parking her car in the street outside Sheila's house Annie gets her bag from the boot and walks to the front door. She rings the doorbell then pushes the door open calling as she enters the passage, 'Hello there. Where are you Sheila?'

When there is no answer she walks towards the kitchen and opening the door finds Sheila seated at the table, a cup of coffee held tightly between her hands and a rather woebegone expression on her face. As Annie comes into the room she puts down the cup and stands to give her friend a hug, apologising as she does. 'Sorry, I didn't hear the bell. My thoughts were a million miles away. Sit down love and I'll get you a coffee.'

'You were looking so sad. What's up? Not having second thoughts about leaving Scott and the kids for a week of girl-time are you?'

Sheila puts Annie's coffee on the table and sighs. 'No it's not that. I'm really looking forward to having some time away with you three, and Mum's helping out with the kids so I know they'll be alright,'

'So what was it then that was causing you to look so down in the mouth when I came in?'

'Oh, I had a row with Scott last night and we didn't get a chance to sort things out this morning.'

Annie grins. 'Well believe it or not the same thing happened with Joel and me. We had a humdinger of a row and he deliberately avoided seeing me this morning before I left. I was so furious I've gone berserk with the credit card and bought the two most expensive pairs of bathers I've ever owned. Probably the two most expensive items of clothing I've ever owned. They're absolutely gorgeous and I feel a whole lot better. It's amazing what a little retail therapy can do.'

Sheila laughs. 'Good on you girl. You've always skimped on yourself as far as clothes go. I think it's great that you've finally lashed out and spoiled yourself a bit.'

'This may be the start of a whole new me. I've spent years scrimping and saving so the kids could have everything they wanted and so continual improvements could be made to the farm, and now I feel Joel hasn't ever really appreciated me enough. Despite the retail therapy I'm still pissed off with him.'

'Well I feel the same way about Scott at the moment so it's probably a good time to get away from them. Let them stew in their own juices for a while and see how they get on without us. So, finish that coffee while I get my case from upstairs and then we'll hit the road.'

When Sheila opens the boot of her car to put in their cases she sees the wine. Scott had bought it home the previous evening and left it in the garage. Despite their argument he had thought to pack it in the car for her before he left to play golf. She thinks, 'How sweet of him,' but then decides it was the least he could do, considering how he has been behaving during the past few months.

While Sheila manoeuvres her silver BMW out of the garage and onto the street she turns to Annie and asks, 'Would you like to park your car in the garage? There's plenty of room for Scott to fit in behind yours.'

'No I don't mind it being on the street. I can't imagine anyone wanting to steal it.' As Annie settles comfortably in the passenger seat she is wondering if she should ask Sheila about the row with Scott but then thinks better of it. She hadn't seemed to want to talk about it, and Annie doesn't particularly want to discuss her argument with Joel.

As she is thinking this Sheila checks the dash board clock and says, 'Only ten thirty. We should be at the beach house by lunch time.

Remembering their conversation at the hotel Annie says, 'Georgie will already be there because she was going up yesterday, as soon as she'd finished the shopping. She thought Jenny might be lonely there by herself and was going early to surprise her'

'Yes I know, but I don't know whether that was wise.' Sheila looks across at Annie, a frown on her face. 'I actually got the impression Jenny wouldn't have minded being alone for a while.'

Annie looks worried. 'Do you mean she doesn't really want us there with her?'

'I'm not sure. I don't know whether I read her wrongly, but she was very quiet when it was first suggested.'

'Now I feel terrible because it was my idea. I thought she shouldn't be alone.'

'Don't beat yourself up about it. You suggested it and then Georgie and I joined in. I'm sure Jenny's okay about us coming, it's just that at the time I felt we'd sort of railroaded her into something she hadn't necessarily planned on doing.' She looks across at Annie's worried face and says, 'Cheer up love. It was a great idea and we're going to have a wonderful time. Now push play on the CD player.'

The song 'I Had the Time of my Life,' bursts forth, filling the car with music and bringing a smile to Annie's face. 'Where on earth did you get a copy of that CD? Don't tell me you've kept one all these years.'

'Nah!' Sheila grins. 'I actually found it at the market plus a whole lot of others from the Eighties and I couldn't resist them.'

Annie joins in tentatively with the chorus, but then they replay it and sing all the words at the top of their voices.

When the song finishes Sheila says, 'Check out what else I've got in that slot behind the gear stick.'

Annie pulls out a stack of CDs and reads then off excitedly, 'Madonna, Prince, Whitney, Crowded House, U2. Oh my God, you've got all our old favourites. Jenny and Georgie are going to love them.'

They spend the rest of the trip playing music, joining in with some of the songs of their youth; the ones they can still remember. By the time they arrive at the beach house they are feeling as young and carefree as teenagers, and all thoughts of worrying or unreasonable husbands have been left behind, at least for the moment.

They put on their favourite just before they get there and drive up to the house singing at the top of their voices, 'We had the time of our lives.' They are so loud Jenny and Georgie hear them from inside the house and come running to greet them. There is a flurry of hugs and kisses before everyone takes something from the boot. Sheila and Annie take their cases and the others follow with the wine.

Once inside Jenny shows them to their rooms and Georgie unpacks some of the bottles of white wine and stashes them in the fridge. While the other two unpack Georgie puts the finishing touches to the salads they had been preparing and Jenny goes out to the deck and lights the barbecue. By the time Sheila and Annie join them lunch is almost ready and Georgie opens the bottle of champagne she bought especially for this moment and pours four glasses.

The Beach House 2011

As they sit beneath the awning in comfortable cane chairs they drink a toast to friendship, to being here together and to the fun they will have in the coming week. Annie looks around at the smiling faces of these her oldest and dearest friends and feels happy and relaxed. Jenny looks just as happy as the other two, and Annie feels reassured that she hasn't talked her into something she didn't want to do.

After finishing their lunch they clear away together, cover left over food, stack the dishwasher and Sheila opens one of the bottles of white wine Georgie had put in the fridge as soon as they arrived.

'Scott and I tried this one last time we were out to dinner and it's superb.'

Jenny gets wine glasses and once they are filled the four women return to their chairs on the deck. This time they don't toast each other, but sit sipping their wine and making appreciative comments on its smoothness and lovely fruity flavour.

Georgie stretches her long tanned legs in front of her and says contentedly, 'Ah, this is the life. It's all so beautiful and peaceful. Do you get up here often Jen, now that you own it?'

Jenny gives a little tight smile. 'Not often enough. When Dad died and left it to me the boys were still quite young and loved it here. Do you remember that summer Annie, when we came up with our kids?'

'As if I'd forget it. It was such a novelty for my lot, and the kids all got on so well together.'

'Yes it was great and I'd hoped to make it a regular thing, but with husbands included. That didn't happen because

Mark never liked being here, called it the boondocks and complained about there not being enough to do. Instead we went where he wanted to go, Fiji, Tahiti, the Maldives, and of course Hayman and Hamilton; anywhere there were beaches and a golf course. Sometimes I'd come up here with the boys for the odd weekend, but in time it became boring for them compared with the places they'd been to. In recent years we haven't used it much at all because the boys nearly always had sport at weekends, and now they have quite busy social lives.

'You could have come on your own or with girlfriends,' Georgie comments.

'Oh, I have. Not with girlfriends. I don't have any really close girlfriends who I'd want to go away with, except for you lot of course. I've come by myself though for the odd weekend and really enjoyed it. Not recently though.'

The others see a shadow pass across Jenny's face, and know she is thinking of the past horrible months of nursing Mark.

To change the subject Annie says, 'Gosh those chops were terrific. Where did you buy them Georgie?'

'At that big food market on the wharf. Sheila told me that was the best place for fruit and vegetables but she didn't mention their meat.'

'Oh yes, I should have told you about that. I think I just assumed you'd go to the butcher we used to go to down the Bay.'

'Didn't know it was still there. Anyhow I got most of what I wanted there, except of course for the deli items and I went to the Wursthaus for them. I really enjoyed it you know, wandering around our old haunts and remembering the fun we'd had in some of those old pubs.'

Sheila grins. 'We did, didn't we? We studied so hard during the week and then really let our hair down at weekends. Partying Friday nights, shopping at the market on Saturday mornings and meeting up with friends for lunch and partying the rest of the weekend.'

Annie has been listening to Sheila's reminiscing with a tight little smile on her face. 'I missed out on all that,' she says abruptly. 'While you three were having fun I was stuck in a little cottage with a baby and had to put up with the mother-in-law from hell on a daily basis.'

Georgie leans forward and touches Annie's hand, 'Yes, you reminded me of that the other night. We spent so much of our teen years together I guess I forget you had dropped out of the group by then.'

'Oh she hadn't really,' Jenny, who doesn't think deeply about other people's feelings, interjects quite sharply. 'She was still always part of our group. Sometimes you came to town and joined us for lunch and coffee in the ref. didn't you Annie, and I'm sure I remember you coming out with us some nights.'

'God Jen, the nights out were few and far between, and I only got to join you for lunch at uni about once a month. And you know, I felt so out of it, especially that first year. There you all were looking young and gorgeous and leading busy lives, studying for your future careers and having a ball at weekends. I'd sit there, pregnant and frumpy, listening to you talk about your exciting lives and feel so jealous and so alien.'

Jenny looks surprised. 'Gee Annie, I had no idea you felt like that. You loved Joel so much and seemed happy about having a baby.'

'And I was fat and my skin had developed dark, blotchy pigmentation and I knew I would never get the chance to study and become a teacher, something I'd wanted to do from the time I was twelve. Sure I loved Joel and was actually happy to be carrying his baby, but I also felt I'd lost so much; my youth, my chance of having a career and my three best friends.' With this Annie bursts into tears and runs into the house.

Jenny looks at the other two in surprise. 'God, I didn't mean to upset her. I had no idea she'd felt that way.'

Georgie stands and says, 'She said something to me the other night at the hotel about missing out on those uni years with us. I think being together again has brought back the bad memories of how she felt then. I'll go and see if I can cheer her up.'

When Georgie leaves Jenny turns to Sheila and says with a shrug, 'I didn't know she'd felt like that. Oh, now I've upset her so much.'

'It's not just what you said. I think, as Georgie says, being together again may be part of it, but she's also had a row with Joel about something. I don't know what's happened between them but she said she feels he hasn't ever appreciated her enough. This morning she bought herself two new expensive pairs of bathers, I think to sort of get back at him for all the years she's had to be careful with money.'

Jenny grins. 'Well let's go and see if Georgie's managed to cheer her up, and then I'll suggest a swim. It will give her a chance to show off those new togs.'

When they enter the bedroom they see their two friends sitting side by side on the bed; Georgie has a comforting arm around Annie's shoulders and Annie is wiping her eyes with a tissue. Jenny runs forward and grabs her hand saying, 'I'm so sorry love. I didn't mean to upset you. I really didn't know you'd felt like that.'

'Oh, I didn't a lot of the time. I'm probably remembering it as worse than it was because I'm a bit pissed off with Joel at the moment.'

'And Sheila tells me you've been out spending his hard-earned money on expensive bathers to get even. Let's go for a swim and you can show us what you bought.'

Annie says defensively, 'They're the first new bathers I've had in years, and you should have seen my old ones.'

Jenny laughs. 'You don't have to explain to us. I think it's great that you've lashed out on yourself for once. Anyhow let's all get changed and have our first swim together in years.'

Once the others leave her room Annie takes the aqua bathers from the top drawer where she had put them earlier in the day. She strips quickly and pulls on the bathers then turns this way and that before the full-length mirror in her ensuite. They look even better than they had in the shop for now the various tags have been removed and she feels they are really hers. For a while she stares at her reflection enjoying the silky feel of the material on her bare skin and the way the cut-outs at the sides flatter her figure. She may not be as cute and petite as Jenny or as tall and glamorous as Georgie and Sheila but she looks good and certainly won't feel like the country cousin in these beautiful bathers.

When she finally comes out of her bedroom the three others are waiting in the lounge room, clad in bathers and with large beach towels slung around their necks. Jenny comes towards her and hands her a towel saying, 'Oh my God, you look stunning. I'm sure I saw that suit being modelled by Jennifer Hawkins in the Woman's Weekly, and you look every bit as good.'

Annie laughs self-consciously. 'Garn, you're overdoing it there girl, but I do feel great in them.'

Sheila puts an arm around her waist and pulls her towards the door, 'Come on you lot. We've waited long enough for this bathing beauty to finish admiring herself. Let's get into that water.'

They make a race of it to the water's edge. Georgie and Jenny run straight in and dive under the gentle waves as soon as it is deep enough for them to swim. Annie and Sheila approach the water more tentatively moaning that it is cold until the other two threaten to dunk them if they don't get under. Soon all four are skylarking around, splashing each other and swimming beneath each other's legs before they settle into a long companionable swim to the point and back. Afterwards they lie damp and breathless on their towels on the hot sand, enjoying the touch of the soft sea breeze playing across their bare skin and the shared feeling of pleasure of being together again in this place.

They spend the afternoon on the beach, talking about anything and everything; jobs children, books and films they have read or seen. Jenny talks about her sons and what they have been doing, but makes no mention of Mark. Sheila and Annie also make no mention of their husbands. It is as though an unspoken agreement has been reached that talk of their partners, both living and dead, is a forbidden subject. Sheila thinks this would surprise Scott for he is one of the many men who are firmly convinced that when women get together they spend most of the time running down their partners.

When the sea breeze freshens and the air begins to cool they return to the house and barbecue some of the gourmet sausages Georgie bought. They eat them between slices of soft white bread after slathering them in mustard or sauce. This is something they often ate when they were teenagers, but now they accompany it with an almost purple, rich Shiraz instead of a west coast cooler and laugh at the memory of how daring they had felt sculling that foul sickly drink.

After finishing the meal they pull on sweaters and shorts over their dry sandy bathers and carry the last of their wine down to the beach where they sit close together on the cooling sand. They watch the sun sink below the horizon in a magnificent display of fiery colours before going slowly back up to the house with their arms around each other and walking in step.

After they say their goodnights and go to their separate bedrooms Sheila showers before bed, not liking the feeling of dried salt and sand on her fine sensitive skin. Annie and Georgie fall straight into bed after cleaning their teeth and rinsing out their bathers. Jenny sits in her room talking quietly to Stuart. He rang as she was getting ready for bed and is saying he wants to see her tonight. Although he understands why she doesn't want her friends to know about them yet he had looked forward to the two of them spending this time together. Naturally he feels miffed and wants her to sneak out and meet him now. She promises to meet him the next night then puts the phone down with a sigh. She loves him and wants to be with him for the rest of her life, but it's all too soon and she doesn't know what to do.

Georgie

Georgie is an early riser. Most mornings when she is home in Sydney she gets up at five thirty and goes for a run. This is the only time when the streets are relatively quiet and she enjoys jogging along the almost empty pavements and watching the sky light up above the tall buildings in her neighbourhood. There is a popular French patisserie a couple of kilometres from her apartment and often she runs to there and buys croissants or a sticky tart for her breakfast. She has always been able to eat whatever she wants without putting on additional weight and many of the women with whom she works envy this about her. They see her eating a substantial lunch and then tucking into a large steak when they go out to dinner. She knows she is lucky to have an efficient metabolism, but she also eats healthily and exercises at the gym two days a weeks as well as taking her morning runs. Her only vice is the sweet, buttery breakfasts she prefers.

Now when she wakes at five thirty to a silent house she pulls on the shorts and sweater that she discarded on a chair the night before and takes her sneakers from the bottom of the wardrobe before slipping quietly out of the house. She puts on the sneakers then jogs across the lawn and down to the beach. The tide is out and the wet sand pleasantly firm beneath her feet as she runs to the rocks at one end of the beach, then turns and runs to the other. Here she takes off her sneakers and walks slowly along the water's edge, enjoying the feel of the cool water brushing against her legs in tiny wavelets.

The morning run has reminded her of home and as she wanders aimlessly along the empty beach she thinks of the past and the many times she shared this morning ritual with Ruth. One of the few things they'd had in common was their love of jogging in the early morning air, breathing in the promise of a fresh, new day. Ruth had also loved the rich French pastries from the patisserie and had gloried in their sweet sensual stickiness. Georgie remembers her looking like a small child at a party, her pretty mouth and rounded cheeks smeared with honey or sugary syrup. Sometimes she couldn't resist licking it off and Ruth would purr in delight. Theirs had been a very sensual relationship and Ruth hadn't understood why it needed to be any different when Sheila and Annie came to stay with them. In retrospect Georgie now sees how having her friends to stay influenced her feelings towards Ruth; made her more critical of some of her somewhat childish and clinging ways, and possibly led her to questioning whether she wanted a lifetime commitment with this woman.

On the morning after Ruth left, Georgie had gone on her usual run, but this time alone for the first time in nearly three years. The plump, jolly owner of the patisserie had said, 'Ah, you're little friend is not with you today. Is she not well?'

Georgie had mumbled something about a flu bug, made her purchases and left the shop with a hurried goodbye.

For the first week Georgie couldn't bring herself to accept the fact that the love affair had ended. During the early days of their separation she felt sure Ruth would get in touch, say it was all a terrible mistake and she couldn't live without her. When this didn't happen Georgie tried to contact Ruth, but she had quit her job as a receptionist without leaving a forwarding address, and hadn't been in contact with any of their mutual friends. Georgie had even driven to the little country town where Ruth's estranged parents lived, in the vain hope she might be there. That had been ghastly. They had stood on the ramshackle verandah and glowered at her from mean slitted eyes and said they didn't have a daughter. As she was leaving the father had shouted after her, 'Good riddance to her and to you. She and youse others lesbians like her are depraved.'

Ruth had told her about her terrible upbringing; of growing up in filth and poverty with two drunken parents who ignored her on the rare occasions they were sober and hit her during drunken rages. She'd escaped as soon as she was able and she told Georgie she had never seen them since. There must have been some further contact with them before the final break that Ruth never told Georgie about. From the father's taunt Georgie gathered she had told them she was a lesbian and so it could only have been after they were together because Georgie had been Ruth's first lover. Or had she been? She wonders why Ruth didn't ever tell her about this final visit to see her parents. Georgie had driven away from that miserable little shanty wondering why Ruth had ever gone back and why she hadn't shared that further rejection with her. What other secrets had there been and how well had she really known Ruth? Is there always some area of your life you don't share even with your lover or best friend?

Following the encounter with Ruth's parents Georgie gave up trying to find Ruth and slipped into a period of depression. She still turned up for work each day, but she was sleeping badly, gave up her morning jogs and stopped bothering to prepare proper meals. Some of her work mates noticed the changes, said she'd lost weight and looked tired and asked if she was feeling alright. She told her two closest friends at work about the break-up with Ruth, and they tried to cheer her up, but Georgie felt they didn't really understand her loss. They were both happily married and shared the misguided concept of many heterosexuals that gay relationships were somewhat more shallow and fleeting than their own.

When Georgie looks back on that time she sees it as a period of mourning. She had lost someone very dear to her and needed time to heal. She also sees that her frantic searching for Ruth wasn't because she wanted her back, but because she badly wanted to know she'd be alright. Slowly she began to enjoy life again and could view the time she'd spent with Ruth as a pleasant interlude. Sure she missed the sex and the feeling of being wanted and needed so much, but there were many things she didn't miss. Once she was gone Georgie realised how many things about Ruth annoyed her; her untidiness, her clinginess, her insecurities, and her rather scatty way of looking at the world. When Sheila and Annie had stayed with them Georgie had been more aware of the faults in their relationship and could see, as if through their eyes, how incompatible they really were. After they left Georgie reverted to turning a blind eye to problems in the relationship; continued to make compromises but when Ruth began saying she wanted them to adopt a baby Georgie had been horrified. Faced with the prospect of being tied forever by parenthood Georgie refused to make this major compromise and Ruth had left.

Georgie knew she had put the loss of Ruth from her life firmly behind her when she jogged to the patisserie for the first time in three months. The owner greeted her effusively. 'It is so long since we see you. We miss you and your little friend coming in for our wonderful pastries.'

Georgie had laughed and said, 'Well I'll make up for it today. I want two croissants and one of your lovely lemon tarts.'

He busied himself with the order carefully laying the goodies in the bottom of a cardboard box and sealing the lid. As he handed it to Georgie he said, 'But where is your friend today? She is not still sick surely.'

Taking the box Georgie answered as casually as she could manage, 'No, she died.'

Now as she walks along the water's edge she smiles to herself as she remembers the shocked look on the patisserie owner's face. He must have thought her so hard-hearted to have been so off-hand about a friend's death. He certainly never mentioned her friend again.

At times Georgie still thinks about Ruth and wonders if they would still be together if she had gone along with Ruth's desire for a child. Now she shakes her head as though to clear away all such thoughts for she knows too many compromises would have been needed to make their relationship work. She had realised the extent of the compromises she was already making when Sheila and Annie visited them. In a funny way at the time of the breakup she put part of the blame for it onto them and she is still carrying a sort of grudge, particularly against Sheila. She knows this is unfair but for some reason can't let it go.

As Georgie crosses the road and walks up the drive she contemplates what she'll have for breakfast. She is suddenly feeling hungry for something sweet and decadent, but knows she didn't include croissants in her shopping. Perhaps there is honey or golden syrup in the pantry that would go beautifully on pancakes.

Sheila

Georgie found both honey and golden syrup in the well-stocked pantry and is busy mixing up a large quantity of pancake batter when Sheila wanders sleepily into the kitchen dressed in a deep green silk dressing gown over matching silk pyjamas. She comes behind Georgie, gives her a peck on the cheek then sits down at the table.

'You're up bright and early. What are you cooking there?' She puts her elbows on the table and leans forward to examine the mixture in the bowl.

'Pancakes. I've been for a jog, and exercise always makes me crave something sweet.'

Sheila stretches languorously. 'Oh I remember now. When Annie and I visited you years ago, you and that woman would go jogging every morning and return with a stack of croissants and tarts.

Georgie turns from the stove where she has been turning a batch of pancakes and says sharply, 'You don't have to call her 'that woman' like that. Her name was Ruth as you well know.'

'There's no need to get so huffy about it. I didn't mean to upset you, but I guess I just didn't take to her.'

'And you made that perfectly clear at the time. You hardly spoke to her, and when you did you spoke down to her.'

'Well frankly I couldn't see what you saw in her. She seemed a total dipstick to me and the way she was all over you was embarrassing to Annie as well as me.'

'Well at least Annie was pleasant to her which is more than can be said for the way you behaved towards her.' Georgie knows she's overacting but the fact that she has

145

just been remembering that visit and the later repercussions makes her hyper-sensitive.

'Oh for goodness sake are you going to carry on about something that happened over three years ago?'

'At the time Ruth was very important to me and I hated the way you were with her, and you're still being insulting about her. I've never criticised your friends or lovers, and she was both to me.'

'Oh come off your high horse. What about the way you were towards Scott. You were forever sounding off about how weak he was and telling me I should ditch him. You were a total bitch about him.'

'Only because of the way he kept you hanging in there for years with one excuse after another. Don't forget I lived through all those ups and downs with you for four years, and it was still going on when I left for Sydney. Of course I criticised him. Most of the time you were so bloody miserable. He strung you along because he was too weak to walk away from that manipulative wife and his precious kids'.

'You never made any attempt to see what a difficult situation he was in and just made things worse for us with your continual harping at me to forget him. You didn't like him then, and you're still pretty cool towards him.'

Sheila knows this last remark is unfair because Georgie had been totally friendly towards Scott when she'd come to dinner. The problem is what Georgie has just said hit a raw nerve for at present she is angry with Scott for allowing himself to be manipulated again and in a terrible way it is bringing back memories of all the angst she went through so many years ago. He allowed himself to be manipulated by his bitch of a wife for years and is now being just as weak dealing with his daughter.

There is a heavy silence in the room when Annie walks in looking fresh and pretty in jeans and a blue tee shirt that exactly matches her eyes. She looks worriedly from one friend to the other. 'I didn't want to wake anyone so I've been reading in my room, but then I heard raised voices. You two aren't arguing are you?'

Sheila says, 'Just a mild disagreement.' She pats the chair next to her. 'Come and sit down. Georgie's making pancakes for all of us.'

Georgie turns back to the pan just in time to save the last batch from burning, and then places the heaped plateful in the centre of the table. She is still angry with Sheila but doesn't want to upset Annie who is a gentle soul and hates any sort of altercation. Sitting down on the opposite side of the table from Sheila and Annie she reaches for a pancake and proceeds to smother it in butter and golden syrup saying, 'Tuck in you two or I'll eat the lot.'

As she is saying this Jenny appears at the door dressed in a pink towelling dressing gown, her blonde hair tousled and still rubbing the sleep from her eyes. 'I thought I smelt pancakes. Why didn't one of you wake me?'

Georgie grins at her sleepy friend. 'If I remember rightly you didn't like being woken early. You and Sheila were owls and Annie and I larks.'

Sheila sighs. 'Not any more. Once you have children you're forced to become a lark whether you want to or not. Unless of course you have a live in Nanny the way Jenny did.'

This has not been meant to sound overtly critical but her repressed anger towards Georgie has put her in a sour mood and her remark sounds more sarcastic than she meant it to. Jenny looks a bit uncomfortable and says defensively, 'I breast fed my boys for their first three months so had plenty of early mornings and quite a few broken nights of sleep. But I guess I was lucky. Sophia, our nanny, was wonderful and took over the early feeds once my babies were weaned.'

Sheila grins trying to take the sting out of her previous remark. 'And you went back to your wicked ways of being an owl. Not that I see anything wrong with being an owl. Deep down I'm still an owl and hope to revert to my natural cycle once Mia is a bit older.'

'Well I'm glad I'm a lark. We early birds get to see the best part of the day when it's all bright and new while you owls are still cocooned in your beds.'

'Not everyone's daft enough to want to go running around in the dark and cold the way you do Georgie.'

Annie senses the mild hostility in Sheila's voice and guesses it's because of the argument she and Georgie were having when she joined them. To lighten the atmosphere she says jokingly, 'Let's finish off these beautiful pancakes then you two owls can fly off and shower and dress while we larks clear up the crumbs.'

Jenny carries her cup and plate to the sink, gives Annie's shoulder an affectionate pat for diffusing the tension she has only just realised is there, and says, 'Good idea love, and then I'll tell you what I've planned for us to do today.'

When Jenny and Sheila return showered and dressed Georgie and Annie are sitting in the now tidy kitchen drinking fresh cups of coffee. Jenny pours two cups from the percolator and says excitedly, 'Today I thought I'd take you to my secret place for a picnic.'

Annie clasps her hands together and says, 'Ooh that sounds exciting. Where is it?'

Jenny laughs at her friend's eager response. 'If I tell you it'll spoil my surprise. You'll find out when we get there. The only hint I'll give you is that you need to bring your bathers. Now drink up everyone then we'll pack a yummy picnic lunch with some of the goodies Georgie got from the Wursthaus. I thought we'd take some of the pates, cheeses and olives, the last of the crusty bread and peaches and grapes to finish off with. And Sheila, you can choose a couple of bottles of wine to go with it.'

She fetches a cane basket from the pantry and hands Sheila a cooler bag for the wine. It isn't long before everything is packed. Sheila slings the wine cooler over her shoulder, Annie carries the bag containing bathers and towels and Georgie and Jenny each take a handle of the picnic basket. Jenny leads them across the road and along the beach to the end where big rocks seem to create a formidable barrier. She continues up a narrow path between the rocks, the basket bumping uncomfortably between her and Georgie and with Annie and Sheila following behind. When they reach the top they see spread before them a wide flat expanse of long yellow grass broken here and there by tall slender gum trees and touches of colour from patches of wild pink heath.

It is still only mid-morning but the sun is hot and Sheila is regretting she didn't put on a hat. Although her freckles have faded she still has to be careful for her skin burns quickly, and she's not sure the sunscreen she applied before they left will provide enough protection. She pauses to put on some more of the roll-on sunscreen she has in her pocket and gazes admiringly around her at the view. It reminds her a bit of an Arthur Streeton painting, one he did near Heidelberg, although in the painting there is a distant view of more paddocks and behind them purple hills and the tiny figures are in long Victorian gowns, not jeans and shorts. Here there is no distant view of land for it ends abruptly at a thicket of she-oaks with a wide blue sky above, but the colours are the same as in the painting and there is the same golden glow in the scene before her.

When the others reach the thicket they wait for Sheila to catch up, and then walk along a narrow path between the trees. Suddenly the ground slopes abruptly before them and they see a steep rocky path leading down to a small crescent-shaped beach. With difficulty Jenny and Georgie manhandle the basket down the slope with Annie and Sheila slithering behind them. They reach the bottom feeling hot and breathless, drop what they have been carrying and lie for a while on the sand, shaded by a large spreading she-oak.

Georgie looks at Jenny and says only half-jokingly, 'I hate to think how we're going to get back up that path with that damn basket.'

Jenny laughs. 'At least it won't be as heavy once we've eaten all the food, and there are footholds that you probably didn't notice on the way down. Now stop your moaning and look around. Isn't it just the most beautiful spot?'

Sheila looks at the small curved beach with rocks and she-oaks at either end. It is indeed very beautiful and very private. The sand is fine and white and contrasts sharply with the dark blue rolling waves that surge in and suck back noisily carrying sand with them, leaving a deep trough at the water's edge. She breathes rapturously, 'It's gorgeous.' Annie sighs, 'Like a picture post card.'

Georgie doesn't seem as taken with the beauty of the place as the other three are. She looks at the breaking waves and says nervously, 'It looks as though there's a bit of an undertow. Is it safe to swim here?'

'I've swum here lots of times,' Jenny answers, wanting to reassure her friend, for she knows Georgie is somewhat fearful of rough water even though she is a strong swimmer. 'There's a slight undertow close to the shore, but if you swim out a bit you get a lovely ride in on the waves.'

Sheila thinks Georgie is being unnecessarily critical of a place Jenny obviously loves and says, 'I think it's absolutely wonderful and the water looks great. I am, however, dying of thirst and pretty hungry so can we eat first and then swim?'

'Yes. I think that's a good idea. I reckon the brie has probably reached that lovely gooey stage where it's at its best.' Jenny opens the basket and takes out a little checked cloth, plastic plates, an array of knives and the food, while Sheila opens a bottle of chardonnay and pours it into the glasses Jenny hands her.

The walk has made them all hungry and they eat ravenously, enjoying the food and the refreshingly cold wine. The brie and pates are perfect on the crusty bread and they finish the meal with the peaches, biting into the soft furry flesh and all finishing up with their hands and faces covered in the sticky sweet juice.

Laughing at the mess she's in Jenny says, 'I need a swim now to get this off me.'

'We have to wait half an hour after eating,' Annie says, and they all laugh and Jenny says 'Yes Mum, otherwise we might drown.'

Seeing Annie's blush at the teasing Georgie says defensively, 'My mother used to say the same thing.'

Sheila also realises Jenny's teasing has made Annie uncomfortable so makes a joke of the situation. 'So did mine, but she didn't say anything about waiting after drinking, so I'll open the bottle of red and we can drink that while our food is digesting.'

After drinking a glass of red each they change into their bathers and run to the water's edge. Jenny and Sheila dive straight in, but Annie and Georgie are more cautious walking slowly until the water is up to their knees.

'Do you reckon this is safe,' Georgie asks Annie as they watch the other two swimming over and under the rolling waves like a pair of dolphins.

'Well Jenny was pretty definite that it is. Let's go girl, and see if we can catch a wave in with the others.'

They swim out, but when Georgie feels the tug of the undertow pushing her further from the shore she starts to panic. She turns towards the shore and is hit in the face by the back swell and splutters as salt water fills her mouth and films her eyes. Jenny is suddenly next to her saying, 'Swim after me and turn when I do.'

It is against what her gut is telling her to do but Georgie obeys, following her friend into deeper water until she turns. Suddenly she is on a wave that takes her on a smooth ride all the way to the beach. She staggers from the water and watches as the other three body surf towards the beach screaming with delight.

Jenny is the first to stand up and she puts a protective arm around Georgie's waist. 'You okay? I thought for a minute out there you were going to panic.'

Georgie laughs. 'What do you mean going to panic? I was scared stiff, and if you hadn't told me what to do I think I'd have drowned. I'm not going in there again.'

Sheila is still feeling resentful and upset about Georgie's earlier criticism of Scott. Her remarks had hit the mark because they echoed something of what she is feeling about him at present herself. These confused feelings now lead her to say somewhat aggressively, 'Don't be such a bloody wimp. You're a good swimmer, and there's no danger as long as you keep your head.'

They all know of Georgie's fear of rough water and the other two don't like to hear Sheila baiting Georgie. Jenny says, 'I should have stayed with you. It can be a bit tricky. Sorry love.'

Annie joins in, 'After so many years of mainly swimming in pools I found it a bit scary too. You two dolphins go and play and Georgie and I'll finish off the wine.'

Sheila turns, runs towards the water and throws her body into the surf. Hearing the other two reassuring Georgie has made her realise how bitchy she must have seemed to be baiting her when they all know of her fear of rough water. Perhaps she should apologise for calling her a wimp and urging her to do something she obviously feared.

When she and Jenny join the others after an exhilarating hour in the waves Georgie and Annie have finished the bottle of wine and packed the basket, and are sitting in the shade of the spreading she-oak talking. They all change out of their bathers and gather everything together. It is decided that on the return trip Jenny needs to carry the least as she will lead the way up the path and help the others find the footholds. She heads off carrying the bottle bag, Annie follows with the bathers and towels and Sheila and Georgie bring up the rear lugging the basket. The hilarity that ensues as they struggle up the steep slope lightens the atmosphere a bit between them, and by the time they reach the top Sheila hopes they are friends again.

It has been a hot day and by the time they retrace their steps across the golden paddock and get back to the beach house all of them are feeling tired, hot and sweaty. They shower and change into light clothes, Sheila and Jenny into sarongs, Georgie into a colourful silk kaftan and Annie into one of her long skirts topped with a tee shirt.

Jenny puts the remaining pates and some cheeses onto a platter and adds slices of ham, sundried tomatoes, olives and small inner leaves from cos lettuces. Sheila opens another bottle of white wine and they sit around the kitchen table eating, drinking and talking, and feeling that sense of weary contentment one has after a day spent out of doors on a summery day.

After the meal they kiss and hug goodnight before heading off to their separate rooms. Georgie and Annie have both been awake since daylight and are asleep as soon as their heads hit their pillows. Sheila is tired, but worries about Scott keep her awake. She thinks perhaps a bit of fresh air will help her relax and opens one of the windows. As she leans on the wide sill watching the moon come out from behind a dark cloud she sees Jenny, still dressed in her sarong stepping silently across the lawn. Just before the moon disappears behind the clouds and plunges the scene before her into darkness Sheila sees a tall figure emerge from the shadowy trees on the boundary and Jenny run into his outstretched arms.

As she turns from the window Sheila thinks, 'What is our girl Jen up to? Could she really be having an affair with that man Frank, and sneaking out to meet him?

She gets back into bed and settles down with the soft breeze from the open window brushing across her hot, slightly sunburnt face. What she has seen has driven all immediate worries about Scott from her head and soon she sleeps.

Jenny

From her bedroom window Jenny can just make out the dark shape of Stuart sitting on the garden seat at the bottom of the lawn. She waits until the house is quiet and she is sure her friends are asleep before slipping silently out the front door and running across the lawn. He turns as she approaches and stands to greet her gathering her into his arms and kissing her passionately on the mouth before saying, 'Oh, you feel so good.'

Her sarong is tied across the top of her breasts and he pushes it down and runs his hands down her sides then up to cup each breast in his strong gentle hands. He bends his head and kisses each breast and she feels her nipples stiffen in response. She reaches for his penis, feels it hard and erect beneath the fabric of his jeans and undoes his zip to release it into her hands. He groans with pleasure as he lays her on the grass and undoes the bow holding her sarong together. For a moment he stands above her looking at her with such adoration it sends shivers through her body. He strips off his jeans and tee shirt before lying beside her, then pulling her on top says, 'You are so beautiful. You can't imagine how much I've missed you and our being together like this.'

She opens herself to him, feels him thrust deep inside her and gives herself over to the rapturous feeling of having him moving within her and the wonderful feel of his strong muscular body enfolding her. She comes too quickly but then he moves so that he is on top. As he continues to thrust deeper and deeper she wraps her legs around him and rises to meet him and feels an orgasm once more flooding through her body at the same time as he comes.

Afterwards they lie facing each other on the warm grass their arms entwined as they kiss gently and lovingly. Jenny has missed this so much; the thought of Stuart and of being with him like this was the only thing that kept her sane during the long horrible months of Mark's illness. Now when she should be feeling free to enjoy their time together, and be able to plan to make it permanent at some time in the future, this pregnancy has complicated things. If she were to have the baby everyone would know she had been unfaithful to her sick and aged husband and her sons would hate her for it. She couldn't stand that.

Unwillingly she pulls away from him and wraps her sarong around her body.

'Don't cover up that beautiful body my darling.' He looks at her with such love it makes her feel soft and pliant. As he lies on the grass looking up at her, at ease with his nakedness, and indeed resembling a young Mel Gibson, the moon comes from behind a cloud and shines on his smooth, tanned body. Jenny gazes down at him adoringly. After years of sharing a bed with an old husband, who despite twice-weekly visits to the gym had sagging flesh and slackness around his stomach, the sight and feel of Stuart turns her on, but they must talk.

She sits on the bench and tries to make a light-hearted start by saying, 'We have to talk so will you please put on your gear so I can concentrate on what I have to tell you.'

He stands and pulls on his jeans before sitting beside her on the bench. 'Now you're looking serious. What do you want to talk about?'

Jenny has been worrying for weeks about how to break this to him, or indeed whether or not to even tell him. Now it comes out in a rush. 'I'm pregnant. It must have happened last time I was up here, when Mark was in hospital. I'm nearly three months gone and I want to have an abortion.'

He looks at her in amazement, 'But why would you want to do that? You told me you'd love to have a baby with me; that once Alec turned eighteen you'd leave Mark and come up here; make a whole new life with me.'

'I meant what I said and that's what I still want to do. I want to marry you and have your baby, but not now. This baby would be born six months after my husband died. What do you think my boys and everyone else would think of me?'

Stuart looks bewildered. 'But you can't kill our baby. Isn't a life we've created together more important than what anyone thinks?'

'It's alright for you to say that. I have to think of my boys. Can you imagine how they would feel learning that their mother was carrying on with another man while their father was dying? They'd be disgusted with me.'

'They're not boys, they're young men. It may be a bit of a shock to them at first, but they'd come round after a while.'

'It's easy for you to be cavalier about them and their feelings. You've never been a parent.'

'And if you have your way I never will be. I don't know how you can put upsetting your sons for a little while ahead of the life of our child.'

'I thought you might react like this. That's why I didn't tell you the other night and risk spoiling our first evening together in three months.'

'How else would you expect me to take this? You're saying that what your precious sons think is more important than our baby; that you'll have him or her killed rather than face a few months of them being upset with you.'

She feels tears welling in her eyes but brushes them away angrily. 'And how can you possibly think you know how they'd react? Despite Mark being a sod of a husband he was a pretty good father and the boys loved him. It could shatter them to learn what I had been doing while he was sick, and they mightn't want to have anything to do with me ever again.'

'I think you're being a bit melodramatic. They're big boys and probably had a fair idea everything wasn't as perfect in the marriage as you and he liked to pretend.'

'And I think you're being deliberately obtuse.' As soon as she has spoken those words Jenny would like to take them back. Stuart has always been sensitive about his lack of education, and will probably take her remark as being a dig at his intelligence.

As she watches his face to see how he will respond he scowls and says angrily, 'You may think I'm obtuse but I know what's most important, or at least what should be.' He takes a deep breath and lets it out in what becomes a long slow sigh. 'If you do this I don't see much of a future for us.'

Before she can really take in what he has implied he reaches down for the tee shirt lying on the grass and pulls it roughly over his head before adding, 'I'm serious Jen. If you get rid of our baby I don't think I could forgive you. It'll ruin everything between us.'

He then turns and walks quickly across the grass and down the end of the driveway. For a long time she continues sitting on the bench hoping he will regret his hasty remarks and return to make up. The moon disappears once more behind the dark clouds and the breeze strengthens. She shivers and puts her arms across her chest for warmth then lowers them until they are over her stomach. It is probably imagination, but she thinks she feels a little lump there and the faintest of movements. 'I don't want to do this little one,' she whispers, and can no longer hold back the tears. Feeling utterly distraught she remains on the seat sobbing and trying to decide what she should do. If she has the abortion she risks losing Stuart and the life they hoped to have together, and if she goes ahead and has the baby she could lose the love and respect of her sons forever.

Eventually she gives up hoping Stuart will come back and walks quickly across the lawn and creeps into the house. She is shivering for she has been so lost in thought she hasn't realised how cold she was becoming. She would love to have a hot shower but fears it will wake Annie who is in the next room. She doesn't want her wondering why she is still up at this late hour. Quietly she searches through the drawer where she keeps her night attire, finds a long warm nightgown and pulls it over her head and down her cold body. Once in bed she reaches for her mobile phone and taps in Stuart's number. It rings and rings then goes to message bank. She listens to his brief instructions to leave a message, but can't think of words that will mend the breach.

After putting down the phone and turning off the light she lies awake for a long time thinking about what she should do. To a certain extent she understands Stuart's reaction, for they have spent many hours during the past three years planning a life together, and having a baby has been a big part of their plan. She has always wanted another child and he has been enthusiastic. If only it hadn't happened while Mark was still alive they could have waited; she would have had time to prepare her sons for the appearance of another man in her life and then the eventual birth of a younger sibling. Now she doesn't have that option unless she has an abortion, but then she risks losing Stuart. In a way she regrets having told him, but it wouldn't have seemed right to plan a life together with such a secret always there between them.

She is suddenly overwhelmed by a wave of hopelessness and sobs into her pillow, very conscious that Annie is in the next room.

Annie and Jenny

As she opens the front door to go for her morning run Georgie sees that Annie is already up and dressed and sitting on one of the chairs on the verandah.

'Beat you up this morning. Thought I'd join you on your run.'

'Good on you girl. I'm going along the beach towards town then over that headland to the shop. I noticed on my way in that the old grocery store has been modernised and thought I'd get some fresh bread. What I brought up must be getting a bit stale by now.' As she is speaking she zips a fifty dollar note into the back pocket of her shorts then sets off down the drive with a long loping stride.

They run along the beach together but when they reach the headland the path is narrow and steep and Georgie takes the lead. By the time they reach the top Annie is panting and red in the face while Georgie is still looking cool and relaxed.

'I thought all the work I do around the farm was keeping me fit.' Annie grimaces and holds her side. 'I certainly can't keep up with you.'

'Don't forget I run practically every day. You're going well, and it's downhill from here.' Georgie sets off again and Annie trails behind her till they reach the shop.

The owner has just arrived and is opening the doors as the two women run up to him. He smiles a welcome then moves around the shop flicking switches and turning on the cash register. As Georgie and Annie look around the small super market he asks, 'Are you looking for anything special ladies?'

'Bread mainly, but I was also wondering if you have croissants.' Georgie looks expectantly around the now brightly lit little shop.

'You'll find what you're looking for on the shelves at the back.' He beams broadly, pleased that he has what they ask for. 'I get a delivery every evening from Joe's bakery down the coast so it's all nice and fresh.'

Georgie picks up a white crusty loaf and a multigrain then says to Annie, 'Can you grab a dozen of those croissants. They may not be as good as the ones I buy in Sydney, but they don't look bad.'

Overhearing her remark the owner says defensively, 'They're the best you can buy in Tassie. Old Joe's been in the bakery business for longer than you girls have been alive, and he's a master.'

'They look delicious.' Annie gives him her best dimpled smile for she is concerned he may have been insulted by Georgie's slightly derogatory tone.

Mollified by her comment and lovely smile he wishes them a great day as Georgie pays and he hands her the bag. Once outside the shop Georgie sets off once more at a steady pace, the shopping bag slung across her back. Even though she is empty-handed Annie finds it hard to keep up with her tall long-legged friend and is panting and holding her side as they enter the kitchen. Sheila turns from the bench where she has been filling the coffee machine and says, 'I thought I was first up but I might have known you two larks would beat me. Did she drag you out for a run Annie?'

'No, I wanted to go, but I hadn't realised I was so unfit. She's a hard lady to keep up with, and now I've got the stitch.'

Sheila grins. 'She's got an advantage with those long legs. Anyhow what's in the bag Georgie?'

Georgie empties the bag onto the table. 'I thought we might need fresh bread, and they also had what is my favourite thing for breakfast, croissants.'

Annie chimes in, 'And we're assured they're the best in Tasmania.'

Sheila pours three coffees while Georgie warms some croissants in the microwave. Once they are all seated and eating Sheila says in a whisper, 'Guess what I saw last night.'

She looks so wide-eyed and eager to speak Georgie says laconically, 'A ghost.'

'Funny. No I was standing by my window after we'd all gone to bed and I saw Jenny sneaking across the grass, still in her sarong, and there was a man waiting for her on that bench near the bottom of the lawn. She ran into his arms and they were cuddling, but then the moon went behind a cloud and I couldn't see any more.'

'My God, I wonder who it was.' Annie looks at Sheila questioningly. 'Didn't you see what he looked like?'

'No.' Sheila shakes her head. 'I thought it might be that guy Frank who she seemed so pally with at the wake, but I couldn't tell. All I saw was the shape of a man and that they were in a clinch and then it went dark.'

'I don't think it's Frank.' Georgie says. 'When I got here on Friday he was driving away very quickly and Stuart, the man who does the garden, was in the kitchen drinking a beer and pouring a wine for Jenny. I got a distinct feeling there was something going on between them, but when I teased her about him Jenny said he was an old friend from when they were kids. Just the same I felt sure she was hiding something.'

Annie looks worried, 'Well whoever it is she was very unhappy after their meeting. I went to sleep as soon as I got into bed, but then woke sometime in the early hours of the morning. I could hear Jen crying and thought of going in to her, but then decided she mightn't want me to know she was upset.'

'Looks like she's catching up on her lost sleep, poor darling,' Sheila says sympathetically.

'I wonder what's going on. When I heard her I thought it might be because of Mark dying.'

Sheila looks doubtful, 'I don't think so. I think she was telling the truth when she told us she was just glad it was over and she wished he'd died sooner. She and Mark hadn't been happy together for years. I used to wonder why she stayed.'

As Georgie helps herself to another croissant she says, 'I guess we'll find out what's going on eventually. Why don't you ask her why she was crying Annie?'

'I don't want her to think I'm prying.' Annie says then adds tentatively, 'I'll see how she is today.'

The three women finish breakfast and are tidying up the kitchen when Jenny comes into the room. She is dressed in jeans and tee shirt. Her hair has been brushed and curls prettily around her face and she has on makeup but it doesn't quite conceal the slight redness and puffiness around her eyes. She slumps into a chair and says, 'Sorry I'm up so late. I had a beast of a night. Couldn't get to sleep.'

Annie pats her shoulder in a comforting gesture, then seeing Jenny's remark about not sleeping as an opening says, 'I woke in the middle of the night and thought I heard you crying. What's wrong love? Is there anything we can do to help?'

Jenny looks around the room at the worried faces of her three friends, puts her head in her hands and sighs, 'Oh, I feel so terrible and I don't know what to do.'

Georgie pours a cup of coffee and placing it in front of Jenny says, 'Come on girl. Drink this and tell us what's worrying you. What are friends for if you can't share your problems with them?'

Jenny takes a sip then says, 'Look sit down and I'll fill you in on my dirty little secret.' When they are all seated she continues. 'Georgie, I think you may have guessed there was something going on between us when you saw Stuart and me together.'

Georgie grins, 'Yeh, you seemed pretty familiar with each other. But then you were so convincing about how you'd been friends for years I thought I was seeing something that wasn't there.'

'Well the bit about us being childhood friends is true. I've known him for years, and we were friends when we were young. Once I hit the teenage years we lost touch. He seemed such a kid and I pretty well ignored him. I actually didn't see much of him until the last few years when he took over the gardening from his father and now we've become very close.'

'You don't have to be coy with us. You mean now you're lovers. There's nothing wrong with that.' Sheila says this a bit impatiently. 'I happened to see you meeting him last night and thought good on you.'

'So what's the problem now?' Georgie takes Jenny's hand and says fondly, 'I think it's great that you've got someone who loves you. We all know Mark wasn't the best of husbands, and how ghastly it's been for you this past year.'

'Did you have a row with him last night? Is that why you were crying?' Annie looks worried, and is wondering if Stuart is miffed about the time Jenny is spending with them.

Jenny is grateful for the way her friends have wholeheartedly accepted the fact that she has been having an affair, but she doesn't feel ready to share with them the news of her pregnancy. She is still in such a quandary. She knows she has to give some explanation for her unhappiness so decides to tell a half truth. 'Yes Annie, we did have a row. Now Mark is dead Stuart's impatient for us to be together. He says we've waited such a long time and can't see why we should be apart any longer. He doesn't care what people might think, but I do, and especially how my boys will be. Last night he stomped off in a mood, and I was upset because he won't even try to see it from my point of view.'

Annie pats her shoulder and says comfortingly, 'I'm sure he'll come round. He'd probably be here today if we weren't in the way.'

'Why don't you give him a ring and invite him to dinner? Georgie and I will cook that lovely piece of pork she bought and we'll all get to meet him.'

Sheila is looking at Jenny eagerly for approval of her suggestion, but having Stuart meet her friends is the last thing Jenny wants at present. The true reason for their disagreement would be sure to come out, and she's not ready to talk about it yet. In recent years she has become adept at lying and now says, 'That's a great idea but he'll be away for the next few days. He's helping a fisherman mate whose crewman is sick.' She forces a smile. 'Let's forget my little problem. I'm sure we'll sort it out when he comes back. Now, what's say we do the valley walk today and cook jaffles near the stream?'

They all agree eagerly and are soon working together getting ready for the excursion. As teenagers they had walked many times through the steep-sided valley that contained rainforest trees. At the base of the valley was a narrow walking track next to a small fast-moving stream surrounded by huge man ferns. It was an oasis of greenery in the midst of what was mainly dry sclerophyll bushland.

Jenny hunts up the old black jaffle irons that haven't been used for years and gives them a thorough clean while the other three make cheese and onion sandwiches and a big thermos of coffee. Before leaving the house they grab sweaters or jackets for, although the day is warm, they know it will be cooler in the valley. They all pile into Jenny's Subaru, after packing the food and a bag containing the thermos and jaffle irons into the boot.

Jenny drives ten kilometres up the coast then turns onto a gravel road that is rough and twisted and the women laugh about the bumpy ride. When they arrive at the parking area at the end of the road Georgie is first out, complaining that she bumped her head a dozen times on the roof of the car. She insists she's riding in the front on the return journey. They unpack the boot then pass through a gate that is the entrance to the valley. As soon as they enter the valley the air temperature drops and they pause to pull on their warm tops. The air is cool and moist and the only sounds are the occasional sharp call of a forest bird and the distant rush of the stream as it flows across its rocky base far below them.

They walk in single file along the narrow track that winds along flat terrain at first then zigzags downwards until it reaches the floor of the valley. The walking is easy but they don't talk much, and only pause to look more closely at a particularly delicate moss covering a fallen log and a patch of fungi, its vivid orange shimmering amongst the surrounding shades of green and brown. They are all enjoying the quiet and peace, and feel that mindless chatter would be out of place.

When they arrive at a clear area next to the stream Annie says excitedly, 'This is where we had our picnics all those years ago, and it hasn't changed at all.'

'Not like us,' Sheila laughs.

'Ah, we're not that different.' As she says this Georgie pulls her backpack off her shoulders and begins to unpack the sandwiches she's been carrying. 'Now let's see if we still know how to make a decent fire.'

While the others go in search of dry sticks Jenny gathers together the rounded stones that have been used by other picnickers and places them in a circle. By the time she has finished this they return with dry ferns and sticks and soon have a good fire blazing away. They put the sandwiches in the jaffle irons then wait until the fire has burnt down a bit before placing them over the embers.

In a short time the food is ready and they sit around on logs eating the hot tasty jaffles and drinking coffee. They are reminiscing about the last time they were there when Jenny says thoughtfully, 'We've all been through so much since then.'

Since the conversation this morning Sheila has been curious to learn more about Jenny's mystery lover, and she is sure the others are too. She sees Jenny's remark as an opening, and asks, 'Talking of what we've experienced, when are you going to tell us some more about Stuart.

What's he look like, how did you become lovers and when do you plan to marry the guy?'

Jenny is feeling so unsure about Stuart and whether in fact they have a future together so to discuss him is the last thing she wants to do. Georgie sees her discomfiture and says, 'I've seen him and you'd think he was a hunk. He looks like a young Mel Gibson.'

This comment has given Jenny a chance to make light of Sheila's questions and she says, 'Yes, he is a hunk and we got together about three years ago. We'd caught up with each other before that though, when he took over doing the garden from his father.'

Annie has been the last to have any suspicions about Jenny's involvement with a man, but now thinks it all very romantic. She asks, 'When did you realise you loved each other?'

'For the first year after we met again it was all totally innocent. We'd talk about jobs I wanted done around the place and sometimes have a drink together after he finished working. Because we'd been friends when we were young, things were always so easy between us. Then one weekend I came up here, by myself as usual, and Stuart took me to that beach we went to yesterday. We swam for ages, riding in on the waves and horsing around like a pair of teenagers. Afterwards we were lying on the beach to dry off and he kissed me.' Jenny grins, remembering that moment. 'And fireworks. I realised I'd wanted him to kiss me for months. Later he told me he'd held back because I was married, but he reckons he's been in love with me since we were kids.'

'How romantic,' Annie sighs.

Sheila is more cynical. 'Why didn't you leave Mark? He wasn't sick then, and you hadn't been happy with him for years.'

Jenny answers defensively, 'I told Mark I wanted a divorce and he threatened to get the best lawyer in town and fight for custody of the boys. They were only fourteen and fifteen at the time, and I was frightened a judge might think they'd be better off with their father. All that happened shortly before I went and visited Georgie in Sydney.' She turns to face Georgie. 'I so wanted to tell you about Stuart and get your advice on what I should do about Mark's threats, but in the end I couldn't. I'd got so used to keeping my problems to myself.'

Georgie has had clients faced with the same dilemma and understands what Jenny was going through. She also thinks Sheila has been unnecessarily aggressive in her questioning of Jenny. Now she says sympathetically, 'I understand why you found it hard to talk about; and it wasn't an easy situation. I've had clients whose husbands' have got custody in similar circumstances and I've had to battle to get reasonable access for them. Now enough of the inquisition. This is meant to be a relaxing day out.'

Jenny flashes Georgie a look of gratitude. 'I'd have told you all about him when things were more settled between us.'

Annie pats her hand. 'We know you would have, and I'm sure you'll make up with him when he comes back from that fishing trip.'

Jenny just says a quiet, 'I hope so.' Then relieved the questions about her and Stuart have ended she says more brightly, 'I guess we'd better think about putting out this fire and packing up. The walk back up will take longer than coming down did.'

171

They pour water from the stream onto the fire then cover the ashes with some of the stones. After repacking their backpacks they set off in single file up the steep narrow path. Jenny has almost reached the top when she hears an agonised cry from Annie who is walking behind her. Looking back she sees she has tripped over one of the vine-like roots that crisscross the path in places. Annie is sitting on the ground, holding her ankle and her face is screwed up in pain.

Coming up behind her Georgie asks, 'What's happened?'

Annie moans, 'I think I've sprained my ankle. I tripped on one of those wretched roots and fell heavily on it.'

Jenny reaches down to help her up. 'Can you walk on it? We're nearly to the top and then we'll be able to check it out.'

Annie stands and takes a tentative step. 'It hurts to put any weight on it, but we can't do anything here so I guess I'll just have to put up with it.'

By the time they reach the top she is in severe pain and hobbles towards a log where she collapses with a sigh of relief. She feels such a twit, so makes light of her predicament. 'I don't suppose any of you girl guides have a bandage with you?'

Jenny digs around in the inside pocket of her back pack and pulls out a small first-aid kit. 'Never go anywhere without it. It's a habit I got into when the boys were young and I'd take them on bush walks. One or the other of them was always getting cut or stung.' She searches through the small pack and pulls out a bandage.

She gently touches Annie's ankle noting that it is only slightly swollen. 'I think you've probably just twisted it, but there's a nasty gash on the side. If you'd sprained it there would be more swelling by now. The bandage will give you some support, but ideally you shouldn't walk on it for a while.'

While Jenny bandages Annie's ankle Georgie says to Sheila, 'If you take my backpack and Jenny takes Annie's, I'll help our invalid back to the car.'

They set off with Georgie supporting Annie as she hops awkwardly along the narrow track. When they reach the car Jenny suggests Annie sit in the back with her foot up, and while Sheila is helping her make Annie comfortable Georgie jumps in the front. 'Hey, this means I get to sit in the front and don't bang my head all the way out,' Georgie jokes, and they all laugh.

By the time they arrive back at the beach house it is late afternoon. After they help Annie onto a couch in the lounge room Jenny unwinds the bandage and checks the ankle. 'It's not swelling so I don't think there's any major damage. How's it feeling?'

Annie tentatively stands up and winces. 'It still hurts to put weight on it, but the sharp pain has gone.'

Sheila looks at Jenny. 'What say Georgie and I cook dinner while you entertain the invalid? It's been years since we messed around in the kitchen together, but I'm sure we haven't lost our touch.'

'Great idea,' Georgie agrees. 'We'll cook the loin of pork with loads of vegetables and make a tarte Tatin for dessert.'

'And a surprise entrée,' Sheila joins in enthusiastically. 'Now come on girl. Let's get cracking.'

While the other two busy themselves in the kitchen Jenny gets out the game of scrabble and sets it up so that Annie can reach it from her position on the couch. Annie is glad that they have this time alone, for learning about Stuart has renewed her concern that they are here at her suggestion. It now seems highly likely that Jenny had planned to come here so she and Stuart could be together after such a long time apart.

She blurts out, 'Jen, I'm sorry we talked you into this.'

Jenny looks up from her letters, a puzzled look on her face. 'Talked me into what?'

'Us coming up here. Obviously you'd have rather come alone so you could spend time with Stuart, but I thought you'd be by yourself.'

'Look love, I did feel a bit miffed initially, but it's wonderful having you all here; just what I needed to take my mind off things.'

'It certainly does that.'

'You said that so vehemently. Sheila told me you'd had a row with Joel and that was part of the reason you got upset on Saturday. What's the problem? I always thought you two had the ultimate happy marriage.'

'I guess we've done alright, but every marriage has its ups and downs.'

Thinking of how unhappy her own marriage has been for such a long time Jenny says rather wistfully, 'But some have more downs than others. I wouldn't have thought you and Joel had many really bad times.'

Annie sighs. 'No, and I don't suppose we have. Except for the first couple of years we've been happy, very happy a lot of the time. It's just that he's become so sort of set in his ways; not willing to see there might be other things in life than the farm. He can't see why the kids might want anything different from the life he's had.' Almost as an afterthought she adds, 'or that I might want something different for that matter.'

Jenny is about to ask her what she meant by her last, rather cryptic remark when Sheila comes into the room carrying two glasses of red wine. 'When Georgie and I shared the flat we always drank while cooking, so we're keeping up the tradition. We've just opened a particularly good pinot that comes from one of the vineyards up this way. Even though you two are loafing around we thought we'd better share it with you.' She places the glasses on the table with a flourish, and says in a very false French accent, 'I 'ope you enjoy the wine Madams. Soon we will serve you an oh so delicious dinner.' With a grin she returns to the kitchen, but before the door closes behind her the delicious aromas of garlic, herbs and roasting pork waft out.

'Gee, those smells are making me hungry. Let's finish this game and then I'll set the dining table with the best dinnerware and cutlery.'

They finish the game and Jenny finds Annie some magazines to read before going off to hunt up out the best china and set the table. As she sits idly turning the pages of a fashion magazine Annie listens to Jenny opening drawers at the dining end of the room and the sounds of laughter coming from the kitchen. She thinks how good it is to hear those two being happy together. They'd seemed a bit distant with each other since their argument on Sunday morning, and it's good to hear them laughing and joking now, for they had always been very close.

When they were teenagers she and Jenny had been very popular with boys and often double dated, whereas Georgie had shown a distinct lack of interest in the opposite sex and Sheila had few admirers. This had led to there being a bit of a split between them; they still spent a lot of time together as a foursome but Georgie and Sheila hung out together when she and Jenny were out with boyfriends.

This changed once she married and the others went to university, for then they formed a trio and she felt left out of things. After Jenny married and had the boys she and Jenny had seen quite a bit of each other and regained their former closeness, while the other two moved into a flat when they were in their early twenties and shared until Georgie moved to Sydney.

Since then this is the first time they have all been together for any longer than an afternoon or the odd dinner, and Annie smiles at the thought that this afternoon they have moved back to the familiar pairings of the past.

As she is thinking this she hears another burst of laughter coming from the kitchen and Sheila comes into the room a bottle of wine in her hands. 'Hi there. Dinner's nearly ready, but I thought you two might like a top up.'

Annie grins. 'I certainly would and I'm sure Jen would too. She's been busy laying out the best dinner ware in celebration of the feast you two are preparing.'

Sheila surveys the table, and from her possie on the couch Annie hears her exclaim, 'Oh, how lovely; and fitting for the meal we've prepared. Now let's help the invalid to the table and we'll serve the first course.'

Annie gets up and hobbles along the room saying, 'I can make it on my own.' She stands for a moment admiring the table. On the dazzlingly white cloth Jenny has set out heavy silver cutlery, crystal glasses and white, gold-rimmed side plates. The centre-piece is an exquisite crystal vase containing beautifully arranged star jasmine and feathery greenery, and the rest of the white and gold dinner set sits on the sideboard.

While Jenny and Annie take their seats at the table Sheila goes to the kitchen and soon returns carrying a platter of golden toasted circles of bread. Georgie follows with a bowl containing a strange black mixture. They place the food before the other two and Sheila says in her atrocious French accent, 'Croutons avec tapenade.'

Annie, who has never seen this dish before, asks what it is and Georgie says, 'It's a favourite of mine. I first had it at a French restaurant in Pitt Street and loved it so much I asked for the recipe. It's made with black olives, anchovies, lemon juice, olive oil and a touch of garlic. We had to improvise with the croutons because we didn't have a baguette. Sheila came up with the idea of cutting circles out of the white bread I bought this morning and it's worked perfectly. Now let's tuck in, or bon appetite as my French friend would say.'

Sheila and Georgie have enjoyed working together preparing the meal and seem to have recaptured the easy camaraderie they once shared. They bring an infectious feeling of gaiety to the room, and as the four friends begin to eat the meal they all laugh and chatter like teenagers. Annie is the only one who hasn't tasted tapenade before and is a bit wary, but when she tries it she enthuses about how delicious it is.

While the other two clear the table and go to the kitchen for the second course Jenny pours more wine and sets out the big dinner plates. The others soon return with Sheila bearing a platter containing the pork surrounded by roast potatoes and tiny white onions and Georgie follows with another platter of asparagus and baby carrots wrapped in prosciutto and sprinkled with parsley. She also carries a jug of gravy or jus as Sheila insists on calling it. With exaggerated finesse they serve the other two before helping themselves to the food. Annie says how lovely it is to be waited on, and Jenny agrees, saying she will certainly return to this restaurant again.

After the main course is finished the chefs clear the table and bring out the tart which consists of caramelised apples artistically arranged on a golden pastry base. This is to be served with whipped cream. When Jenny comments on how attractive it is Sheila says, 'I can assure you it tastes as good as it looks. And I have a lovely sauterne to go with it.'

Jenny places the dessert plates on the table and gets some smaller glasses from a cupboard in the sideboard. When the dessert has been served and the new glasses are filled with the sweet white wine Jenny lifts her glass and says, 'To our friendship, and thank you for a fantastic meal.' They clink glasses and as the others sip their wine she adds, 'And thank you for being so understanding about me not telling you about Stuart before this, but it was all so complicated.'

As she says this she feels a bit hypocritical, for she still hasn't told them about the baby and that is really the most important complication now.

They finish the meal and Jenny loads the dishwasher while the other three go to the lounge room to look through the collection of old CDs Sheila has brought with her. As she finishes tidying up in the kitchen she hears the sound of Whitney Houston belting out the old familiar song, 'I Wanna Dance with Somebody.' When she joins them she sees Georgie and Sheila dancing around the room while Annie watches from the couch, moving her body in time to the music.

They spend the remainder of the evening playing the old CDs, singing along with some and dancing to others. By the time they eventually say their goodnights and stagger off to bed they are all slightly drunk and very tired, for it has been a long and eventful day.

Jenny picks up her mobile from the bedside table and punches in Stuart's number, but once more gets his answering machine. She almost hangs up as she did the previous evening, but is desperate to settle things between them. She says abruptly, 'We need to talk. The girls are leaving on Friday morning but I'll be here till Saturday. Then to soften the message she adds, 'I love you. Please try and understand how I feel.'

Sheila and Annie

After waking early Sheila decided to build on the renewed feelings of camaraderie between her and Georgie and join her on her morning run. On their return they burst into the kitchen to find Annie up and hobbling around the kitchen. Sheila collapses into a chair breathing heavily. 'My god, I got up early just to show her I can be a lark too but I thought we were going for a gentle jog. You'd think she was trying out for the Olympics.'

Georgie grins. 'You're just not fit girl. Annie kept up okay with me yesterday.'

'Only just,' Annie laughs. 'It wasn't easy. I got the stitch twice and was staggering by the time we got back.'

'Talking of staggering, how's the ankle this morning?' Sheila asks.

'It still hurts a bit when I put all my weight on it, but it's nowhere near as painful as it was. I reckon if I take it easy today it will be right by tomorrow.'

As she is saying this Jenny comes into the room, looks at Sheila's red sweating face and at Annie awkwardly trying to make coffee while balancing on one leg and says, 'Sit down Annie, and you two go and shower while I make us breakfast for a change.' Despite not having heard from Stuart she is determined to try to hide her concern from her friends, for she doesn't want to spoil the time they have together.

She gives Annie a bunch of parsley to cut up and sets to work beating together eggs and cream, then adding grated cheese. She pours the mixture into a pot and sets it on a very low heat, stirring it occasionally while she grills bacon and cooks toast. Just before the other two return she adds the parsley to the scrambled eggs and puts it on a platter in the middle of the table. She put buttered toast and the crispy bacon on another large platter and sets out four plates and mugs.

When Georgie and Sheila are seated she pours coffee for everyone then sits down saying, 'Help yourself everyone.'

They are all eating hungrily and praising the food when the phone rings. Jenny looks worried. 'God I hope nothing's wrong. The boys and Mum are the only ones who know the number here, but I can't imagine why any of them would be ringing.'

She gets up hastily and goes to the hall where an old-fashioned phone sits on a small wooden stand. The others pause in their eating; they try not to appear to be eavesdropping on the conversation but they all are. The call is obviously unexpected for Jenny looked worried when she left to answer it.

In a short while Jenny returns, a smile on her face. 'It's Joel for you. Evidently he got the number from the boys last night, but thought it was too late to ring.'

Annie looks flustered. 'Did he say what he's ringing about? Everything alright at home isn't it?'

Jenny hears the panic in her voice and pats her shoulder, 'Yes love,' she says quickly and reassuringly. 'He just wants to talk to you about something to do with Sam. He sounds happy so I'm sure there's nothing wrong.'

Annie hobbles to the passage and the others hear her say in a surprisingly abrupt voice, 'What's up? Why are you ringing me here?'

There is a long silence while Joel is obviously speaking then Annie says, 'Well I'm glad you've finally really listened to him. Now perhaps you'll realise it's what he wants and not something I've been pushing him into.'

There is another silence before she says more softly, 'Of course I forgive you, but I get so tired of you thinking you know what's best for everyone. You don't you know.'

Following another pause Annie says, 'And I love you, but there are still things we need to sort out. I'll be home Saturday. See you then. Bye.'

When Annie returns to the kitchen the others are eating and pretend they haven't heard her half of the conversation. Jenny and Sheila know there has been some problem between Annie and Joel and Georgie knows what the disagreement has been about. From what they've overheard it would seem that things should be settled between the two, but Annie isn't looking as happy as they expected her to.

Jenny looks up questioningly. 'Everything okay love?'

Annie sits back down and sighs. 'Yes, it's sorted. I've already told Georgie about this. For months Sam's been trying to get Joel to see that he doesn't want to work on the farm. He's a bright boy and wants to study architecture or engineering at uni, but Joel has refused to take his ambitions seriously. The other day Sam asked me to intervene which I did, and Joel and I ended up having an awful row before I came up here.'

'So everything's good again.' Georgie is happy the problem is sorted because she hadn't known what to think when Annie had complained to her about Joel. She'd always thought him such an easy-going gentle man and couldn't imagine him being difficult.

They are all surprised when Annie answers. 'Sam's problem is over, but I still don't feel everything's sorted. During these past few years Joel has seemed to become so set in his ways.' She gives a sad little shrug then continues.

'Oh, I don't know. Perhaps it's me. Perhaps I've become too picky or want more than is reasonable to expect.'

Sheila pats her hand. 'I'm sure you'll sort it all out when you get home. Obviously Joel's took notice of what you told him. I just hope Scott has taken my advice by the time I get back'.

Georgie had sensed that something was wrong between Sheila and Scott when she'd been at their place for dinner, but Sheila hadn't wanted to talk about it. Now she asks semi-jokingly, 'Well are you going to let us in on what's going on between you and Scott? You said the other night when I was at your place you'd tell me when we got up here, but so far all you've done is bite my head off when I criticised the way he treated you in the beginning.'

'Yes, I did over-react didn't I? When you said that about Scott being weak and easy to manipulate it hit home because that's the way I've been feeling about him lately. His daughter Vicki has been harassing him since her mother died; ringing him up at all hours and ranting drunkenly about how he's to blame for her death.'

Annie looks bewildered. 'How could he possibly be to blame? She died of cancer didn't she?'

'Yes, but according to Vicki the cancer was caused by the stress Scott put her through by leaving her. I felt sorry for Vicki to start with for she obviously wasn't coping with her grief, but it's gone on for so long it's affecting Scott's health. He's also become so bad-tempered with the kids. He used to be a great father, but now he picks on them for the least little thing and they are becoming quite frightened of him when he's in one of his miserable moods.'

'So that's what you and Scott rowed about?'

'Yes Annie. I told him I'd had enough and if he didn't do something about it I would. We didn't get a chance to talk in the morning because Mia woke us up, and I didn't want to continue the argument in front of the children.'

'Perhaps he'll have dealt with it while you're away,' says Annie optimistically.

'No, I don't think so. As you said Georgie he was weak and easily manipulated by that first wife of his and I don't think he's changed.'

Jenny has seen Scott more than Georgie and Annie in recent years. She stands and puts her arms around Sheila's shoulders and says, 'He's a good man though, and you know how much he loves Mia and William but Vicki's his daughter too. He only stayed with his first wife for so long because she convinced him it was best for the children. He will always love his first son and daughter and it must be hard to see Vicki suffering now.'

Sheila shrugs. 'I know it is, but I just wish he'd do something about it. Now, that's enough of my problem. What have you got planned for us today?'

'Well, it's another sunny day so I thought we'd spend the morning on the beach, then veg. out on the deck this afternoon and go out to dinner tonight. There's quite a good restaurant attached to the motel in town, and it will give me a chance to thank you properly for the beautiful meal you two cooked last night.'

'Lovely,' enthused Annie, 'I'll get a chance to wear my one decent dress.'

Jenny

For Jenny it had been a bad start to the day for she expected Stuart to ring this morning and he hadn't. When he failed to call by seven-thirty she had rung him again only to get the answering machine once more. She'd left a brief message, 'Please call me tonight,' and pressed the off button. Where can he be at this time of day? Has he gone off somewhere in a sulk, or is he sitting at home listening to the phone ring and deliberately ignoring her?

Although she hasn't suffered from full blown morning sickness she has felt slightly seedy at the start of each day for the past two months. Today is no exception and she tells herself she probably shouldn't be drinking, but then what does it matter if the baby is affected as she's going to kill it anyway. She has deliberately not thought about it as a baby until now because she couldn't see any other alternative but to abort it. Having talked to Stuart and seen his reaction she is confused.

Determined to forget her worries and have a good time with her friends, she showered and dressed in a bikini and sarong before joining the others in the kitchen. They had all been enjoying the breakfast she cooked when Joel rang. She'd have thought his call would have made Annie happy, but obviously there is something still bugging her, something she's not telling them. Sheila has finally told them why she is unhappy with Scott so that's one less secret between them. Jenny thinks Sheila's being a bit hard on the poor guy, but then she doesn't have to live with him and his current moods. No-one ever really knows what goes on in other people's lives, not even the lives of your best friends.

When they asked what she had planned for the day Jenny decided now would be a good time for a meal out. It should cheer them all up and be something to look forward to during the day.

While the others change into bathers Jenny fills the dish washer and tidies the kitchen, and soon they are all heading for the beach. Annie is still limping but says the ankle is so much better than it was. Although the waves are only small they have enough force to put her off balance, so she only swims for a short while then sits on the beach reading while the others cavort in the water. She finds it difficult to concentrate on her book for her mind keeps returning to Joel's phone call. He had been so sure she'd be thrilled that he'd finally listened to Sam; couldn't understand why she had still been short with him. Well he'll find out when she gets home.

After a long swim the others join her and lie on their towels to dry out. The day is hot and by mid-morning they are all feeling slightly sunburnt, despite slathering each other with sun screen.

Sheila says, 'I really don't think I can take any more sun.'

Annie agrees. 'I'm definitely feeling overheated. Remember how we used to lie in the sun practically all day?'

'All part of being young and foolish,' Jenny says with a grin. 'Let's go back to the house and make long cool drinks and sit in the shade.'

They gather together towels and sun glasses and walk across the hot sand and road, sighing with relief once they begin walking on the cool lawn. When they reach the house they take turns under the outside shower and then go to their rooms to change into light clothes. It is almost lunch time so Jenny lights the barbecue and puts the last of the chops in a marinade of olive oil, lemon juice, garlic and rosemary. She whips up a green salad of mescalin, cucumber, green capsicum and spring onions and puts it in the fridge, then turns her attention to the drinks.

By the time the others return she has four long cold gin and tonics sitting on the glass-topped table on the deck.

Sheila collapses into one of the cane chairs and takes a glass saying, 'Oh yum, my favourite tipple.'

They sit around the table chatting and enjoying their drinks. After the glare of the sun on the beach it is a relief to be in the shade of an awning that runs the length of the deck on this side of the house. Jenny checks the barbecue then gets the chops from the kitchen and puts them on to cook.

Annie sniffs the air. 'Isn't that the most wonderful smell, lamb, rosemary and garlic?'

"It's sure making me hungry,' Georgie moans. 'Would you like me to make a salad to go with it?'

'It's already made and in the fridge, but I haven't dressed it yet. Would you mind putting on some olive oil and lemon juice and bringing it out?' Jenny turns the chops then goes to the kitchen for plates and cutlery.

Georgie places the salad on the table saying, 'Look at this, girls. I don't know how Jen puts together a beautiful salad like this in no time at all.'

Jenny laughs as she puts the chops onto a platter and places it in the middle of the table. 'One of the things I love about being up here is that I get to mess around in the kitchen. At home it's very much Trudy's domain and I feel like an interloper if I so much as make the boys a quick snack. The only time I get to cook at home is at the weekends'

Annie looks surprised. 'I thought Trudy just did the housework; I didn't realise she did most of the cooking as well.'

Jenny can almost read Annie's thoughts from the expression on her face. 'I can see you wondering what I do with my time. Well I can tell you; not a lot. For the first few years after Mark and I married I was busy with the boys as well as continuing to do a lot of the marketing for the firm. I'd hoped to work full-time once the boys went to school, but by then Mark had found a bright young thing, female of course, with a Masters in Marketing to take my place.'

Sheila looks surprised at Jenny's glum expression. 'But you've done a tremendous amount of entertaining for the firm and were very involved in the charities for which Mark got most of the kudos.'

'I've done what Mark wanted me to do, not necessarily what I'd have chosen.'

'I always thought you were happy being the hostess with the mostest. And when we were girls you always said you'd rather be a rich man's darling than a young man's slave.'

Tears form in Jenny's eyes but she brushes them away and says angrily, 'You know damn well I haven't been his darling for ages. During the first few years of our marriage he was great. He included me in the business, and was so pleased when I gave him children, something neither of his previous wives managed to do. The good years didn't last long though. He was incapable of being faithful and soon started sneaking around having affairs. In recent years he hadn't even bothered to be discreet about them. I've been his hostess and the mother of his children; apart from that I've just been his bloody chattel.' Now the tears can no longer be brushed away and run freely down her face. 'I should have left him years ago, before I started the affair with Stuart, but I was too damn weak.'

Sheila puts her arms around her and the others reach across the table and hold her hands. For a long time they are silent then Annie says gently, 'Well now you can choose exactly what you want to do.'

Jenny looks at the worried faces of her friends and sighs, 'If only I knew what that is.' She wipes away the tears. 'Oh, sorry for carrying on like such a twit.' She frees her hands and stands. 'We're meant to be having fun; must be time for another drink and then I'll ring the restaurant and book us a table.'

They spend the remainder of the afternoon chatting about films and books and food; nice safe unemotional subjects for the other three don't want Jenny to get upset again.

Getting ready for their night out reminds them of so many evenings long ago. Jenny curls up the ends of Annie's hair and insists on giving her the full make-up treatment, something Annie rarely bothers with now. Sheila and Georgie brush each other's hair and everyone admires the outfits they have each chosen to wear. Georgie wears a white silk pants suit, Sheila a long burnt orange skirt with a cream, low-necked blouse and Jenny a short black cocktail dress. Annie is so glad she packed her patterned dress for she knows it suits her and she looks as classy as her three friends.

Jenny drives them the short distance to the restaurant and they walk from the car park arm in arm. They feel young and glamorous as they walk through the still warm night, enjoying being together and carefree, at least for the moment.

They enter the small foyer. There is a polished timber reception desk on one wall and next to it is a door that evidently leads to the bar for a rowdy noise can be heard whenever the door is opened. On the other wall is a sleek modern couch covered in dark blue suede and next to that is the door to the restaurant. When Jenny leads them into this room they are greeted by an attractive woman whose straight shoulder-length blonde hair and deeply tanned skin is complimented by a long dark blue silk kaftan. She greets Jenny with kisses on both cheeks and says, 'It's so good to see you stranger. I heard a couple of days ago you were up here with some friends and was pleased to see you'd booked in for dinner.'

Jenny grins. 'So the local grapevine's still working efficiently. These are my oldest and dearest friends, Annie, Georgie and Sheila.' She turns and puts an arm around the blonde. 'And this is one of my newest friends, Charmaine. She and her husband Craig bought the motel when they were here on holiday and moved from Brisbane about four years ago. They've done wonders with it and Craig is a top chef so I can assure you you'll have a great meal.'

Charmaine beams at the praise. 'Let me show you to your table. I've given you the one at the back of the room near a window.'

Once they are seated Annie looks admiringly around the room. 'I love the décor. The dark blue carpet with the white walls looks so smart. And those gorgeous paintings add just the touch of colour needed to bring it all together.'

Sheila agrees approvingly. 'They certainly are stunning. They remind me a bit of the paintings Brett Whitely did of Sydney Harbour.'

'Actually Charmaine's the artist and they're all inspired by places around here. She'd made quite a name for herself up north. Had a couple of solo exhibitions, but since coming down here she hasn't had much time to paint. She's hoping to get back to it now that the motel and restaurant are up and running the way they wanted.'

As Jenny is speaking Charmaine returns with a bottle of cold water and the menus. She pours water for everyone then says, 'As Jenny knows we specialise in fresh fish. Tonight we have crayfish, just off the boat, and some really lovely trevalla so our specials tonight are crayfish tails topped with a creamy sauce for entrée and trevalla parcels for mains.'

'Sounds great to me.' Jenny says enthusiastically. 'I've had Craig's fish parcels before. The fish is always so succulent and his flavours are superb.'

'I haven't had Tassie crayfish for years and trevalla is my favourite fish so I'll have the same. What about you two?' Georgie looks across the table at Annie and Sheila who have been reading the menus.

'I'll have the crayfish entrée too, but I'll have flounder for the main.' Sheila puts aside the menu and takes a sip of water.

Annie continues to study the menu. 'It all sounds so wonderful. I'll have the same entrée as everyone else, but I think I'll go for the flathead. Dad used to take the boys and me fishing when we were kids and that was what we mainly caught. They're still one of my favourites.'

Jenny orders a local chardonnay and Charmaine takes the menus and leaves with a smile.

'It sounds as though you've been a regular. I'd got the impression you were a bit reclusive when you stayed up here.' Sheila looks enquiringly at Jenny.

'Generally I was, but I met Charmaine on the beach shortly after she and Craig arrived. She was painting and we got talking about their plans for the motel and restaurant. We've become good friends and when they first opened I'd often come here alone for dinner and we'd sit and chat when all the other diners left. After I told Mark I wanted a divorce and he found out I had a lover Stuart and I dined here together a couple of times, but I always felt a bit uncomfortable being in public with him.'

Sheila says curtly, 'Once Mark knew about you and Stuart I don't see why you'd worry about being seen together. Mark certainly wasn't always that careful about being seen with his women.'

Jenny looks flustered. She is upset by both Sheila's tone and her reference to Mark's affairs. 'I didn't want the boys finding out. They are still friends with some of the kids they played with when they used to come up here, and I thought it might get back to them.'

Annie thinks Sheila is being unnecessarily mean by mentioning Marks philandering. Although they had all known he had been unfaithful for years, until today Jenny had never confided with them about it. Obviously it had been something she'd hoped wasn't public knowledge, but Sheila's remark made it clear it was. She is glad when Charmaine appears with the entrees and the conversation turns to appreciation of the food.

The remainder of the meal passes happily. They all agree the crayfish is superb and enjoy their various mains. After ordering coffees and liqueurs Jenny excuses herself to go to the toilet. Annie stands and says, 'I need to go too.'

She follows Jenny across the dining room to a door that opens onto the back of the foyer. They cross to another door that leads to the saloon bar and Jenny laughs, 'Quite a route march isn't it. You wouldn't want to be in a hurry.'

As she says this she looks towards the main bar on the other side of the dividing counters and her smile disappears. Annie notices her changed expression, peers across at the noisy, smoke-filled room and asks, 'What's up? You look as though you've seen a ghost.'

'Oh it's nothing,' Jenny answers as she pushes open the door and moves quickly to the first cubicle. She is glad that by the time they meet at the wash basins Annie seems to have forgotten the incident.

When they return to their table the coffees have arrived. They all agree it is the perfect end to what has been a really lovely meal. On the short trip home Sheila comments on how rare it is to find such a top restaurant in a country town, and the talk turns to other memorable meals they have enjoyed together. Once they arrive back at the beach house they kiss and hug goodnight and go to their bedrooms, for they are all feeling tired and slightly drunk.

As she shuts her door behind her Jenny breathes a sigh and slumps disconsolately onto her bed. Stuart had been in the bar laughing and joking with some of his friends. She is relieved Annie doesn't know what he looks like, for she would have had to come up with some explanation of why he was there when he is meant to be away fishing.

She had looked forward to taking her friends out for the evening but it hadn't gone as well as she'd expected. She feels they are all a bit miffed at her for not telling them about Stuart sooner, for when they were young they told each other everything. She hadn't told them about Mark's infidelities either and Sheila's rather caustic remark tonight hurt. Sheila had made it clear she, and probably the other two, had known about her marital problems. Some stupid sense of pride had kept her from telling her closest friends about the heartache and embarrassment she was experiencing but her silly sense of pride had made her keep it to herself. Now she realises they had probably known in any case.

She'd learnt about the first affair shortly before she and Annie spent that holiday up here with their kids. Heartbroken and confused she'd needed to talk about it to someone, but somehow Annie didn't seem to be the one. Outwardly she had so much more than Annie. She had completed her education and worked in an exciting and rewarding job, had married her wealthy boss and now lived in a beautiful house. Their two sons attended the best private school in the state. For years she'd felt sorry for Annie battling to help Joel make a success of their farm while their children attended a mediocre country school; now she envied her, for she would always have the security of Joel's love. Was it some sort of false pride that had stopped her confiding her heartbreak to her friend? She isn't sure; it's so long ago and she hardly remembers what the young disillusioned Jenny really felt.

That first one had been the worst. Fiona, bright young and ambitious, first replaced Jenny as marketing manager and shortly afterwards became his lover. Someone in the office sent Jenny an anonymous letter telling her of the affair. When she faced Mark with the letter he'd pretended it was just vicious gossip and she pretended to believe him.

She had kept her heartbreak to herself. Throughout the years of their marriage she knew there were other women, heard whispered rumours and learnt to recognise the tell-tale signs that he was having yet another affair. She learnt to turn a blind eye to his womanising. She knew

Mark loved her in his limited way and he adored their sons. Once when they were both slightly drunk after a dinner with friends she suggested, only half-jokingly, that they divorce. He had looked at her stunned and said, 'I'll never divorce you. You're the mother of my children.'

She had felt trapped but lacked the will to fight her way out of her comfortable trap. Thinking back to the conversation she overheard years ago between her mother and aunt she realised she had spent years despising her mother for what she too was now prepared to accept for the sake of peace.

Falling in love with Stuart had seemed to be the first pure and honest emotion she had experienced in years, but she'd lacked the strength to live up to it. She's given in to Mark's threats of fighting her for custody of their sons and allowed him to sully that relationship. What should have been open and honest became a secret, from their sons and her friends. Now her friends know about it, but not the dilemma she faces.

Tonight she was upset to see Stuart laughing and joking in the bar with his friends. Her initial reaction had been one of shock and anger at seeing him looking so light-hearted and happy after the ultimatum he'd given her. Their future together is in the balance and he was out enjoying himself. In retrospect she knows this reaction was ridiculous, for she had also been out with friends apparently having a lovely evening. No, what is really worrying her is that he hasn't answered her phone calls.

She reaches for her phone and taps in his number. Once more it rings and rings then the message bank clicks in. She knows Stuart doesn't check his phone often, but he should have got her earlier messages by now. All she can think to say is, 'Why don't you answer my calls?' She puts the phone on the bedside table and slowly begins to undress.

Georgie

Georgie is woken by a steady banging noise and opens sleepy eyes to see where it's coming from. When she'd opened her window before going to bed she mustn't have latched it properly for now it is swinging in the wind. She gets out of bed quickly, secures the latch then gazes at the wild and windy view before her. From her room at the back of the house she can see across the back lawn to the line of trees that edge the property. They are swaying furiously in the strong wind and above them the sky is a strange pearly yellow filled with dark scudding clouds.

'Not much of a day for a run,' she thinks as she walks to the chest of drawers next to her bed and pulls out track pants and matching top. Knowing how changeable Tassie's weather could be she packed both summer and winter clothes for her trip down, but this is the first day she's needed her warm gear. As she dresses she wonders if Sheila will join her again today for a run. In Sydney she usually runs alone, but during this week she has enjoyed having company even if Annie had had trouble keeping up and Sheila had moaned a bit. Georgie had been very upset by their argument earlier in the week, but cooking together and then Sheila joining her for a run seems to have brought them closer together again. Possibly having the argument was a good thing because it brought out grievances they both had, but there is still something not quite right between them; something unsettled. As she pulls on her joggers and ties the laces she thinks about friendships and how important these three women have always been to her. Even though sometimes two or three years pass between their meetings there is always the same feeling of familiarity and affection once they are together again. Perhaps it's true that the friends you make when you are young are the most important.

She walks silently along the passage, and as she steps out onto the verandah feels slightly disappointed that Sheila isn't there waiting to join her. As she sets off at a steady pace down the drive she thinks Sheila is probably wise to stay snugged up in bed, for there is a strong cold wind blowing that makes running unpleasant and difficult. She decides to stay on the road away from the worst of the sea winds and heads north running parallel with the beach until she reaches the top of the slight rise that leads to the headland. She pauses and looks out to sea. The water is a dull grey colour. Large waves are crashing onto the beach and further out the wind catches at the water swirling it into a mass of white foam. She vaguely remembers her father calling this phenomenon 'white horses' and wonders when they could have been at a beach together. She has no memory of him ever taking her anywhere or of spending time with her except as two people forced by circumstances to live in the same house. It could be that his final rejection of her blotted out anything good they may have shared.

She continues along the road, but when the first drops of rain begin to fall turns around and heads back to the beach house. By the time she reaches the drive she has run two kilometres in cold pelting rain and is soaked to her skin. Heading straight for her bedroom she strips off her sodden clothes in the ensuite and luxuriates under a hot shower until she begins to feel normal again. She dresses in dry undies, jeans, a warm sweater and thick socks before heading to the kitchen in search of a warming cup of coffee.

Annie is already seated at the table drinking a coffee and leafing idly through a magazine. She looks up as Georgie enters the room and says sympathetically, 'You must have got soaked. I saw you setting off, but thought you'd turn back before the rain hit. Sit down and let me make you a coffee.'

Georgie waves her to stay seated and says, 'Nah, you stay where you are. It's my own stupid fault I got so wet, but I didn't expect it to rain that hard. It was almost like a tropical storm.'

As she says this there is a sudden rumbling noise, loud enough to make Annie jump. 'My God, what was that?'

'Looks like we're in for a thunderstorm,' Georgie says as she picks up her coffee cup and walks outside to the verandah. She moves around to the front of the house and looks at the wild water and the dark scudding clouds. A bright flash of zigzag lightning brightens the grey world before her and is followed by another roll of thunder. Georgie has the same feelings about thunderstorms as she has for rough water; a combination of fear and fascination.

'What are you doing out here in the cold?' Annie comes and stands next to her, nursing her cup of coffee between her hands and shivering in the cold morning air.

'You should have seen the lightning. It lit up the whole bay.'

As she speaks an enormous double zigzag descends from the thick clouds and seems to land with a sizzle in the water. It is closely followed by thunder that is so strong it shakes the verandah.

'Another minute and we'll be in the middle of the storm,' Annie says nervously. 'I think we ought to get inside.'

The slight fear in Annie's voice breaks into the rapt fear and fascination Georgie has been feeling and she follows her back into the house. As Annie secures the door

Georgie realises her heart is thumping as hard as it would after a five kilometre run. She thinks how stupid it is that she has so little control over her emotional response to the wilder side of the natural world.

Annie sees that her friend is looking strained and says cheerfully, 'I reckon it's my turn to cook breakfast today, and I'm going to do what we call farmhouse breakfast at home; eggs, baked beans, bacon and sausages.'

'Sounds fine to me,' Sheila says as she enters the kitchen. 'Do you need a hand?'

Annie has already turned on the grill and is pulling out a pot and pans from the wide drawer under the sink. 'Just help yourself to coffee, and then you can go and wake up our stay-in-bed friend. Tell her breakfast in ten minutes.'

Sheila pours a coffee and then walks along the passage to Jenny's room. She knocks then opens the door saying, 'You awake yet Jen?' She sees the bed is empty but hears a noise that sounds like someone vomiting coming from the ensuite. She slides aside the door, sees Jenny leaning over the vanity basin in her nightdress and asks, 'You okay Jen?'

Jenny had woken feeling nauseous, as she has a few mornings lately, but has not actually vomited until today. She splashes water on her face then turns to Sheila and forces a grin. 'Just trying to wake myself up. You lot are all such early risers.'

'Well I've been sent to tell you that breakfast is in ten minutes, and Annie is cooking what she calls a 'farmhouse breakfast', eggs, sausages, baked beans and bacon, so you'd better be feeling hungry.'

Inwardly Jenny groans at the thought of a hearty breakfast. All she really wants is coffee and dry toast, but she'll have to pretend to enjoy it. Perhaps she'll be able to get away with just eating a little of each, although the thought of sausages and baked beans is nearly enough to make her vomit again. After Sheila leaves the room to return to the kitchen Jenny looks in the mirror over the vanity basin. She sees her reflection, white-faced and tense, and once again feels nauseous as the smell of frying sausages wafts through from the kitchen. She doesn't remember feeling like this when she was pregnant with the boys. Perhaps that was because she was so much younger then, or it may be because she was so happy about having them. Her feelings about this pregnancy are altogether different and at times she thinks the baby is punishing her for not wanting it. When she turns from the mirror to begin to dress she shakes her head as though trying to get rid of this melodramatic, foolish thought.

As she joins the others in the kitchen Annie is placing a platter of sausages and bacon in the middle of the table next to a steaming bowl of baked beans. She turns her flushed cheerful face to Jenny. 'The toast is cooked and I'm taking orders for eggs. Do you want one or two?'

Jenny forces a grin. 'One will be plenty for me, but I am hanging out for a coffee.'

She helps herself to a coffee and then sits at the table next to Georgie. 'It's a howling gale outside. I don't suppose you went for a run this morning.'

'Well I did as a matter of fact. I got drenched, but was back before the worst of it hit.'

'It's definitely going to be an inside day for us today. We'll get a chance to see some DVDs of films from the 80s that I've managed to dig up.'

Georgie, who has always been an avid film buff, asks eagerly, 'What have you got?'

'Well I tried to find ones we'd enjoyed together when we were young. There's Fatal Attraction.'

Before she can continue Sheila says, 'Did we really enjoy it or just like being scared'.

Jenny says defensively, 'It's a terrific film. I actually saw it again a few years ago on television and Glenn Close's acting is fantastic.'

Annie has served the eggs and now joins her friends at the table. 'I reckon I'll still be frightened out of my wits by it. From memory it has a pretty violent ending so I demand the right to scream in the appropriate places.'

Georgie laughs. 'You always did overreact to scary movies and we don't expect that you've changed. What else have you got Jen?'

'Nothing scary. I've got 'Dirty Dancing of course.' She grins as they all cheer. 'And another old favourite, 'The Witches of Eastwick.'

'I loved that film,' Sheila enthuses. 'Wasn't Jack Nicholson something else? So ghastly but somehow attractive in a totally creepy way.'

'Anyhow,' Jenny continues, 'I thought as it's such a wretched day we could make a fire in the lounge and sit around watching old films and be slobs for a day.'

'Sounds wonderful to me,' Annie says eagerly. 'Do you have any popcorn Jenny?'

Georgie says, 'I saw some in the pantry when I was putting the food away, and on Sheila's advice I bought marshmallows that we can toast on the fire.'

Jenny forces herself to eat an egg and a small rasher of bacon with her toast. The others are happily demolishing the pile of sausages topped with generous serves of baked beans. She is pleased they don't seem to notice how little she eats or that she is less than enthusiastic at the thought of popcorn and toasted marshmallows.

As soon as breakfast is finished Sheila goes to the lounge room to make the fire, Georgie hunts out the popcorn and puts it in the microwave and Jenny and Annie pack the dishwasher and tidy the kitchen before joining Sheila. She has the fire going and already the room is feeling less chilly. Jenny puts on the first DVD and she and Annie settle themselves on the couch, Georgie sits in an armchair and Sheila stretches out on the floor with her head resting against the couch. The furniture is in front of the fireplace but angled towards the large television set in the corner of the room. Georgie has placed a large bowl of popcorn on a small table but it is ignored because they are all feeling full after their big breakfasts.

Jenny has chosen to put on 'Fatal Attraction' first, perhaps to see if her friends, seeing it again, enjoy it as much as she had. What strikes Georgie is how different it looks on a smaller screen. Although the television set is quite large there is no comparison with how it had looked on the big movie screen. When they were teenagers none of them had seen a big city and the shots on the big screen of Glenn Close and Michael Douglas wandering through the rather sleazy city streets had been captivating. From where she is seated Georgie can see her three friends and she notes how avidly they watch the rather frantic sexual grappling of the pair. To her it looks rather odd and slightly unpleasant, in much the same way the depiction of sex between homosexuals most probably appears to the other three.

She puts aside these thoughts and is soon immersed in the film. It is quite engrossing and extremely well-acted. As Jenny had said Glenn Close's depiction of an unbalanced woman who stalks her lover when he wants to break things off with her following a one-night stand is impressive. As the film comes to it's very violent end, Annie screams and hides her eyes from the violence and Jenny pats her shoulder and says facetiously, 'There, there. I'll tell you when it's safe to open your eyes.'

Georgie laughs, 'You haven't changed a bit Annie. Still our sensitive little one.'

As she says this she gets up and stretches for the film had been so engrossing she hadn't noticed her feet becoming numb. She now feels the need to move around so goes to the window and looks out. Rain continues to fall heavily and she can hear water rushing along the front guttering and pouring into the rainwater tank at the side of the house. Usually when it rains so hard the wind drops but it is still blowing with gale-like force from the sea. In front of her she can see huge waves crashing onto the beach beyond the flattened marram grass, and the trees that line the sides of the property are heaving and twisting. The thunderstorm has passed, but as she watches she hears a loud cracking sound and a large branch falls onto the sodden lawn.

As she turns from the window she says, 'It's certainly set in for the day. I'll open some wine and we'll get pissed.'

Sheila says, 'Good idea,' and heads to the kitchen to find a bottle.

'Let's make toast. I saw pate and cheese in the fridge while I was making breakfast.' Annie follows Sheila and Jenny goes after her saying, 'There are some old toasting forks in the bottom of the pantry cupboard.'

Left alone in the lounge room Georgie moves to inspect the fire. The coals are glowing brightly in the front and she puts a log on the back to make sure it keeps burning. Soon the others return to the room laden with plates of food, a couple of bottles of wine and glasses and long forks made of twisted wire. Jenny puts slices of bread on the tines and props the forks up in front of the fire. The bread cooks quickly and soon they have a plate full of toast. They help themselves to toast and spread the slices liberally with butter topped with pate or cheese. Sheila opens the wine and pours each of them a glass before settling herself once more on the floor with a contented sigh.

She takes a bite then says appreciatively, 'Oh, this tastes so much better than when you cook it in a toaster.'

Annie nods. 'When I was a kid we used to have crumpets cooked on the fire for Sunday tea during the winter. It was one of my brothers' favourite meals.

'I remember seeing forks like those at my grandmother's house and wondering what they were used for. My father, of course, would never have allowed such an informal meal. He was shocked when he heard of people eating meals in front of their television sets, and would be appalled to see us lounging around picnicking like this.'

Sheila looks at Georgie sympathetically. 'He was a stickler for doing everything correctly wasn't he? I used to feel sorry for your mother.'

'So did I, but she should have stood up to him more.'

Annie notices the set expression on Georgie's face. She is reminded of their conversation at the hotel and Georgie's comment about the duty visit she had to make to her mother's. She asks rather warily, 'How was the visit?'

'Not as bad as expected. I've seen so little of her for years so we were pretty stiff with one another to start with, but things improved. She's better now Dad's not around.'

'So she's coping alright on her own?' Sheila asks this in an off-handed way, more to be polite than from any real concern. She had always thought Georgie's mother a little mouse of a woman who was dominated by the unpleasant bigoted father.

'She's doing okay except for the fact that the house needs a coat of paint. I've offered to get that done for her and surprisingly she's accepted.' Georgie suddenly thinks of the photo and says, 'Incidentally do you all remember how I used to think I was adopted?'

Sheila grins. 'As if we could forget.'

'You were always going on about it; every time you had a run in with them you'd say it.'

'Yeah, I know I did. But I didn't tell you that I once asked Mum point blank if they'd adopted me.'

Annie looks concerned. 'Oh gosh, what did your mother say?'

'She got terribly upset; cried and carried on and said how thrilled she'd been when she held me in her arms for the first time. When I managed to calm her down she said she knew I didn't look anything like her or my father but that I took after Dad's sister who had died when she was young. I didn't quite believe her; that's why I never told you about her.'

'And what's brought this up now?' Sheila asks.

Georgie scrambles to her feet, says, 'Hang on a minute', and leaves the room. When she returns she is holding an envelope and she pulls the crumpled photo from it and gives it to Sheila saying, 'What do you think. This is my long lost aunt, Joanna.'

Sheila stares at it for a moment then hands it to Annie, but not before saying, 'My God, it could be a photo of you.'

Jenny peers over Annie's shoulder to get a look. 'It's amazing. The only difference is you wouldn't be seen dead in those daggy clothes.'

'Talking of being seen dead, what happened to her?' Annie is still holding the photo and now passes it back to Georgie.

'She drowned. Evidently went swimming with friends at a surf beach, swam out and just disappeared. Mum never met her but Dad told her Joanna was very beautiful and clever but had always been unhappy. He told Mum she'd committed suicide because she was a lesbian.' Georgie looks at the photo fondly. 'I'd have loved to have known her. I'm sure we would have been close. I feel kindred with her just looking at this old photo.'

'Well you certainly look like her; just don't go following her example by suiciding,' Jenny says.

Georgie once more looks at the photo and says seriously, 'I'm sure she didn't take her own life deliberately. She looks too positive to do something like that. I think she had my fear of rough water and was just testing herself; trying to overcome the fear and then got into difficulties.'

'God, that's such a wild supposition. As if you could know what she had planned.' Sheila stands and to refill everyone's glasses and takes another look at the photo as she pours wine into Georgie's glass. 'Just because you look like her doesn't mean you know how she felt.'

'Well I think it does.' Georgie says this defensively as she slips the photo back into the envelope. 'As soon as I saw this I felt a bond with her. I just wish she'd lived. It would have saved me a lot of angst while I was growing up.'

The others are silent, for they are all remembering the time when they were young and how hard life had been for Georgie back then. She was so clever and beautiful but her life was made difficult by having parents from whom she felt alienated and a society that hadn't yet come to accept her right to be sexually different. Annie feels the gaiety that had filled the room begin to disperse as they watch Georgie return the photo to the envelope and put it in the pocket of her track pants. She looks sad and they all feel they've let her down in some way, but are not sure how.

Suddenly her face brightens as she leans forward and picks up one of the DVDs they haven't yet watched. She holds it up and says, 'Well Jen, I guess this is the one we've all been waiting for. Let's open another bottle of wine and settle down and enjoy it. You lot can all perve on Patrick Swayze and I'll enjoy the music and dancing.'

She puts on the DVD then sits back in the arm chair and Annie relaxes. Sheila pours them all a glass of wine before taking her place on the floor again. As the film unfolds they feel transported back in time to when they were girls, the time before the adult world and all its problems impinged on their lives. They sway in time to the music and thrill to watching a young Patrick Swayze dance his way into the heart of a young girl who, as they were back then, is poised on the thresh-hold of adulthood. When the film ends they sigh in unison and all have silly grins on their faces. They are feeling slightly drunk, having demolished three bottles of wine during the afternoon. Annie suggests that perhaps they should have something to eat to soak up all the wine they've consumed. They gather in the kitchen and trip around each other as they fill plates with crackers and cheeses and bowls with nuts, olives and clumsily cut slices of apple.

When they return to the lounge room they spread the food on the coffee table in front of the fire. Sheila opens yet another bottle of wine and they eat and drink and talk about the film. Sheila toasts the marshmallows and they all agree they are better cooked than raw but still don't go very well with wine.

Outside the storm continues to rage but they are warm and snug. Georgie looks at Jenny and Annie giggling together on the couch, but Sheila has become quieter and is gazing into the fire as she sips her wine. She has seen the different ways in which her friends are affected by alcohol many times before and is a bit concerned by Sheila's silence, for she is inclined to become melancholic after drinking too much. The other two are happy drunks and are now laughing about a boy Jenny dated in her teens.

'You were pretty keen for a while there.' Annie teases. 'Reckoned he was the sexiest thing on two legs.'

Jenny giggles. 'I did, didn't I? The trouble was so did he. He already had an ego the size of a house, but after some girl told him he looked like Tom Cruise in Top Gun he became unbearable.'

'He was forever combing his hair and poncing around in that leather jacket and aviator's sun glasses.'

'When we went out I'd catch him looking at himself in every window we passed.'

'I was glad you ditched him pretty quickly.'

'Yeah, and he didn't like that at all. He'd been used to being the one who did the ditching.'

Georgie is tired but feels quite sober. She has always had the ability to consume quantities of alcohol without getting drunk. Generally this is an advantage, but at times she finds the drunken conversations of those around her rather tedious. Right now the prattling on of her two friends is beginning to annoy her. She stifles a yawn and says, 'I guess it's time we thought of going to bed.'

As she begins picking up the empty plates from the table Jenny stands rather unsteadily and says, 'Yeah, I guess we should hit the sack.' She gives Annie a hug, kisses the top of Sheila's head and gives Georgie a gentle pat on the arm before saying, 'Leave that. We'll tidy up in the morning.' She says a cheery goodnight and leaves, closely followed by Annie. Georgie continues taking the plates and glasses to the kitchen, loads the dishwasher and puts the empty bottles in the recycling bin. Having been brought up in a house where it was considered almost criminal to go to bed without first tidying everything up the habit has stayed with her. She looks around the tidy kitchen with satisfaction before returning to the lounge room, where Sheila is still slumped on the floor gazing at the fire. She sits on the couch and puts a hand on Sheila's shoulder. 'You okay? You've gone awfully quiet.'

When Sheila turns Georgie sees tears forming and beginning to spill down her cheeks. 'Listening to those two talking about their boyfriends reminded me of how miserable and insecure I was so much of the time back then.'

'Aw honey, that's such a long time ago. We were both pretty lost during those teen years, but hey, look at us now.'

'That's the thing. I was insecure then and deep down I haven't changed. This business with Vicki is ruining our lives, but Scott won't do anything about it and I'm not willing to force him. I'm afraid I'll risk losing what I've got, so I put up with his vacillating ways as I always have. You know watching 'Fatal Attraction' again reminded me a bit of how I felt during the months before Scott finally got around to filing for a divorce.'

'Oh, for goodness sake, she was a nut case. You're not going to try and tell me you ever felt as crazy as that.'

'Not quite, but after you went to Sydney I suddenly felt so alone. I began to think there would always be some reason why Scott's children would need him to be around and that he would always put them first. I even began to wonder if he was just stringing me along. I think I went a little mad.'

'Oh love, I didn't know that. Why didn't you tell me you were having a rough time?'

'I don't know; false pride I guess. Don't get me wrong. I didn't get to the stage where I would have thought of slitting my wrists or start sneaking around looking in the windows of Scott's house, but I did become terribly depressed and cried at the drop of a hat. Anyhow I gave Scott an ultimatum; either he filed for divorce or we were finished and he finally set the wheels in motion.'

'Good for you. It was about time.'

'You'd been telling me for years that I should ditch him if he wouldn't prove he loved me by leaving his wife.'

'I know I probably came on really strongly about it at times but I was less analytical then. Since then I've learnt that we all make compromises. The thing is to know when the compromises you make are being too damaging to whom you are and what you have a right to expect from those closest to you. Look how Jenny spent years trying to ignore Mark's infidelities, and the sadness that must have caused her; and Annie has evidently put up with things Joel has done that have made her unhappy but she hasn't spoken up for fear of having an argument.'

'You don't seem to have made many compromises though.'

'Oh yes I have. My affair with Ruth involved a lot of turning a blind eye to things about her and our relationship that I knew weren't really what I wanted. I had a go at you the other day for the way you behaved towards her, but in fact you did me a favour; made me face up to the fact that there were too many differences between us.'

'I didn't mean to cause trouble.'

'You didn't but your attitude towards Ruth helped me realise just how many compromises I was making in order to keep a relationship going that was doomed to failure. The main thing is to know when you've compromised too much and only the people involved can make that decision.' A look of sadness crosses Georgie's face and she sighs. 'Sometimes that takes a while to know. You have to decide whether this business with Vicki is causing too much damage to you and Scott and the children. Now enough of these sad thoughts. It's time we went to bed.' She pats Sheila's shoulder and moves to the door before turning and saying, 'Come on. Things will look brighter in the morning.'

When she is in her room Georgie pulls the envelope from her pocket and once more studies the photo of her long-lost aunt. Despite having spent the last half hour trying to cheer Sheila up she is still feeling pissed off with her. Her derogatory comment earlier that Georgie was making a 'wild supposition' when she said she understood Joanna had hit home. She would have liked her friend to at least try and understand how overpowering her feeling of kinship with Joanna is.

In a way she feels let down by all her friends. None of them seemed to understand how important knowing about this aunt and seeing how alike they are has given Georgie a sense of belonging she has lacked all her life.

She runs a caressing hand over the photo as she gazes at the young smiling Joanna standing on a rocky shore, her hair blowing in the wind. She was too strong and vital to have committed suicide. It is far more likely she shared Georgie's fear of rough water and was trying to overcome the fear by swimming on that fateful day.

She props the little photo up against the vase on the bedside table so it is the last thing she sees before putting out the light and snuggling down into the warmth of the duvet.

Jenny

Jenny wakes with her head throbbing and stomach churning. She barely makes it to the vanity basin before vomiting green bile into the white enamel. As she turns on the tap to wash the disgusting mess away she sees that her hands are shaking. When she feels the spasms begin to subside she lowers herself to the floor and sits there shivering as the cold seeps through her thin nightdress. Her hands go automatically to cover her stomach as though to comfort the tiny creature inside her, and she thinks how absurd she is being. Either she must think of it as an unwanted burden to be got rid of as soon as possible or as a baby who must be nurtured and cared for properly while it is in her womb, not abused by the quantities of alcohol she has consumed this week. She is so confused, and the ominous silence from Stuart, as well as having to keep her condition secret from her friends isn't helping.

She rises unsteadily from the floor, turns on the shower taps and stands under the stream of hot water, glorying in the feeling of warmth returning to her body and the thumping in her head diminishing. As she is beginning to dress there is a loud banging on her door and Annie rushes in, her hair awry and bright splotches of red on her cheeks. 'Georgie's gone swimming.' She says this breathlessly before collapsing onto the bed.

Jenny turns from her wardrobe where she has been getting a warm sweater from one of the drawers. 'What's the panic? It's probably fairly cold after all that wind and rain yesterday but she's pretty tough.'

'No, you don't understand. The water's still rough and she's not just swimming near the shore. I got up too late to go for a walk with her so thought I'd wander down to the beach to meet her on her way back. She'd stripped off her trackies and was wading out in her undies, and when I called to her she just kept going.'

'Why are you in such a panic? She probably didn't hear you.' Despite trying to sound reassuring Jenny's heart thumps as she finishes dressing quickly and takes Annie's hand. 'Where's Sheila?'

'She's down on the beach. She started swimming out after Georgie but had to turn back. Said it was too rough. When I left she said to tell you to call the nearest water police.'

Jenny punches is the number on her mobile, explains briefly that a friend is in difficulties in the sea and describes their location. As she pushes her phone into the pocket of her jeans she tells Annie the water police are on their way. She pauses briefly to grab two towels from the cupboard in the passage before running after Annie down the drive and across the road and the strip of sandy foreshore to the beach.

Sheila has pulled a sweater on over her bathers but is shivering as she stands staring anxiously out to sea. Jenny wraps a towel around her saying, 'They're putting out the boat but said it will take at least twenty minutes to get here.'

Jenny looks across the rough waters and can just make out Georgie's dark head and the flash of her arms as she is buffeted by the strong waves. 'What does she think she's doing? She was alright last night wasn't she?' Jenny's concern makes her voice break and she feels tears rolling down her cheeks.

Sheila's face is ashen as she turns from the sea. 'She seemed okay, but I was pretty drunk and feeling sorry for myself. I vaguely remember her trying to cheer me up. I doubt if I'd have noticed if she was upset about anything.'

'Georgie doesn't show much about how she feels. That photo of her aunt is pretty important to her and perhaps we didn't listen enough to what she was saying about it.'

'What do you mean Annie? Do you think that photo had something to do with this?' Jenny waves her arms in the direction of the sea.

'I'm sure it has. There was something about the way she said she thought she knew how her Aunt Joanna had felt.'

'But she didn't believe she committed suicide so why is she doing this?' Sheila is looking out to sea trying to keep sight of Georgie. Suddenly her face lights up and tears spring into her eyes. She grabs Annie excitedly by the arm and yells, 'Look, she's turning. I'm sure she's coming back in.'

The three friends stand on the sand, arms around one another and watch as the dark head comes slowly closer and closer to the shore. They don't dare take their eyes away from the small figure as it battles against the waves but keeps on coming. As Georgie nears the shore they all rush forward until the water is over their waists. When she reaches them they crowd around her crying and laughing at the same time. Georgie laughs and shouts, 'I did it, I did it,' as she staggers onto the sand. Jenny wraps her in a large white towel just as a white and blue power boat appears around the point.

'That's the police boat.' Jenny watches as it speeds across the waves. 'I'll have to let them know everything's okay.' She grimaces as she pulls her ruined phone from the pocket of her soaking wet jeans. 'Not on this though,' she says with a laugh.

'Why'd you call them?' Georgie looks at her, a slightly bewildered expression on her face. 'I wasn't in any danger you know.'

'How were we to know?' Sheila snaps crossly. 'You've never gone out that far before, and especially not in waves like these.'

'And you didn't even look around when I called you.' Annie looks concerned. 'I guess I panicked and then got the others stirred up.'

The boat is now a short distance from the shore and it rocks erratically in the swells for the police on board have slowed their engine. In the bow a man with a hailer calls, 'Everything okay?'

The four women wave and shout and Jenny points at Georgie. Eventually the men on board realise they aren't needed and rev up their engine before turning and speeding out of the bay.

'I'd better ring their headquarters and explain,' Jenny says. She looks ruefully at her phone. 'I'd say this is ruined. Let's go up to the house and get dry, then I'll ring on the land line.'

The four women run to the house. They are all soaking wet and the cold wind has set their teeth chattering and numbed their bodies. Although they are still baffled by Georgie's behaviour, uppermost in their minds is the thought of getting warm so they all head to their separate rooms to shower and change.

Jenny had stripped off her wet clothes and stood under the shower for a long time, glorying in the feeling of being warm once more. As she begins to dry herself she notices blood staining the white towel. She thinks she must have scraped herself on a shrub and not noticed it in her rush to reach the beach. Looking down she sees blood running down her leg, but there is no cut or abrasion; it is coming from inside her. Desperately she pats at the blood with the towel as she realises what this might mean. Is she miscarrying? What should she do?

She pulls on panties, wraps her dressing gown tightly around herself and lies on the bed. She has a slight nagging pain in her lower back. Perhaps if she stays perfectly still the pain and the bleeding will stop. Tears begin to trickle down her face. She so badly wants to see Stuart; wants his arms around her and to hear his voice assuring her he loves her no matter what. This has been the first morning since their argument that she hasn't checked her phone, and now it lies damaged and useless on her dressing table where she put it while taking off her soaking wet clothes. If he tries to get in touch with her the line will be dead, and she doesn't feel she can ring him on her land line with the others around.

She gets up and checks to see if the bleeding has slowed. There is a stain on her panties but the blood is already drying. This must be a good sign she tells herself as she pulls on fresh panties. She thinks about using a tampon but is afraid that may increase the bleeding so hunts up the sanitary pads she keeps for days when her periods are extra heavy. She finishes dressing, and then remembers she should call the police station. They are understanding and assure her it's better to be safe than sorry. Now she is near the phone she is tempted to ring Stuart but fears the others will hear for the door is slightly ajar. She enters the kitchen where they are already sitting around the table drinking coffee. Obviously Sheila and Annie have been quizzing Georgie because as Jenny enters the room she is saying, 'I don't see what all the kerfuffle was about.'

'I got so scared when you didn't turn round when I called you.'

Georgie says defensively, 'But Annie I didn't even hear you.'

Sheila asks angrily, 'What about when I swam out after you. I was shouting at the top of my voice. You must have heard or seen me.'

'Well I didn't. It didn't even occur to me that either of you would be up. In fact it was something I wanted to do by myself.'

Jenny pours herself a coffee and sits at the table next to Georgie. She puts her arm around her and pulls her close. 'I guess what we want to know is why did you want to go swimming on such a fiendish morning. You've always been frightened in rough water and you went out today of all days.'

'And you went out so far.' Annie is nearly in tears as she says this.

'Shit! Why don't you all get off my back?' Georgie stands up and moves to the sink. 'It's something I needed to do.'

'But why did you go out so far?' Annie begins to sob. 'When you just kept swimming and swimming I thought you must be going to drown yourself.'

Georgie looks genuinely bewildered. 'For God's sake Annie, why would you think I'd do that?'

'Don't sneer at her.' Sheila puts a comforting arm around Annie. 'We were all frightened you were doing what your aunt did. You told us last night you felt you were like her in other ways besides just looks.'

'I don't just think I'm like her, I'm sure I am. Seeing that photo gave me a feeling of how I came to be the person I am. If you'd really listened to what I said Sheila you'd know that I'm sure Joanna didn't deliberately drown herself any more than I would.'

'So what were you doing going out in that wild sea?'

'Fighting my fear once and for all. You all know how I've always been scared in rough water even though I'm a strong swimmer. Well once I saw Joanna's photo and heard about her death I knew she'd felt the same way. Today I've done what I think she was trying to do but unfortunately for her she didn't make it back to shore. In a way I feel I've exonerated her memory as well as freeing myself from a stupid and irrational fear.'

'Well it's a shame you couldn't let us in on what you planned to do.'

'And I think it's a shame you described something about which I felt strongly as a 'wild supposition'. I used to think you knew and understood me Sheila, but now I have my doubts.'

'Oh let's not argue anymore.' Jenny says impatiently. She is feeling upset and worried enough without having to listen to this childish backbiting. As she sips her coffee the phone rings. Her heart jumps. Has Stuart finally tried to answer her calls only to be unable to reach her on her damaged mobile? She takes the phone from the wall and says breathlessly, 'Jenny speaking.'

On the other end of the line a male voice says, 'Hi Jenny, Joel here. Can you get Annie for me please?'

She tries to hide her disappointment by saying a cheery hello to Joel but knows she sounds abrupt when, in answer to his question about the weather 'up there', she says, 'I'll get Annie for you. She'll fill you in on the storm we've been having.'

When Jenny tells her it's Joel Annie says rather sharply, 'I wonder what he's ringing about now'. She shuts the door to the passage before answering the phone and the other three sit in silence, all of them wondering what can have brought about Annie's changed attitude to her husband. In the past she had always spoken so lovingly about him, but now she seems quite critical and doesn't seem overly pleased about him ringing her again. When she returns only minutes later she has a set look on her face. Jenny asks tentatively, 'No problems at home?'

'No, he just wondered if I'd be coming home earlier as the weather's been so bad.' She pours herself another coffee, sits back down at the table and sighs, 'God, you'd think I'd be able to have a few days away without him fussing.'

Jenny looks at her three friends sitting glumly around the table. Georgie and Sheila are angry with each other and Annie is obviously cross with Joel. She is edgy and unhappy herself and feels she just can't be bothered with trying to make things right. She'd like to tell them to all go away and sort themselves out, but instead she puts on her most winning hostess smile and says, 'Let's make French toast for breakfast and watch the 'Witches' in front of the fire.'

Sheila volunteers to make the fire again and the other two set to work beating eggs and milk, heating up butter in the biggest pan and hunting up brown sugar and cinnamon. Jenny makes another pot of coffee and soon they are all settled around the fire feasting on the plate of French toast that Jenny has placed on the coffee table and waiting eagerly for the DVD to begin.

As the film unfolds the other three watch with amusement as the three witches are drawn into the opulent and bizarre world of the devil. Jenny is inattentive; she finds it difficult to concentrate on what is happening on the screen for she is worried about the bleed. She would like to go to the toilet and check if it's stopped altogether, but doesn't feel she can interrupt the others enjoyment by asking them to pause the film. If it hasn't stopped completely by the end of the film she'll ring her doctor and ask if bleeding like this at three months is normal.

When the final credits begin to scroll up the screen Annie sits back, a bemused look on her face. 'I'd forgotten so much, particularly how revolting Jack Nicholson was.'

'I think I had too.' Sheila looks pensive. 'I remembered him as being reasonably attractive. I think that was because all the women succumbed to him. And another thing, when I was young I didn't realise he was meant to be representative of all men and the way they manipulate women.'

'I think you're reading something into the film that wasn't there.' Georgie looks at Sheila and sighs in an exaggerated way. 'He was the devil, not an ordinary man.'

'I know that but there was the other aspect. Probably because you don't know about men/women relationships you didn't get the nuances.'

'Perhaps I didn't, but I do think I understood what the film was about.'

'Well did you get that all the women had been damaged by men before he came into their lives. They describe themselves as disintegrating, disappearing or being in so much pain. They had lost their feelings of self-worth because of the way men had treated them in the past. That's why they were so vulnerable to someone who seemed to understand them.'

Annie says diffidently, 'I thought they actually willed him into existence. They all wanted a man who understood them and that's why the devil had such power over them. He understood what they wanted and fulfilled a need each one had.'

'But they were needy because men had made them so unhappy. One of them even says, 'Let them have their way and the pain stops. Georgie didn't understand that because she's never been in the situation where a man's made her unhappy.'

'Don't talk about me as though I'm not in the room Sheila. Quite frankly I think you're overanalysing what was meant to be a sexy, supernatural romp with a twist at the end. And I think your interpretation is based on how you're feeling about Scott at present.'

'And how is that?' Sheila glares angrily across the room at Georgie.

'Certainly not happy. You've been angry ever since you got here and you've taken your anger out by being bitchy to me on several occasions.'

'What do you mean?'

'Well, insulting Ruth for one thing, calling me a wimp when I didn't want to go back into the water the other day as well as sneering about the way I feel connected to Joanna. And you've had a go at Jenny a few times. You've mentioned at least three times how Mark was unfaithful to her. As if she wanted to hear that again and again.'

'My, you have saved up your venom, 'Sheila retorts viciously.

'Stop it you two. Do you want to spoil everything?' Annie looks close to tears.

'I'd say Sheila's pretty well done that already.' Georgie stands and walks to the window.

Jenny's immediate concern is to check whether the bleeding has stopped and she has only been half listening to the argument. Hearing Georgie's remark makes her think how childish and petty both the two women are being. Now she says angrily, 'Annie's right. Why don't you both grow up? You're beginning to sound like the witches did when they had their falling out.'

Georgie turns from the window and sighs. 'You're right Jen. We were sounding like them, but they managed to sort out their problems and I can't see that happening here.'

'What do you mean?'

'We've spent the past days pussy footing around. We've skated over the surface instead of really confiding in each other. Sheila's told us about Scott's problem but not why she's let it go on for so long, Annie is obviously very unhappy with Joel about something more than Sam's future education and you, Jenny, have told us about Stuart but you're holding something back. You've been so tense I get the impression there's something bigger than a lover's tiff that's worrying you.'

Annie nods her head in agreement. 'Georgie's right. Although it's been lovely being with the three of you again I've felt there's been something missing. Sure we still care for each other but we've been holding back, keeping our innermost feelings and secrets to ourselves. When we were young we didn't do that so we were closer.'

'Are you sure you're not idealising things Annie?' Jenny says defensively. 'Yes we were close but we didn't tell each other everything. Do you remember when we played truth or dare up here? If I remember rightly you chose to take the dare rather than reveal what you and Joel were getting up to.'

'And if I remember rightly you three made me pay dearly for choosing the dare over truth.'

Georgie has moved from the window and once more joins the others around the fire. She looks serious as she says, 'We certainly punished you for keeping that part of your life separate from us. We expected you to share with us what you were feeling, and that's the big difference between how we were then and how we are now.'

Sheila has been silent since Georgie's criticism of her. Although she had found her remarks hurtful, she also recognises the truth in what she's said. It is true that she's let her anger towards Scott spill over into her relationship with her friends. Now she looks towards Georgie and says, 'You're right Georgie. What you said about us pussyfooting around is true. On the surface we've had a happy time together, but when someone's been upset it's been glossed over. It's as though we no longer really care if one of us is bothered or unhappy. We've not been willing to confide in one another about what is worrying us or going wrong with our lives. Because of that we haven't been giving each other support and understanding the way we used to.'

'You say that now, but when I tried to tell you how I felt bonded with Joanna you sneered at me Sheila.'

'I know I did, and I'm sorry Georgie.'

Jenny listens tensely. She knows what is being said is important, but something else is drawing her attention away from really taking it all in. She thinks she feels blood trickling down her leg and feels a fearful and unexpected sense of loss. Without a word of explanation to the other women she rushes from the room, heads straight to the toilet and pulls down her panties. There is fresh blood on the sanitary napkin but it doesn't seem enough to signify the beginnings of a miscarriage, or she hopes it isn't. This had never happened during her other two pregnancies, but she seems to remember reading somewhere about break-through bleeding. The trouble is she can't remember what was written about it. She needs to talk to her doctor, needs to be either reassured or prepared for what may be happening within her body. One thing she now knows without any doubt is that she wants to keep this baby; wants it to stay safely inside her womb until the time is right for him or her to emerge. The other thing she knows is that she wants to share what is happening to her with her friends; wants and needs their love and advice and support.

Truth or Dare

When Jenny returns to the lounge room to join her friends only Annie remains, staring dolefully into the fire. She puts an arm around Annie's shoulders and says, 'All on your lonesome. Where are the other two?'

'Georgie's gone out to the veranda, probably watching the storm, and Sheila's in the kitchen. She said something about opening a bottle of wine to cheer us up.'

'Somehow I think we need more than wine. What the other two said before is true. We have changed towards each other; have become wary of sharing the important things that are going on in our lives.'

'I know what you mean, and I think we've been holding back because now we have other people in our lives who are more important. We've been so concerned about protecting the privacy of those relationships we have distanced ourselves from each other.'

As Annie is saying this Sheila comes to the door of the lounge room and stands there, a bottle of wine in one hand and a tray in the other. She asks diffidently. 'Is this a private conversation or can anyone join in?'

'Don't be silly Sheil. What you and Georgie said is true. The things we've been keeping from each other are pulling us apart and we need to bring them out into the open. You sit down and I'll go and get Georgie.'

Jenny goes out to the front verandah where Georgie is sitting on the top step gazing out at the flattened marram grass and stormy seas. When she sits down next to her Georgie turns and says, 'Sorry about letting off steam like that. You've been through a horrible few months, and the last thing you should have to listen to is Sheila and me sounding off the way we did. I shouldn't have let her sarcastic remarks get to me.'

'Don't apologise love. I'm glad you spoke up. What you said about us pussy footing around each other was true. I know I've only told you all part of what's been happening in my life, and you were right, there is something more than a lover's tiff that's been making me tense and confused.'

'Do you want to talk about it?'

'Yes I do. But right now I want you to come inside so I can tell you all together about what I've been going through during the past week.'

As Georgie stands and puts an arm around Jenny's waist she says, 'You sound so serious. Let's go.'

When they join the other two Sheila walks towards them with a glass of wine in each hand. She hands one to Georgie saying sheepishly, 'Peace offering.'

Georgie takes the glass and grins, but when Sheila offers Jenny the other glass she shakes her head saying, 'Better not, in view of my condition.'

'What do you mean?' For a moment Sheila stands still holding the proffered glass out awkwardly in front of her, then what Jenny has said sinks in. 'Are you saying what I think you are?'

'Yes, I'm pregnant. I'm sorry I didn't tell you all sooner, but I've been so confused and worried about it. Listening to Georgie and Sheila talking about the way we've been behaving towards each other during the last few days made me realise what we're losing, and I want back what we had. I so badly need to share this problem with someone, and who better than you three. I need your help to sort my way through the confusion and fear I'm feeling right now.'

'Oh Jen, sit down and tell us all about it?' Annie pats the space next to her on the couch. 'Obviously you're not happy about being pregnant.'

'I wasn't. That's why I had the row with Stuart. I wanted to have an abortion and he said if I did it would be the end of things between us. Now I may be losing our baby and that's made me realise just how much I want to keep it. Oh, I'm in such a mess.'

'What do you mean you may be losing it?' Sheila sits on Jenny's other side on the couch and takes her hand. 'Have you had any symptoms?'

'I started bleeding this morning and had a bit of a pain in my back. There wasn't much blood and I think it's slowed now, but I'm frightened something's going wrong. This never happened to me when I was pregnant with the boys.'

'I had some breakthrough bleeding when I was pregnant with Mia. Naturally I panicked, but my doctor said it was nothing to worry about. Evidently it's quite common during the first three months, something to do with hormone levels. How far along are you?'

'Nearly three months. I know to the day when I conceived because it was the only time Stuart and I were together during the past six months. Mark was back in hospital for some quite experimental treatment the doctors thought might extend his life. He was in isolation during that time so I took the opportunity to come up here.'

'If you're still bleeding at all I think you should get it checked out though.' Annie looks concerned. 'Ring your doctor and see if you can get an appointment tomorrow. I'll come with you to make sure you're alright on the trip down.'

'Thanks Annie, I'd like that. I'll ring now and see if she can fit me in tomorrow.'

When Jenny leaves the room the others sit in silence until Annie whispers, 'That's why she was crying on Monday morning. They most have argued about the baby when Sheila saw her in the garden. I should have gone in to her and asked what was wrong.'

'She wouldn't have told you then. It's only the fear of losing the baby that's made her realise she wants to keep it.' Sheila looks thoughtful. 'I wonder if they've talked since then.'

As she is saying this Jenny comes back into the room a relieved smile on her face. 'She'll see me tomorrow morning at ten; said it's probably nothing to worry about but she'll give me a check-up and an ultra sound. And no Sheila, Stuart and I haven't talked since Sunday night. I've rung him and left messages but he hasn't called back so I don't know what he's thinking at present. He was terribly hurt that I wanted an abortion; couldn't or wouldn't understand how much it would shock my sons to learn I'd been carrying on with another man while their father was dying. He said our baby was more important than how they might feel. I see that now, but it's too late.'

'Why's it too late? Ring him and tell him you want the baby now and don't care what anyone thinks,' Georgie says matter-of-factly.

'And what happens if I have a miscarriage? He'll probably think I did something to cause it. No, I'll wait until I'm sure the baby's alright.' She smiles at her friends. 'I feel so much better now that I've told you lot about it.

We'll have to leave pretty early in the morning Annie, probably no later than eight.'

'That's okay with me, I'll be ready. Then I'll spend the day with you and catch up with you Georgie at the hotel in the evening.'

'Sheila and I will tidy up here before we leave. What do we do about the washing; sheets and doona covers and towels?'

'Just leave everything in the laundry. A local woman comes in and cleans up for me now Stuart's mother's too old to manage it. All you two need do is make sure there isn't any food left that could go off.'

'Talking of food, I'm hungry.' Georgie grabs Sheila's hand and says. 'Let's go into the kitchen and whip up a couple of frittatas.'

While the other two are busy in the kitchen Jenny turns to Annie and says, 'Thanks for offering to come with me. If it's bad news I'll be glad to have a shoulder to cry on.'

'Let's hope it doesn't come to that. The doctor was reassuring wasn't she?'

'Yes, but she also said it was better to make sure all is well. I think she's mainly concerned because of my age. Once a woman's forty there are more likely to be problems.'

'Lots of women have their babies in their late thirties and early forties now though. Compared with the mothers of today we were both so young when we had our kids. I'd had my three by the time I was twenty-three and you'd had your two boys by then as well.'

'You sound almost sorry you had your babies when you were so young.'

'I am in a way. It meant I didn't get the chance to do anything else before I became a wife and mother. I regret that now.'

'Even though I've been pretty wrapped up in my own problem I had noticed you haven't been your usual cheerful self. It's not just about Sam not wanting to work on the farm is it?'

'No, that's sorted, but seeing the way Joel was first about Phoebe wanting to study on the mainland and then this business with Sam has made me realise how he only sees things from his point of view.'

'I think we all do that to a certain extent, but how's that affecting you. You and he have always been so in tune with what you wanted out of life.'

'It may have seemed that way, but really I've always just gone along with what Joel wanted.'

'But it looked as though you were happy doing that. I've always thought what a lovely life you've had, with a husband who adored you and work you shared.'

'But it wasn't necessarily the life I wanted. Don't get me wrong; I still love Joel and couldn't imagine life without my kids, but I feel I've had no say in what I've done so far. Our future was mapped out for us. When we were just kids ourselves we became parents and Joel had his life's work that he has continued to love. I took it on as mine also, but now I want to do something different and I'm sure Joel won't understand why.'

As Annie is saying this Sheila and Georgie return to the lounge room each carrying a large plate. They place these on the coffee table and Sheila says, 'We've made two kinds; mines potato and smoked salmon and Georgie's is spinach, bacon and cheese, and you have to try both.'

'Yum, they smell delicious; and you three don't have to hold back on the wine just because I'm not drinking.'

Once the food is served Sheila pours more wine and says only half -jokingly, 'You two seemed to be having a very serious conversation when we interrupted you; no more secrets I hope.'

'I was just telling Jenny I want a change; want to do something different.' Annie looks around the circle at her friends and smiles. 'I don't know why I didn't talk to you all about this before. I guess I thought I'd be being disloyal to Joel if I told you I wanted something different from the life I have with him.'

'You're not going to 'fess up to us that you're having an affair are you?' Sheila asks this teasingly expecting to see Annie blush as she still does when embarrassed.

Instead Annie laughs. 'Of course not you dope. Despite the way I've complained about him I still love him; I just don't want to spend the next half of my life working on the land and in the kitchen. Actually since Jamie started working with Joel I've almost become redundant. I mainly help with the pruning and picking in the vineyard and next year Phoebe will have finished college and will take that over. Also next year Jamie and Betty are getting married. She's a lovely girl and I'm sure she'll be happy to help out with the cooking.'

'So what do you want to do with all this new-found leisure?'

'What I want to do Georgie is go to uni and do the Bachelor of Education I planned to do twenty odd years ago. When I got married Mum said I could always go back later and become a teacher, and her words have stayed with me as a sort of beacon. Now I want to do it.'

'Ah, so this is the other problem you alluded to a week ago when we were at the hotel. Why didn't you tell me then? I think it's a marvellous idea.'

'The main reason I didn't was because I haven't spoken to Joel about it yet. I've put it off because I know he's not going to understand why I want to do this. He's been bad enough about Phoebe insisting on going to college and Sam wanting to do something other than work on his precious land. I reckon he'll find it even harder to come to grips with the fact that I might want to do something different.'

'For goodness sake Annie, I can't see why you've put off telling him when it's so important to you.' Sheila sounds quite exasperated. 'This is Joel you're talking about. He wouldn't stop you doing anything you wanted to do.'

'No, he'll just say I should do what I want, but he'll be hurt and go quiet and then I'll feel I'm being selfish.'

'But that's absurd. Do you mean to say you've put off telling him about something that's so important to you simply because he'll sulk?'

'When you put it like that Sheila it does sound ridiculous. I probably didn't explain properly. The thing is Joel and I don't know how to have an adult disagreement. I think it's because we married so young. Back then we agreed about everything and I guess expected to go on that way. Later when problems arose, as they always will, we didn't know how to deal with them in an adult way.'

'So, what did you do?'

'Pretended they didn't exist or weren't that important, and hoped they'd go away.'

'And how's that worked for you?' Sheila says this quite belligerently and Georgie gives her a warning look.

'I guess it's meant we've had a very peaceful life on the surface, but it's also meant things were buried that should have been discussed. It's led to me not speaking up when I should have and often suppressing the anger I felt towards Joel. I've carried this anger within me for so long; the anger I felt when he didn't stick up for me against his mother and the innumerable times he was too tired or too busy to take an interest in what was going on in the kids' lives. I guess the way he's acted lately, as though he knows what the kids and I want from life, has caused it to come bubbling up, and quite frankly I haven't known how to deal with it. Being away from him for these few days, and now talking to you three about it, has done a lot towards getting things into perspective for me. I'm definitely going to sit him down and tell him what I plan to do as soon as I get home.'

'About time I would have thought.'

Georgie has been listening impatiently to Sheila's rather aggressive questioning of Annie. Despite not wanting to risk the harmony they have felt cooking together she can't resist saying, 'You're being pretty hard on Annie, but you've always made allowances for Scott to avoid an argument. You did it all those years ago when he strung you along and you're still doing it. You want him to behave decisively with regard to Vicki but you're afraid to push him.'

'That's not true. I told him if he didn't tell her to stop calling by the time I got back I'd deal with her.'

'But you won't do anything because you're still too insecure to force him to do something he finds difficult. You'll let him drag it out because you want him to prove that you and your children are more important than Vicki.'

'You don't know everything. He may have already fixed the problem.'

'Well, why don't you ring him and find out?' Georgie knows that by daring Sheila to do this she is forcing her to face her insecurities, but she wants her friend to realise she has a right to be heard. Her intentions are good but she sounds harshly critical when she adds. 'Perhaps then you'll stop being so scratchy. You've been pretty dismissive about the way Annie avoided facing up to her problems, but you've done the same thing.'

Sheila stands and saunters across the room calling back from the door, 'I'll ring him now.'

'You certainly put her on the spot. I thought you two had made up.'

'Oh Jenny, so did I, but when she got stuck into Annie about what she should do she annoyed me. It's obvious that the phone calls from Vicki are upsetting the whole family. Scott looked terrible the night I went to dinner at their house and he was very moody, and the fact that he doesn't put a stop to it is really getting to Sheila. She's hoping he'll deal with his daughter's neurotic behaviour, but deep down she knows he's not strong enough. She's putting up with a bad situation and hoping it will go away, yet there she was criticising Annie for doing much the same thing.'

'It's easy to see what other people are doing wrong,' Annie gives a little sigh. 'And it's also so easy to keep quiet about what you really want and expect just for the sake of peace. I know I've done that, and it's led to a situation where I'm angry with Joel, but he doesn't understand why because I haven't spoken up enough.'

As Annie is saying this Sheila re-enters the room her mobile phone clutched tightly in her hand. There are bright red splotches of colour on her cheeks and she seems tense and angry. Hearing Annie's remark she says, 'You and me both. Obviously I hadn't made it clear enough to Scott what I expected of him, but I have now. I told him again if he hasn't put a stop to those calls by tomorrow I'm reporting Vicki to the police for harassment.'

'Gee that's going a bit far isn't it?' Annie looks worried. 'Perhaps you could talk to her?'

'That wouldn't do any good. We've never got on that well so I know she won't take any notice of me. Anyhow Georgie I'm glad you stirred me along to see if he'd done anything, and I'm hoping he'll sort her out tonight once and for all. Now that's dealt with let's open another bottle of wine and I'll mix Jenny a nice non-alcoholic drink and we'll drink a toast to no more secrets between us.'

For Jenny it's been a long and worrying day. There has been the fear for Georgie battling her demons in the wild seas, her own fear of losing the baby and of telling the others about her pregnancy as well as the conflict between them all as they shared their confidences. She remembers back to the last time they were all here together and how they'd played truth or dare. Today has been similar in that they have exposed their innermost secrets to each other. Georgie has faced her fear and won, and Annie is now determined to speak out about what she really wants to do with the rest of her life. Sheila has made it clear to Scott she will no longer accept his vacillations and hopefully he will settle the problem between him and his daughter tonight.

The other three are getting mildly drunk and Jenny feels slightly out of things. She thinks the bleeding has stopped but her back is aching and she still fears all is not right. She is anxious about seeing the doctor tomorrow for she now knows this little life growing inside her is more important than anything else, even the disillusionment of her sons. She would dearly love to talk to Stuart and tell him about her change of heart, but must wait until she knows what is going on inside her body. What will happen between them if she loses the baby? This is something she is not prepared to think about tonight. Instead she thinks of how good it will be to have Annie with her when she sees the doctor tomorrow. She gives her an affectionate hug before saying, 'I'm off to bed. I'm so glad you're coming with me tomorrow.'

Annie hugs her back. 'I'll be up bright and early. See you then Jen.'

As she walks along the passage to her room Jenny hears the laughter of her friends and thinks how good it sounds.

Farewells

After two stormy days the winds have abated and the rain ceased. Georgie runs along the beach glorying in the clean fresh smells that follow such weather. It is as though the whole world has been cleansed. She breathes deeply and exhales a sigh of contentment. While she runs she thinks over the previous day; remembers her own triumph in the sea as well as the secrets that were exposed and the argument that erupted between her and Sheila. Hopefully the problems facing her three friends will be sorted out soon, if not today. On such a gorgeous day one could not help but feel optimistic.

As she crosses the road and runs up the driveway she sees Sheila slamming shut the boot of her car then getting into the driver's seat. She runs forward and asks breathlessly, 'Where are you off to?'

Sheila turns on the ignition and says briefly through the open window, 'Home.'

'Why are you leaving so early? Nothing's happened to one of the kids has it?'

'Not to my kids. Vicki's tried to commit suicide. Scott rang a while ago in a tizz. Evidently she took a lot of pills and then rang him. He's spent the night at the hospital.'

'Is she okay?'

'I gather she's feeling pretty sore from having her stomach pumped out but she's fine. Scott's sounded a mess though. Blames himself for being tough with her, and by inference it's my fault for telling him he had to put a stop to her calls.'

'That's so unfair.'

Sheila shrugs. 'Tell me about it, but what's fair? Anyhow I'm off. He got the kids up in the middle of the night and dumped them on Mum and Dad before speeding off to save Vicki. I need to get home to reassure William and Mia everything's okay and to give my parents a break. See you.'

She gives a brief wave of her hand before starting the engine and driving away leaving Georgie feeling slightly stunned by the abrupt farewell. She also feels guilty. If she hadn't egged Sheila on to take a stand perhaps none of this would have happened. Her previous feelings of optimism drain away and she feels apprehensive when she enters the kitchen. In her experience once one thing goes wrong others often follow. She is pleased to see Jenny and Annie sitting talking quietly together as they drink their morning coffee.

Jenny looks up and says, 'Did you see Sheila before she left?'

'Yes. She was just getting ready to drive away.' Georgie pours herself a coffee and sits at the table. 'She was pretty short with me. Perhaps she blames me for daring her to make that call.'

'Oh, I don't think so love.' Annie pats her hand. 'She was just in a hurry to get home; wanted to make sure Mia and William haven't been too upset by what's happened, and to let her parents catch up on some sleep.'

'Her leaving so early means you'll be here by yourself to pack up. Is that okay?' As she says this Jenny drinks the last of her coffee and puts the cup on the sink. 'We really must get going soon if we're to make the appointment on time.'

'Of course it's okay. By the way, how are you today? No more bleeding in the night?'

'No, it seems to have stopped, thank goodness, but I won't really be confident my baby's alright until I've had a thorough check-up.'

After they finish breakfast Jenny and Annie pack quickly. Georgie and Annie arrange to meet later that day at the hotel and Jenny says she'll be at the airport tomorrow to see Georgie off. As she watches the car disappear down the drive Georgie checks her watch, only eight am, they should make it to town in plenty of time for the ten o'clock appointment. She returns to the kitchen, stacks the dishwasher and turns it on before stripping all the beds and putting the sheets, pillow cases and doona covers in the laundry. With these chores completed she decides to have another coffee before tackling the fridge and sorting out what food should be thrown out. With coffee in hand she goes and sits on the front verandah. Without the others around the place feels eerily quiet, but also rather peaceful.

At times she dreams about living the life of a hermit in some beautiful isolated spot where the problems and noise of other people would not impinge, but really she knows it wouldn't suit her. She likes quiet times by herself but she also enjoys company, dinners and visits to the theatre and galleries, entertaining friends in her home and weekends away skiing or snorkelling. She also enjoys her job. Although some clients can be a pain in the arse she gets on well with most of them and gets satisfaction from helping them. For the moment though she is enjoying being alone for it has been unusual for her to spend such an extended time in the company of others, and there have certainly been a fair share of emotional dramas.

She closes her eyes and is thinking how quiet it is when she is startled by a voice calling, 'Hi there. Georgie isn't it?

Georgie opens her eyes to see Stuart walking up the drive. He is dressed more formally than the last time she saw him. Today he has on grey slacks and a navy polo-necked sweater and his longish hair is neatly combed. She is surprised to see him here and is not sure how to greet him. Jenny had said he hadn't wanted to talk to her since the night she told him she wanted to abort the baby. She'd also made it clear to the three of them she didn't want him knowing about the threatened miscarriage until she knew the baby was safe. Now, faced with him standing here before her, she's not sure what to say.

He looks a little nervous as he asks abruptly, 'Jenny around?'

To buy time while she thinks about how much she should tell him she answers rather too heartily, 'Hi there. No I'm here on my lonesome. Take a seat and I'll make you a coffee.'

Before he can either refuse or accept she makes a hasty retreat to the kitchen, makes his coffee and pours herself a refill. When she returns to the verandah Stuart is sitting on the top step so Georgie hands him his coffee and sits beside him.

As soon as she sits he says, 'I've just noticed Jen's car is missing. Where's she gone so early in the morning?'

Deciding not to beat around the bush Georgie answers rather aggressively, 'If you must know she's gone to town for an appointment with her doctor.'

Stuart turns and looks at her, a worried look on his face. 'She didn't go by herself did she?'

'No, Annie went with her.'

'It should have been me. I should have gone with her.'

'Yes, you should have, and you probably could have if you'd seen fit to answer her phone calls. I gather she rang you several times and you didn't call her back. She hasn't known how you're feeling. Evidently you made it pretty clear you didn't want to have anything more to do with her if she had an abortion.'

Stuart looks so thoroughly miserable Georgie finds herself feeling almost sorry for him, but he hadn't stood by Jenny when she needed his understanding and support. She hardens her heart and says, 'She's feeling very insecure about you at the moment.'

He sighs. 'I don't blame her for feeling that way. I was pretty shocked when she said she wanted an abortion; told her there wasn't any future for us if she went ahead with it. Since then I've done a lot of thinking. I can see now how hard it would be for her, telling her boys she's pregnant to me when their father's only just died.'

'Well why didn't you answer her calls?'

'For the first couple of days I was confused. It shocked me that she'd even think of getting rid of our baby. I was still coming to grips with the idea when I went to the pub on Tuesday night. There were a lot of the young local guys there, some of them about the same ages as Jen's sons. Listening to them talk made me remember how black and white things are for you at that age. It helped me see why Jen was so worried about how her boys would react.'

'Well you still didn't call her?'

'I needed to clear my head, so I went surfing up the coast by myself. Sitting out in the water waiting for a wave I had a lot of time to think. I'm upset Jen has to get rid of our baby, but I understand now why she feels the way she does. I also know I want to be with her no matter what. I love her so much. I can't imagine life without her. When I got back late Wednesday night I rang to tell her all that. I got her messages and asked her to ring me but she didn't call me back. Then I tried to call her yesterday morning but her phone was dead.'

Georgie grins. 'Yes her phone suffered a severe case of water damage, but that's another story. What do you plan to do now?'

'If you can let me know which clinic she's gone to I'll head off. I want to be there for her when she wakes up.'

It suddenly occurs to Georgina that Stuart has assumed Jenny's appointment with the doctor has been for an abortion. She can't resist teasing him a little. 'Oh she won't be put to sleep.'

He looks horrified. 'They'd have to. They couldn't possibly do that to someone who's awake.'

'They do all the time. Ultrasounds are painless.'

'What do you mean?'

'I mean that Jenny is having a thorough examination to make sure the baby is alright, including an ultrasound.'

'So she's not having an abortion?'

'No you dope, and if you'd rung her sooner you'd have known what was going on. She had a bleed and some back pain and got frightened that she might be going to miscarry. It made her realise just how much she wants to keep the baby.'

'Oh, and now you say she might be losing it. I have to be with her. Can you tell me where the doctor's surgery is?'

'I'm afraid I don't know. Anyhow by the time you get to town they'll have left. The appointment was for ten. I reckon they'll go home afterwards so you could catch up with Jenny there. You do know where she lives don't you?'

'Yes. I've never been inside but I know where it is.' He looks a bit abashed. 'I guess this sounds soppy, but sometimes when I've been in town I've driven past her house just so I could feel close to her. I really do love her Georgie, more than I can say.'

Georgie almost feels like giving him a hug. Instead she slaps him on the arm and says, 'Well go tell her that you big lug. I'm sure she'll be pleased to see you. I think she's been feeling you've given up on her.'

As she watches Stuart stride off down the driveway Georgie smiles to herself. There can be no doubting how he feels about Jenny. Of course that doesn't mean it will be all smooth sailing from now on. Hopefully the baby is alright but if it is there is still the problem of telling Jenny's sons and how they will take the news of their mother's pregnancy.

As she sips the last of her coffee Georgie wonders what will happen to her three friends during the next couple of days. This business with Vicki seems to have caused a lot of Sheila's insecurities to resurface. Georgie now feels badly about stirring her about how she has compromised too much as far as Scott was concerned, and then last night she virtually dared Sheila to make him take a stand with his daughter. The stupid woman's suicide attempt has complicated things. When Sheila left she seemed so angry, not least of all with her. Who knows what will happen there.

Georgie is more confident Annie and Joel will sort out their problem, but then she's always had such a soft spot for Joel so can't imagine him being difficult. She finds it really hard to understand why Annie has put off telling him what she wants to do. Perhaps he is no longer quite as amenable as he was when they were all so young. Tonight she'll get a chance to talk to Annie about this, but today may have been the last time she sees Sheila for a while. Georgie would like to sort things out with her, apologise for stirring her so much, but unless Sheila comes to the airport tomorrow this won't happen.

'Well, time to sort out this food,' she says aloud as she stands and walks to the kitchen where she rinses the two cups, before beginning the tedious business of clearing the refrigerator. This finished she puts the garbage bag in the wheelie bin and trundles it down the driveway to the kerbside. After a quick check through the house she gets her case and stows it in the boot before locking the front door and putting the key in its hiding place.

As she drives away she is already planning what she will do with the rest of the day. She should get to town by midday at the latest. She thinks she'll call her mother and arrange to take her to lunch somewhere nice. In a funny way the feeling of affinity she has with Joanna has helped Georgie feel a bit closer to her mother. Perhaps because it's put to rest her long-held belief that she was adopted she can at last accept that she is truly the daughter of her strangely alien parents.

Later in the morning when she books into the hotel Georgie asks for and is given the same room as the one she shared with Annie. As soon as she has settled in she rings her mother and arranges to take her to lunch. Her mother sounds so thrilled at the idea Georgie feels a touch of guilt about the way she has virtually ignored her over the years. She determines to try and be a better daughter.

With the lunch arrangement made she then rings Jenny to find out how she got on at the doctor's, and to see if Stuart has managed to catch up with her. Jenny answers in a rush. 'The baby's fine and Stuart's with me at the moment. I'm so relieved Georgie. Stuart arrived shortly after we got back from the doctor's and said he'd talked to you and knew what I'd been going through. Oh. I love him Georgie. We're both so happy, and we're telling the boys tonight.'

Georgie wishes them good luck and rings off then dials Sheila's number. The phone rings until message bank comes on. She's not sure how Sheila is feeling towards her at present so leaves a rather stilted message, saying she hopes things are okay and would she ring her when she gets a chance.

Later at lunch she tells her mother about how she and her friends spent the first few days at the beach house; describes the secret beach, the lunch in the bush beside a creek and their evening out at the restaurant. She also tells her about her swim and that she now feels she has conquered her fear of rough water. She doesn't tell her how the swim ties in with her feelings about Joanna for she knows her mother wouldn't understand. For the same reason she doesn't talk about Jenny's love life and pregnancy or Sheila's and Annie's problems for she is sure her mother won't approve of any of their actions or plans, and she doesn't want to hear her criticising her friends. Despite her new found intentions to be a better daughter she knows there will always be a barrier between them.

When they arrive back at her mother's house she walks her to the door and kisses her on her papery powdered cheek. Her mother thanks her profusely for the lunch and says how much she enjoyed it. The love and gratitude in her mother's eyes makes Georgie squirm, for it has been a small enough daughterly gesture and right now she just wants to get away. She is looking forward to returning to the hotel and catching up with Annie again. As she drives away she thinks how strange it is that she feels closer to a dead aunt than to her living mother.

She scarcely has time to slip out of her shoes and pour herself a glass of white wine from the mini fridge when there is a knock on the door, and as Georgie opens it Annie steps inside. She gives her a hug then crosses the room at a rush, flops down on one of the lounge chairs and says with a sigh, 'What a day! Is there any more of that wine?'

Georgie laughs at her friend's flustered appearance. 'You look as though you could do with a drink.'

'I certainly could. I've just come from Sheila's and things aren't good there.'

Georgie pours the wine and gives Annie a hug after placing the glass on the table. 'What's up? Vicki's okay isn't she?'

'Oh yes, she's alright, but things are pretty tense between Sheila and Scott. He came home while I was there. They didn't say much to each other because the kids and I were there, but from what Sheila told me he blames her for what Vicki did, and she's totally pissed off with the way he's handled the whole situation. They've obviously got a lot of sorting out to do, so I made a quick getaway to my car and came to the hotel. I wasn't sure whether you'd be here until I checked at reception. Did you catch up with your mother again?'

'Yes, I took her to lunch and she seemed to enjoy it.' She sighs. 'I don't know. I wish I could feel something more for her than filial responsibility, but I don't. Anyhow enough about me. I'm dying to hear what happened at the doctor's and whether Stuart arrived at Jen's house while you were still there.'

'Everything went well at the doctor's. Jen had an ultra sound and then a thorough check-up. The doctor was lovely, totally reassuring. Evidently Jenny is very fit and there are no problems with the baby. She'll do another ultra sound next month just to be sure, and she'll be able to tell Jen the sex of the baby by then.'

'And what about Stuart? When did he arrive?'

'Not long after we got back to Jenny's place. He got there looking sort of flustered and carrying the biggest bunch of red roses I've ever seen.'

'So everything's sorted there is it?'

'Well between those two it certainly is. I left them alone in the lounge-room and went out to the kitchen to make coffee. When I came back they were twined around each other on the couch. They seem to be totally besotted and really looking forward to having a baby together. Their only problem now is breaking the news to the boys, and that's a big one. They're going to tell them tonight, so hopefully we'll find out how that's gone tomorrow.'

'You have had an eventful day. Now let's go down and treat ourselves to a good dinner and a bottle of champagne. Then we'd better have an early night. My plane leaves at nine and I have to be at the airport by eight so we'll have to get up pretty early in the morning.'

The next day, after a rushed breakfast Georgie drives her hire car to the agency in town and Annie follows in her car. Before leaving town, at Georgie's request, they do a detour around the wharf area before heading across the bridge and on the highway to the airport. They are both still sleepy, so don't talk much as they make the brief trip.

While Georgie checks in Annie parks her car then re-joins her friend in the coffee shop. As she sits down

Georgie says, 'I bought you a flat white. That's what you drink isn't it?'

'Lovely thanks. How're you going for time?'

Georgie checks her watch. 'Still half an hour till I have to go. Thanks for bringing me to the airport Annie. I know you're probably keen to get home and I do appreciate you being here to see me off.'

'As if I wouldn't. You don't get down here that often and I miss you, you know. And as far as being keen to get home I'm not so sure. Of course it'll be good to see Joel again, but I'm not really looking forward to telling him what I want to do.'

'You never know, he might be alright about it. Just make it clear to him how important it is to you.'

'Oh I will. You know talking to you three about it has made me determined to finally do what I've thought about for years. '

'Well something good has come out of the holiday.'

Georgie says this so ruefully that Annie is surprised into saying, 'Why do you say it like that? Most of the time it's been great. I thought you were enjoying it as much as I.'

'Lots of it I did enjoy. I loved being with the three of you again and we had some great times, but I'm not happy with the way Sheila and I have been. She's going through a tough time and I goaded her too much. We've always been such good friends, but now we seem to rub each other up the wrong way. She was so angry when she left. I think she probably blames me for talking her into making that call to Scott.'

'Look at the moment she's just angry, and mostly I think with herself. And she'll stay that way until she sorts things out with Scott.'

Georgie checks her watch again. 'Twenty minutes till take-off. It looks as though Jenny isn't going to make it to say goodbye. I wonder how they got on last night.'

As she is saying this they hear a shout and see Jenny running along the departure area with Stuart close behind. She arrives in a rush and puts both arms around her friends. 'I'm so glad we got here in time. It took longer getting through the city than expected.'

'The main thing is you're here. Annie and I are longing to know how it went with the boys last night.'

'Not as bad as I thought it would be.' Stuart has been standing back and as she says this Jenny pulls him forward and winds her arm through his. 'Actually Stephen said they'd known for years about their father's philandering, but hadn't let on because they were trying to protect me. Alec said when a friend of theirs' told them he'd seen me at dinner with another man they thought it served their father right if I'd found someone else.'

Stuart looks down at her fondly. 'They are both so mature and obviously love their Mum. The thing they're finding hard to come to terms with is the baby.'

'They weren't as shocked as I'd expected though.' Jenny grins. 'I think they're mainly surprised at the thought of their mother not being too old to get pregnant, but I'm sure they'll get used to the idea.'

Suddenly a voice comes over the loud speakers and through the static Georgie hears the call for passengers for her flight to start boarding. Annie and Jenny take an arm each to escort her to the security counter. There is the last minute flurry as she removes her shoes and places her carry-on bag on the moving counter. She kisses Annie and Georgie and gives Stuart a friendly hug saying, 'Look after our girl won't you.'

He grins broadly and says, 'You bet.'

Before passing through the security gate she glances around the crowded room. It has been a vain wish but she had hoped Sheila might come to see her off. She collects her shoes and bag and with a final wave to her friends begins walking across to the doorway where the hostess is checking in the passengers. She is nearly there when she hears her name being called and sees Sheila running along the long departure lounge. Ignoring the shouts of the guard Georgie goes back through the security gate and runs barefoot to greet her. As they hug she feels tears trickling down her face. She chokes, 'I didn't think you'd come.'

Sheila is crying too. 'I had to take the kids to Mum and Dad because Scott is still with Vicki. Looks like I only just made it in time. I couldn't let you leave without saying goodbye.

'When you didn't call me back I thought you were still angry with me.'

'I'm not angry with you; in fact I'm grateful. You helped me see I've compromised too much as far as Scott is concerned, but not anymore.'

'Just don't do anything rash. You've loved Scott for most of your adult life and I know all about the compromises you made during those early years. The thing is you thought he was worth it then, and he's still the same man. He'll always love his first children and worry about them, but he adores you and Mia and William.'

'I realise that, but this business with Vicki has brought back all the insecurities and anger I felt when he put her and David before me.'

'I know love, and you have to work through that. Despite what I've said I don't really think you've made too many compromises. To me it seems that what you and Scott have together is worth fighting for, but only you can make that decision.'

'Well right now I'm wondering whether it is worth fighting for. You know he'd been told Vicki was out of danger when they contacted him but he still frightened our poor little kids by getting them up in the middle of the night so that he could rush to her bedside. He's continued to put her first and now he's also blaming me for what that neurotic bitch did. At present all I want is him out of my life.'

Georgie sees a guard approaching and says hurriedly, 'I understand how you must be feeling but don't make any rash decisions. Please, please keep in touch and let me know how you're making out.'

Sheila gives a big grin. 'Of course I will, that's what friends are for'. She gives Georgie an extra tight hug then steps back and with a gentle finger wipes the tears from her friend face. 'Oh God I miss you. Make sure you come back soon.'

The guard puts a hand on Georgie's arm and says roughly. 'If you don't come now the plane will go without you.'

He ushers her once more through the gates, and soon she is through the exit and must run across the tarmac to the waiting plane.

She finds a seat near a window and scarcely has time to fasten her seatbelt before the plane begins to taxi along the runway. It turns at the end and commences its run for take-off. As it passes the terminal Georgie peers out the little porthole window. The last sight she sees is her three friends standing outside the terminal together their arms around each other as they watch her go.

Georgie smiles to herself. They all have so much going on in their lives at present, but put their problems aside to come and see her off. She thinks of Sheila's last words and whispers across the ether to the three distant figures, 'See you soon.'

Biography – Barbara Knight

After many years as a teacher, housewife and mother I completed a Bachelor of Arts at UTAS, majoring in English Literature and History in the 1970s. I followed this with a graduate Diploma in Librarianship and worked in public libraries for sixteen years before my retirement.

During retirement I spent several years attempting to become partially self-sufficient by fishing and growing a huge variety of vegetables and fruits before turning to the more cerebral pursuits of writing and painting.

I am an avid reader, a long term member of book discussion groups and have been writing seriously for many years. I have had six short stories published in anthologies or magazines. I have also written a number of novels and a memoir.

www.ingramcontent.com/pod-product-compliance
Lightning Source LLC
Chambersburg PA
CBHW070553120726
47909CB00007B/2331